# Roll of the Dice

## KAYLA MARTIN

Roll of the Dice

A Murphy Family Novel (#2)

Kayla Martin



Published by Black Willow Bay Publishing LLC

Copy edited & proofread by Kristen Hamilton

www.kristensredpen.com

Cover design by Paige Moreland (@lpm_draws)

Family tree & chapter images by Jordan Burns (@joburns.designs)



Print ISBN: 979-8-9900332-5-2

Kindle ISBN: 979-8-9900332-4-5

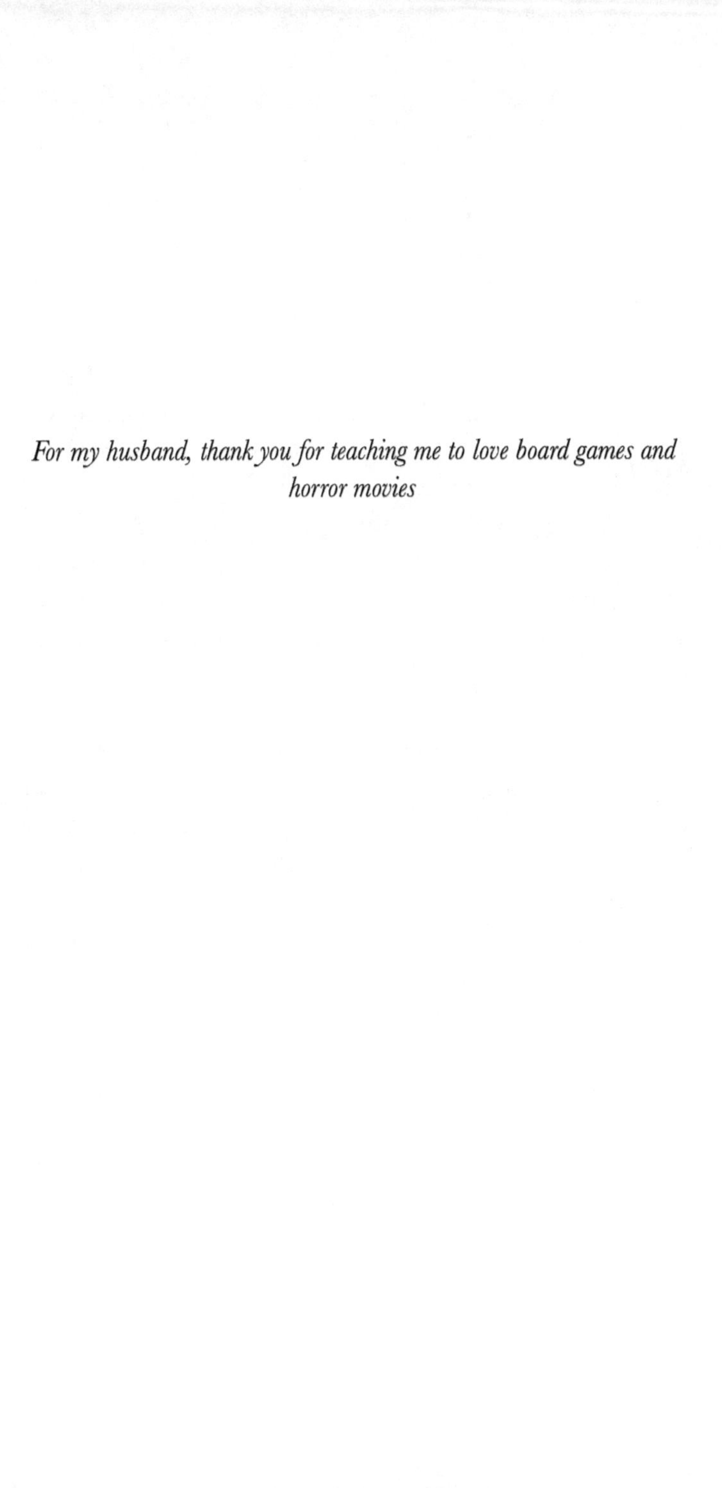

*For my husband, thank you for teaching me to love board games and horror movies*

# AUTHOR'S NOTE

Dear Reader,

*Roll of the Dice* is the second book in the Murphy Family series. The first book, *A Thousand Sunsets*, is available now if you would like to read it first. However, as an interconnected standalone series, it is not required to read them in order. Do whatever you want!

Please also be aware that this story contains multiple open door romance scenes that have on-page consensual sexual intimacy. If you are interested in knowing which chapters these scenes happen during you can visit the Dicktionary before the acknowledgments.

This story covers the following topics: underage drinking, learning disorders (brief discussion), parent death (off page), and grief. I hope I have done these topics justice based on my own experiences and through the guidance of my alpha and beta readers. As always, your mental health is the most important thing, please take care of yourself first before anything.

All my best,
    Kayla

# PLAYLIST

Over the course of writing this book music was used to get in the right headspace. The songs on this playlist represent the overall story and vibes of *Roll of the Dice*. If you enjoy book playlists you can find it on Spotify by searching "Roll of the Dice".

**Cinderella** by Play
**feel something** by Bea Miller
**bad idea!** by girl in red
**girlfriend** by Bea Miller
**Teeth** by 5 Seconds of Summer
**Being Your Friend** by Katherine Li
**What A Time** by Julia Michaels, Niall Horan
**Dress** by Taylor Swift
**chance with you** by mehro
**idfc** by blackbear
**Don't Blame Me** by Taylor Swift
**Do I Wanna Know?** by Arctic Monkeys
**hate u love u** by Olivia O'Brien
**Shameless** by Camila Cabello
**Starving** by Hailee Steinfeld, Grey, Zedd
**Birthday Suit** by Kesha
**Juno** by Sabrina Carpenter
**I Think I'm In Love** by Kat Dahlia
**Collide** by Rachel Platten
**Perfectly Wrong** by Shawn Mendes
**Rock Bottom** by Hailee Steinfeld, DNCE
**hate to be lame** by Lizzy McAlpine, FINNEAS

**Supermarket Flowers** by Ed Sheeran
**War of Hearts** by Ruelle
**In The Stars** by Benson Boone
**When I Look At You** by Miley Cyrus
**New Year's Day** by Taylor Swift

# MURPHY FAMILY TREE

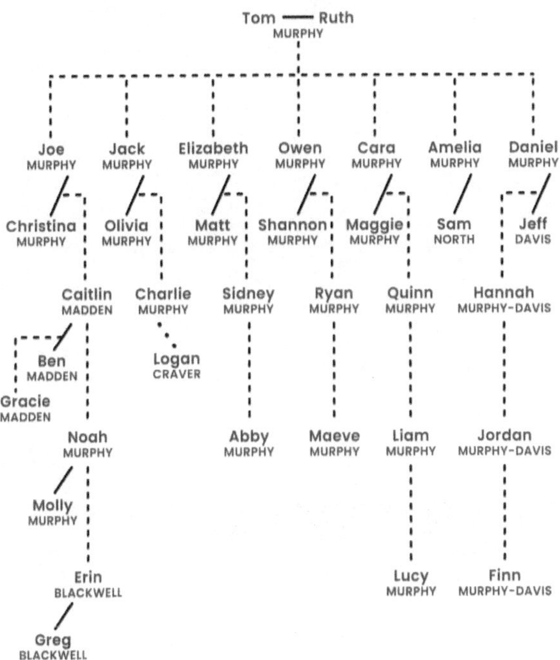

## ONE

## MAEVE

I'm running late, really fucking late.

Whoever decided 8:00 a.m. college classes should be a thing should be arrested. It's the first day of junior year and I'm already ringing it in poorly. Hannah, my cousin-slash-roommate, was no help this morning when she left and didn't wake me up after I snoozed my alarm. I love the girl, but sometimes I want to kill her.

I told her my Managerial Finance class started at eight and made her promise to wake me if she saw me still asleep, but she clearly forgot. Her bed was made when I unearthed myself from my covers and ran past her room on my way out the door, so she must have seen me sleeping when she left. I'm curious where she went since her classes don't start until after lunch and she isn't a morning person.

My head is currently home to a construction site after spending the weekend celebrating the start of the semester with our sorority sisters. I'm regretting the final shot I had last night with every step I take. I could go for a burger right now, or bacon—anything greasy would do the trick— but I didn't have time to grab anything this morning besides aspirin which hasn't worked its magic yet. I want nothing more than to crawl back into bed and skip today.

Running through campus is my only solution if I want to make it to at least some of my first class. It didn't help that I couldn't find a parking spot when I got here, so I had to park in the furthest lot.

The campus is small enough where I can usually walk anywhere in ten minutes, but since I'm late I had to park in the overflow lot—adding another five minutes to my already running pace. Luckily, it's sunny today, so at least I'm not rushing to class in the rain. My gaze rakes over the sky to make sure no rain clouds have appeared out of nowhere.

When I make it to the center of campus, I'm greeted by the familiar large courtyard with multiple intersecting sidewalks connecting the old brick buildings. While the aesthetic of the brick exterior and scattered trees is appealing, being inside them is another story. Since they were built in the early 1900s the lack of air conditioning and upgrades is apparent during long lectures. The courtyard is the best part, and one of my favorite activities is to sit in the grass and relax. Last year, Hannah and I finally invested in a hammock that can hang between trees, and it's especially nice once the leaves start to change, but it's still too early for that. Hustling down the sidewalk I make sure to watch out for the crack in the sidewalk that tripped me last semester and hold back a pained groan when I see one of my sorority sisters heading my way.

I look around at my options: grass to my left, grass to my right, and the start of the next path too many feet away to reach without running. *Fuck.* I have no time to get there to avoid her, but if I pass her she'll stop me. She's earned her nickname—Chatty Casey—for a reason. One time she trapped me in a corner for thirty minutes talking about which type of fish she should buy, while I stood there trying to politely exit and step away from her. She wouldn't let me, and kept stepping into my path. I have exactly zero time to get sucked into a conversation with her right now, but I don't have a choice as she closes in.

"Maeve, I'm so glad I caught you." Casey blocks the path in front of me, oblivious to how I'm midrun and panting.

"Hi, yeah, I'm running late. I don't—"

"That's fine, I won't be long. I've been thinking about your event this semester and it would be fun if we did a sexy car wash. What do you think?" Casey tilts her head and peers at me with her big blue puppy dog eyes. I don't have the time to inform her why that's a horrible idea as I shift back and forth on my feet. Then I'd definitely miss class.

There's no way I'm subjecting the sisters to one of the most demeaning activities for our fundraising event. I'm steering us away from the stereotypical sorority events, and a car wash would set us back decades.

"Thanks, Casey. But I already have an idea, and I really need to go." I step into the dew-covered grass to get around her and pick up my pace, yelling behind me, "I'll see you later, have a good first day of class."

Finally pushing my way through the doors of the building where my finance class is, I catch a glance at myself in the window. My long brown hair is already falling out of my claw clip and my Mu Eta Psi T-shirt and pink sweatpants combo aren't what I expected to be wearing on the first day, and I notice I grabbed the shirt with a sauce stain that I've been meaning to treat. Fucking pasta. I had a whole plan to hit the ground running this semester, but now it's all shot to hell. Tomorrow I'll get up early, get ready, and grab coffee. At least I don't have another class until tonight, so I'll have plenty of time to stop at my favorite café on campus to help me survive the rest of today.

As I'm rushing through the silent halls, my phone starts going off—I have to remember to silence that—and I drop my backpack to the floor to retrieve it. I tossed it in my bag in my rush this morning, and now it's lost to the depths with all the extra pens I threw in.

I finally find it at the bottom and swear under my breath when I see it's my mom calling. If I don't answer now, she's going to keep calling and leave at least three voicemails. I'm already late so I might as well get it over with. I should have set multiple alarms for today.

"Good morning, Mother," I groan into the phone, biting down on my thumbnail and getting a mouthful of nail polish as I scrape it with my teeth. I struggle to hide my cough while bending down to grab a piece of fruity gum from the side of my backpack. I've been a notorious nail biter since I can remember, but the stress of talking to my mother always makes me forget I get my nails done to combat this, with gum acting a second defense.

"Sweetie, oh good you picked up. I wasn't sure if you would be in class or not. Didn't you say you had an early class?"

"I did, yes. Why are you calling me?" I already regret answering.

"Well, when I have great news I can't wait to share it. I was going to leave you a voicemail," she says and her pitch is too high for a Monday morning. It only makes my headache worse. "I've found you a date for Charlie's wedding. He's my hairdresser's cousin's coworker's grandson and he sounds perfect for you."

Yup, definitely regret answering. Since my cousin's wedding invitation came two months ago, my mom has been on a relentless quest to find me a date. She even RSVPed me with a plus one without asking. I'm grateful for my mom, but her constant push for me to follow in her footsteps and be married right after college is getting exhausting. When she was my age she was already engaged to my dad, and she keeps repeating how she "wants me to be happy like her" like there's only one way to be happy. She doesn't understand why I want to focus on starting a business of my own when I could use the school's diverse student population to find a soulmate. It's like she can't stop herself from helping.

"Sweetie, did you hear me?" she asks.

"Yes, and for the hundredth time, I don't want to bring anyone to the wedding," I tell her through gritted teeth. It's not that I'm not interested in dating, but I don't need to babysit someone at a family wedding. I want to let loose and have fun, get drunk with my cousins, and dance until my feet hurt. If I bring some random date I'm going to have to introduce them to everyone and I'll be worried if they're having fun all night.

"It's too late to change your mind, I already sent the RSVP in." I'm pretty sure that's wrong, but I don't want to fight her on it. Leave it to my mother to make my decisions for me based on what she wants.

"I didn't ask—"

"You'll love him, I'll send you his picture," she interrupts me.

"Please don't." I lean against the wall, finally outside the room I'm supposed to be in and I'm twenty minutes late. "Mom, I need to go to class. Please stop trying to find me a date."

"Sweetie, if I don't find you a date then who will? You're going to get wrapped up in excuses and forget to do it." She sounds like I've asked her to stop breathing.

"If I agree to find a date by the end of September will you stop?" I ask, willing to do anything to end this conversation, including agreeing to bring a date.

"Fine, but if you can't find one I'm setting you up with my hairdresser's cousin's coworker's grandson," she huffs.

"Deal," I say and end the call, silencing my phone. She still sends the photo of this random guy, whose name I don't know. He's the definition of an average white boy, with brown hair and brown eyes. Looking at the picture only makes me annoyed and further cements the fact that I don't want my mom picking some random date for me. I'd never hear the end of it if I ended up following her plan even though I'm trying not to. Falling in love isn't something I'm interested in right now.

With all the things I want to get done this semester, adding a relationship doesn't fit in. My to-do list is already a mile long and it's only the first day.

I slip my phone into my pocket, contemplating if it's worth it to go in since I'm already so late. I figure it can only go up from here so I take a deep breath before stepping into the classroom.

All eyes are on me the second I'm through the door and I can feel the professor's glare burning a hole through me. In the past two years, I've never been late for class. In my defense, I've also never had a class that started before ten, but I'm sure the students I recognize from previous classes will give me shit. I turn toward the professor and she doesn't seem as mad as I had initially thought.

"Ms. Murphy, I presume?" she asks and I nod. "Glad you could finally join us, please take a seat." She hands me a syllabus and points to the far side of the room, where there is one seat left.

I take it from her and move as quickly as I can without running, waving at a few people I recognize. I'm unsure what I did to deserve this morning from hell, but it somehow gets worse when I get to the only empty seat and see the familiar face of a tall lanky redhead dressed in all black sitting behind it. My stomach drops, and my gum almost falls out of my mouth. The last time I saw him was over the summer, and we were fighting over the ending of *Titanic*, and if Jack could have survived. He refused to listen to any of my arguments or resources including a deleted scene clearly showing Jack not being able to fit on the door without it sinking. He always finds things to fight with me about, no matter how tiny there are, like what type of pizza is best. Any conversation I have with him always ends up in some type of disagreement.

I return the scowl on his face with one of my own, attempting to play it cool and act unsurprised to see him as I roll my shoulders back. He seems to be in his usual perpetually annoyed state, the furrow of his eyebrows is more drastic compared to the summer. I bet I could stick a penny between them and it would stay.

It's bad enough I have to see him every summer during my family vacation. Since the year he got a lifeguard position at our favorite campground, he's been a thorn in my side. For five summers he's learned how to push my buttons, and I can't help but push his back. He was supposed to stay in the Thousand Islands where he belongs.

He's not supposed to be here.

He doesn't even go here.

Or I thought he didn't.

## CONNOR

I'm so fucked.

Maeve? It has to be *Maeve*? It's not that I don't like her, she's just the absolute *most*. She's loud, in clothing and personality, and I get a headache anytime I'm around her. Not to mention, she's always glaring at me and challenging what I'm saying. She's always playing defense in a game I didn't sign up for. We've never agreed on anything in our lives. Although, I do enjoy how easy it is to push her buttons and the flustered huff she always lets out mid-argument. There's also the fact that she bares a striking resemblance to my first—well only—girlfriend, and I would rather not be reminded of that trainwreck of a relationship.

When I saw her walk into the classroom my stomach dropped and I hoped she had the wrong room. She was already late and the only remaining seat was directly in front of me. Which meant if she was in this class, she would see me.

Luckily, she didn't see me right away, and I had time to collect myself before she came over. I couldn't see her face during class, but I could tell she was mad. There was something about the tilt of her head that said "if I turned around right now you would be dead."

When I was researching schools to transfer to I kept feeling drawn to Genoveva State University, and I didn't know why. I must have heard her and her cousins mention it one of these past summers, and it stuck with me. Now I'm wishing I had picked literally any other school. Or brought it up this summer so I could still transfer before the semester started.

For the rest of class I couldn't pay attention to anything, all I could focus on was how Maeve was going to make this semester so much worse for me. Maybe I still have time to switch classes, or schools, maybe states. Hell, could I find a school in Canada? It wouldn't be hard to move home and cross the St. Lawrence River. When the professor dismissed us, Maeve gathered her things and practically ran out of the room.

I'm going to have to see her again for this class in two days, and hopefully by then she'll move to simply ignoring me instead of glaring at me. With my luck she's going to assume I followed her here and give me shit about it, and I'd rather not start every week fighting with her. For now, all I can do is hope I don't run into her again before Wednesday.

Heading to one of the campus's many cafés, I try to figure out where my next class is. I should have become more familiar with the campus before the first day, the tiny map on my phone isn't much help and the page refreshes any time I zoom in.

I'm looking down when I push open the door and see a cup of iced coffee go flying by my feet. I hear, "What the *fuck*?" before I register that I've opened the door into someone, and not just anyone, but Maeve.

I should apologize for opening the door into her, but the venomous look she's giving me triggers the opposite reaction. "Listen, maybe if you weren't running out the door you would have seen me opening it."

"So this is my fault?" She gestures to her now coffee soaked shirt and pink sweatpants. Her shirt is clinging to her and I have to focus on not staring at the clear outline of her belly button and other parts of her. I've seen her in plenty of bikinis over the past year, but there's something about standing in the middle of a café that feels like I shouldn't be able to see this much. Thankfully, she's wearing a bra, but it must be thin because I can still see the faint outline of her nipples.

"Yeah, it is. You're too busy giving depressed Barbie to watch where you're going." I stand taller, crossing my arms and towering over her with my six-three height, while gesturing to her appearance. The spilled coffee making the bags under her eyes and her messy hair more prominent, like the fake Depressed Barbie commercial from the movie. She's just missing the blonde hair to complete the stereotype.

"Fuck you, Connor. Get out of my way." I see a flash of pain in her eyes as she goes to move around me. I'm being an ass and there's no reason for it.

"Wait, let me buy you another one," I say, reaching out and grabbing her arm before she gets too far away from me.

She freezes and squints her eyes, pulling her arm out of my grasp. "Why?"

"Because I feel bad?" I don't understand why she has to question this. I'm trying to be nice.

"Fine." She turns around and heads toward the line. I have no choice but to follow her, and we stand silent in the slowest line I've ever stood in. The silence only magnifies the sound of other students talking, keyboards clicking, and the hiss from the espresso machines as coffees are being made.

When we finally get to the counter Maeve orders a large iced coffee, a breakfast sandwich, and muffin before stepping to the side and informing the barista I will be paying. I glare at her, wanting to make her smirk disappear by pretending I forgot my wallet, but my dad taught me better than that. Instead, I place my order of a large black coffee and we step off to the side to wait.

The staff here must be focusing on food because Maeve's breakfast sandwich and muffin are out before our coffees. She takes both and stuffs them into her bag without saying thank you. I don't blame her, I wouldn't thank me either. I shouldn't have been looking down at my phone when I walked in here, but I'm never going to admit that to her.

Maeve is shifting on her feet next to me, unable to stay still, her gaze anywhere but at me. It feels weird to be standing here with her. Usually we are surrounded by her ten plus cousins and the other lifeguards from the campground. I've never been in a situation where it's only us, and I have no idea what to say to her. I know so little about her, besides the fact that she likes pink and gum—and apparently iced coffee.

I'm about to bring up the weather—clear skies and warm—when Maeve breaks the silence. "Are you really not going to offer me your hoodie so I don't have to walk around with coffee on my shirt?"

"Would you take it if I offered?" I ask, guilt forming in the pit of my stomach that I didn't think of this first, but not willing to admit I was wrong.

She contemplates my question, before shifting on her feet again and answering, "No."

I'm saved from replying to her sass by her cousin, Hannah, walking in. Compared to Maeve, she's much easier to talk to. She's nice to me and it always seems like she's up to something with her siblings—they're triplets and have chaotic triplet energy. Her blonde hair is cut shorter than the last time I saw her, and she's got the biggest smile on her face as she approaches us.

"Hi, Hannah." I wave at her, grabbing our coffees from the counter as my name is called out.

"Hi, Connor? What are you doing here?" Hannah asks, brows furrowing as her eyes bounce between us.

"He, unfortunately, goes here," Maeve groans, taking the iced coffee from my hand. Our fingertips brush and she flinches at the touch.

"Nice, that should be fun." Hannah nods and turns to Maeve, looking her up and down. "What happened to you?"

"That was my fault," I chime in before Maeve can chastise me. "I ran into her when—"

"*Meow.*"

I'm cut off mid explanation when a loud meow comes out of Hannah's large purse. Her eyes go wide and she freezes, keeping her eyes locked on me.

"Hannah," Maeve says, and I can hear the disapproval in her voice.

"Hm?" She glances at Maeve, her lips in a straight line.

"What was that?"

"What was what?"

"The meow."

"What meow?" Hannah looks around for the sound that clearly came from her purse.

"The. Meow. That came from your purse." Maeve points to the purse with her iced coffee, her words coming out in a hiss.

Watching them is like a tennis match I can't tear my eyes away from, not even if I wanted to. I probably shouldn't be here for this moment, but if they start fighting someone is going to have to break them up. I'm no stranger to holding Maeve back from a fight—two summers ago I held her back from kicking someone's ass at a party. I wish the memory of my arm wrapped around her waist and her body pressed against mine didn't linger around so long, but she always had an annoying way of sticking around when I least wanted it.

"Oh that? It's nothing." Hannah's voice brings me back to reality as she waves her hand nonchalantly, reaching into her purse and pulling out a tiny orange kitten.

"Hannah!" Maeve shouts and steps closer to her and the little orange ball in her arms. "We aren't allowed to have pets in the building. Why would you get a kitten? When did you get a kitten? Is this why you were up early today?" Maeve's questioning comes out so fast I can hardly keep up with it.

The crease between her brows is clear evidence she isn't a fan of the idea of hiding a kitten. I've never been a cat person, but I might be if it makes Maeve mad.

"It's kind of cute," I say, and I'm immediately met with Maeve's glare accompanied by her frustrated huff. I have to bite my tongue and fight a smile so I don't laugh; I've never been able to push someone's buttons as easily as hers.

"It's fine," Hannah chimes, adjusting her hold on the kitten to pet its head. It leans into her hand and starts purring. "I've kept plenty of secrets before, we'll be good as long as Mr. Linley doesn't find out. And yes, I picked her up this morning."

"Come on, Maeve, let her keep it. You love things with

claws. What's her name?" I ask, returning my attention back to the kitten before Maeve decides to hit me. The kitten lifts her head to sniff my hand before giving it a small head bump as I scratch her chin.

"Connor, if you could kindly fuck off that would be great. This doesn't concern you," Maeve snaps and I might be two buttons away from her getting ready to fight me. I probably shouldn't push her too far on the first day of class.

"Right." I pull my hand away from the kitten and back up to safety. "I'll be leaving then, guess I'll see you both around campus."

"Over my dead body," Maeve mumbles.

"It was good to see you, Connor. Sorry Maeve is grumpy today. And her name is Greta," Hannah calls after me as I exit the café.

## THREE

## MAEVE

Hannah and I sit in my car in silence as I drive, except for the meows still coming from her purse. The universe is testing me today, and now I have to go home, change, and come back to campus, all while managing not to murder someone in the process.

My T-shirt still clings to my stomach and I'm grateful I didn't order hot coffee, or else Connor would be in a hole right now. Once he left, Hannah asked if she could borrow my car for the afternoon since she needs to go to the pet store. It turns out she and Brittany, another one of our sorority sisters, saw an ad for a local family looking to rehome two of their kittens, so they went to pick them up this morning. Since Hannah doesn't have a car of her own —and either walks to campus or catches a ride with me or a sister from the Mu Mansion—my car is her best option.

The Mansion is the apartment building where the majority of our sorority sisters live. We aren't technically supposed to have the big sorority houses like larger campuses or the ones in movies, but we found a work around by all moving into the same building. It's five stories with ten apartments, and two years ago our sorority sister Cristina's father bought the whole building making it easy for us to fill the place with Mu Eta Psi sisters.

He's a good landlord and lets us get away with a lot, but he has a no pets rule. Cristina graduated last year, so she won't tell on Hannah or Brittany, and Hannah already agreed to take on any fines we might get when this inevitably blows up in her face. Since she's the oldest triplet, she's a big instigator, always encouraging her brothers to do dumb shit that ultimately lands them in trouble. But she's always been good about taking responsibility for things when it's her fault. She's always pulling spontaneous stunts like this, but she'll short circuit if anyone suggests changing her plan.

As much as she's a pain, I'm lucky to have her at the same school as me. Coming from a big family, the probability of us all going to different colleges was high. Our parents were skeptical about us being roommates, worrying that we would get sick of each other, but it's like living with a sibling. We fight sometimes, but it never lasts for long. And I'd rather be living with someone who's sleeping habits I know from countless sleepovers instead of learning about a stranger.

Finally in the apartment I drop my bag and spin to face my cousin, who has pulled the kitten out of her purse and is holding her up toward me.

"Pwease don't be mad at me," she says in a voice I assume is meant for the cat. She knows me too well and targets my weakness for baby animals.

I roll my eyes and take the kitten from her, tucking her close to my face. Her little nose sniffs my ear and it tickles, while her paws rest on my neck to keep herself steady.

"I'm not sure what I'm more mad about because there are a lot of options. Connor showing up here unannounced, me being covered in coffee, or you getting a secret cat." I pause and she's nodding, waiting for me to continue. I'm used to her stunts, so I'm honestly not surprised she ended up getting a pet that we aren't supposed to have. "What hurts the most is that you didn't take me with you to get her."

A wave of relief washes over Hannah's face, making me laugh as she runs at me and squeezes me tight. "You're so right. Next time I go get a pet I'll take you with me no matter what," she says into my shoulder.

She backs away and I hand her Greta. "I need to wash off and change, then can you take me back to campus before going to the store?"

"Absolutely of course, thank you thank you." Hannah jumps around and makes Greta do a dance in her arms.

Thirty minutes later I'm in the original outfit I had planned for today. It's a pink floral sundress that I can still get away with wearing since it's the end of August. The capped sleeves are my favorite feature, and I paired them with a small wedge sandal. Putting the final touches on my eyeliner I finally feel ready to take on the day like I was supposed to this morning. I will not let being late, spilled coffee, and Connor fucking O'Shea ruin my first day. Heading out into the living room, I sit on the couch across from Hannah, who has a sleeping Greta curled up in her lap.

"How long until you need to be back?" she asks.

"I don't have class again until tonight, but I need to go to the office to get information for the fundraising event, so no more than an hour cause you know how long they can take. Plus I want to start researching internship options." I sigh and glance down at my phone to confirm I'll have plenty of time to get my errands done. It's early to start looking for internships, but I'm determined to find the best fit for me that will help me learn how to start my own event planning business. Ideally, I want to find one for next semester here and one for summer at home to gain as much experience as possible so people trust me with their events.

"Not a great first day so far?" she inquires.

"Ohmygod I didn't tell you the best part." I sit up and lean closer to her. "Shannon called me about the wedding again and is now trying to set me up with someone's grandson? I can't remember, but she sent me a photo." I pull up the messages with my mom and toss the phone at Hannah. We've gotten into the habit of referring to our parents by their first names, since yelling "Mom" in a room with our family makes them all turn around. Now it's easier to say everyone's first names so there's no confusion.

She looks at it, shrugs, and tosses it back my way. "Why won't she leave you alone?"

"I don't know, I was so desperate to get off the phone that I told her I would find a date by the end of September if she would stop. And now I have to come up with a plan of how to do that."

"You could bring one of the sisters?" she suggests.

"Thought about it, but I need more than just a friend date," I say, since I'm not interested in dating any of our sorority sisters.

"Explain," she says.

"Well, I'd love for her to get off my back for more than the wedding. If I want to focus on finding an internship I'm going to need her to stop pushing people on me. I don't have time to add 'deflect Shannon's comments' to my to-do list."

She furrows her eyebrows at me in confusion. "How could you do that?"

"I'm going to lie to her, and you're going to help me." I

point at her, standing up and starting to pace. Hannah watches me with concern as I start laps around the room. "Hear me out. If I find someone to be my date then what happens when I bring them?" I pause and look at her.

"You'll get a million questions," she nods, starting to understand where I'm going with this.

"I'll get a million questions," I confirm. "Is this new? Who is this? Am I keeping them around? If I hire someone to be in a fake relationship that could buy me months of Shannon-free nagging. After the wedding I'll bring them up in conversation and then after a few months I'll tell her how we broke up."

"Wait so you're going to hire someone for months?" Hannah is back to being confused.

"That's just it, I'm not. I only need them until the wedding. I'll stock up on photos and since they're here no one else in the family has to know we aren't actually dating. Do you know how much work I could get done without her constant calls and unsolicited friends' grandsons?"

"You could finally pick a business name and logo." She points out with a raise of her eyebrows. I've spent the summer texting her all kinds of names and logo ideas for my event planning business, needless to say I have not settled on one.

"I could finally pick a business name and logo," I shout, throwing my hands up in the air and falling back onto the couch. Greta pops her head up at my movement and moves off Hannah's lap toward me. "But I don't know where to start with all of this," I say, placing Greta on my lap, she starts purring when I scratch under her chin and there's no way I'm letting Hannah get rid of her.

"Why don't you post about it on the bulletin board outside the Veva Café?" she asks, bringing up the campus's infamous 'Seeking' board. It mostly has ads for people searching for roommates, jobs, or the occasional help moving.

"That's brilliant. I'm going to write it now." I hand Greta back to her and find our craft bin to make a poster. Pulling out a bright sheet of construction paper and some colored markers, I write out what I'm looking for.

WANTED: WEDDING DATE

I (20F) am looking for someone to attend my cousin's wedding with me on Nov. 1. Convincing my mother we are in a relationship is a _must_.

Will pay in food, willing to discuss terms.

Open interviews at the Veva Café August 26 12pm-2pm.

Look for the girl in pink.

SERIOUS INQUIRIES ONLY PLS

I have Hannah proofread it before slipping it into my backpack and heading out the door.

## CONNOR

Standing outside The Learning Center doors, I'm unable to bring myself to cross the threshold. I have no reason to be scared to go in there, but something is telling me to run far in the other direction.

Deciding to transfer here after finishing two years at community college was easy, according to my parents. My grades weren't the best, and it was clear I needed some help. The Learning Center here has some of the best tutoring options for everyone, at least that's what my advisor told us. My dad didn't understand why accounting didn't come easily to me. He graduated top of his class, started his accounting job right out of college, and he's been there ever since. Meanwhile, I'm playing the good son and taking the easiest career route I possibly can. I figured since we were so alike already that accounting would be easy. Then I could graduate and interview at his firm, working side-by-side with him like we always talked about. I should be grateful I have this sitting in my lap, but I only feel like I'm letting him down by not being good enough. We're usually on the same page with everything. We like the same board games, video games, and movies. It's frustrating that this doesn't come as easily to me as it does to him.

He threw me a curve ball last semester when he saw my grades were less than ideal. I remember him standing in the kitchen cooking dinner while I sat at the counter with my head down. *"Connor, you need to apply yourself more,"* he had said. *"You're smarter than this. If you don't keep your GPA above a 3.5 then I'm not going to be able to interview you when you graduate."*

I could switch majors and find something else to do, but I've already sunk two years into this accounting degree. I keep telling myself I don't need to be passionate about accounting to be good at it. I mean, is anyone passionate about accounting? Jobs are only jobs, I'll have plenty of time to do things outside of work, but I want something stable that allows me time for myself and family. When I eventually have kids I want to be like my dad, always home for dinner and there during the holidays. Teaching my kids games and showing them movies that my dad showed me.

When I got accepted here I agreed to get a tutor no matter what, to make sure my semester started off as strong as possible. But I can't find it in myself to admit defeat yet. I don't need help, I can do this on my own. I've never needed a tutor before, so why start now? It's only math, I'm sure I'll be able to figure it out.

I adjust my backpack and turn around, leaving The Learning Center behind me to head back to my apartment since I'm done with classes for the day. The idea of going back there isn't any better, though, because my roommate hates me.

I didn't know anyone here, and couldn't afford an

apartment on my own, so I ended up finding someone who needed a roommate through the college's transfer Facebook group.

When I get back to the apartment my gut tightens at the sight of my roommate's car in the driveway. He doesn't say much to me, and I get the feeling that he isn't in the market for any new friends.

"Hey, man," I greet him when I walk through the door to find him on the couch watching something I don't recognize.

He doesn't say anything, throwing his hand up in a weak wave and turning up the TV. Message received, loud and clear.

I make myself scarce, heading to the kitchen to grab a drink. When I open the fridge, half the things are now labeled with scotch tape that all say 'Brad Smith.' Guess we won't be sharing any food either. I roll my eyes and grab a can from a box of Mountain Dew that I'm going to have to label as mine.

I wish I had worked harder to find a roommate, because it sucks having no clue where to start when it comes to making friends. At my previous school I was a part of a small gaming club—if a group of four guys playing board games every two weeks counts. Here, the clubs and any other school activities don't start for a few more weeks. Until then, I'm essentially alone.

I retreat to my room to play my Nintendo Switch and rest. I ignore the plastic bins full of my clothes as I enter my room and grab my Switch from the nightstand and fall onto my bed. The screen comes to life as I select *Slay the Spire*. I'm about to start a new game when I feel my phone vibrating in my pocket and pull it out to see my dad is calling.

"Hey, Dad," I answer and hit the speaker button, setting the phone next to my head so I can talk and play at the same time.

"Glad I caught you, how was your first day?" he asks, the happiness in his voice bringing my mood up. I can always count on him to make my day better, and I'd give anything to be at home with him playing a game or watching a movie. Ever since I can remember, board games, video games, and horror movies have been our thing. We're always on the lookout for new expansion packs, releases, and vintage memorabilia. It drives my mom crazy when we stay up until two in the morning determined to finish a game as a horror movie plays in the background, but that's only when she doesn't join us. We're big fans of the classic Universal Monster horror movies, and my dad has a whole VHS collection of them in the basement where our VCR is.

All the things I could tell him about today run through my head, but the only thing that flashes through my mind is Maeve and her various pissed off expressions. I don't feel like explaining to him how I fucked up and picked a school where the only people I know are two camping regulars, one of which hates me.

"It was good, I didn't get lost," I say instead, hoping he doesn't ask me about my specific classes.

"That's great. And did you sign up for a tutor?" he asks, and I can hear the tilt of his head toward me, waiting for an answer. I can't tell him I took one look at the door and turned around. I need to make it through the first few quizzes to see if I really need help. Then I'll go back and sign up for one.

"Sure did, it was super easy." The lie slips out of me easier than I expected. I don't like lying to my dad, and my stomach twists in knots. We never keep secrets, but I need to do this one thing without his help.

"Perfect," he sighs into the phone. "I also sent you that expansion pack for *Eldritch Horror that* we've been searching for, check it out and we can play next time you're home."

*Eldritch Horror* is one of our favorite cooperative board games. We rarely win and it always takes us several hours to complete. Brad will have no interest in playing, but I hope whatever club I find is open to it since it's not a game you can win easily by yourself. I've played as multiple characters alone, but that's not as fun compared to playing with someone else.

"Sounds like a plan, everything good at home with you and Mom?" I ask. Today is Monday which means they'll have some type of chicken meal planned for dinner.

"Everything is peachy, cooking chicken parm tonight and looking forward to it," he says and I smile at how predictable my parents are. Part of me misses living with them and the comfort of it, but I'm also glad to be on my own for the first time.

We talk for a few more minutes about their plans for the week and other upcoming game releases. He tells me about how my sister, Morgan, and her wife are doing in New York City. Morgan moved there after college, and with our eight year gap sometimes it feels like I'm an only child. I looked into schools near her, thinking it would be smart to go to school near my family, but none of them felt like the right fit. Mo and I have always had a weird relationship with the age gap, but she's always there for me when I need her.

By the time we wrap up our phone call, my mood has started to turn around. It feels good to talk to someone today who actually likes me. I wish any other camper was in my class instead of Maeve, because they would have been easier to talk to.

Tomorrow, I'm determined to have a better day. I'll have all new classes and hopefully Maeve won't be in any of them, but I'm going to have to see her on Wednesday again in our finance class. I do my best not to think about her, her hazel eyes, or wet clothes clinging to her body for the rest of the night.

# FIVE

## MAEVE

It's been over a week since I posted the wedding date ad to the bulletin board. I've heard a few people bring up the flyer, but no one has figured out it was me yet, and I wasn't planning on broadcasting that fact.

They're all about to find out now though, since it's almost time for me to commandeer a table in Veva Café. I'm waiting for my iced coffee and I can see everyone looking around and whispering more than usual. It feels like all of their eyes are on me, which I don't usually mind, but right now I want to get this over with. Maybe this was a bad idea and I can sneak out of here before anyone starts asking questions. I could take the poster down later when no one is around and pretend this never happened. But then I'd be subject to a date of my mother's choosing. She's already sent me several more options since our phone call, and I politely informed her I was serious about handling the situation myself. I considered blocking her number, but Hannah said that's a bit dramatic.

I find a spot in the corner and sit against the wall, giving me the perfect view of the café, luckily there's no one else in here wearing pink. I'm keeping an eye out for anyone who looks lost right as a tall timid guy steps in front of my table.

He must be a few inches over six-feet, dark hair, and staring down at his feet as he whispers, "Are you the one looking for the wedding date?"

"I am, I'm Maeve. Have a seat please." I gesture toward the empty chair across from me. I pull out my notebook with a carefully crafted chart of questions and space to fill in names. I'm not about to pick the first person who shows up; I have to make sure they're the right fit or this whole thing blows up in my face.

He sits down and makes himself comfortable, pushing the table toward me as he spreads his legs out under it. I have to grab my iced coffee before it spills all over me; I don't need another coffee disaster this month.

"Right, so do—"

"How much can you pay me?" he cuts me off and it seems all his timidness is gone now that he's sat down.

"I can't pay you, I said I can pay you in food," I reply, attempting to keep the annoyed tone out of my voice.

"Fine, it also said you were willing to discuss terms." He rolls his eyes and leans closer to me. "That's code, right?"

I can feel my blood starting to boil under my skin, and it takes everything in me not to reach across the table and slap this guy. He hasn't even introduced himself and now he wants to know if I'm willing to trade sex for a date? This was such a bad idea.

"No," I say as I collect myself. "It's not code. But I'm also not interested in whatever you might have planned, please leave." I point with my pen toward the café doors and cross my arms.

"Seriously?" he groans. "This was such a waste of

time, I don't want to be your date anyway, you're such a bitch." He stands up from the table and storms out, and I only have time to take three deep breaths before someone else is walking up to the table.

The next two hours go similarly. Everyone either wants to get paid in cash, or wants me to fuck them. One girl asked if I was willing to let her practice her stick and poke tattoos on me, while another wanted me to watch her pet bird for the entirety of December. My iced coffee is long gone, replaced by gum so I don't bite my nails as this whole situation gets worse.

I'm struggling to focus on the guy in front of me right now. He seems fine, and he hasn't asked me for money or sex. He's telling me about his high school track and field stats, which is a red flag that he peaked in high school, but he's my last interview of the day. If I don't pick this guy, I'm going to have to find someone else or be stuck with my mom's pick.

His ramblings are going in and out of my ears as I pop my gum and check my phone to make sure I haven't gotten any emails from my internship prospects. Over the last week I've sent out countless emails introducing myself to various companies and event planners, but no one has emailed me back yet. I'm going to have to start calling them to check in if I don't hear soon, and that's the last thing I want to add to my to-do list.

Glancing up from my phone, I catch sight of Connor standing near the pickup counter as the guy in front of me continues to boast about high school. I make the mistake of making eye contact and see Connor's already staring at me. He smirks and gives me a small nod and I feel my face heat. I don't need him here to witness this, it'll only be something he can make fun of me for later.

We've done a good job over the past week at not

speaking to each other. Unfortunately, seats have been final since the first day, so he still sits behind me twice a week. There's a 100 percent chance he's going to ruin our lovely silent streak and bring this up tomorrow during class.

I bring my focus back to the guy in front of me, reviewing my notes to remember his name—Justin. He's still talking so I let my gaze drift back toward where Connor is, but he's not there. I don't know why I care if he's still there or not, but I look around to see if I can find him.

Finally, I spot him with a coffee in his hand and heading right at me. His smirk looks more devious than before and my heart starts to race, but probably not as fast as Justin's record. He better not be coming over here right now.

Before I can wrap up this interview, Connor grabs a chair from the table next to us and pulls it up. Sitting right between me and Justin he rests his elbows on the table and takes a sip of his coffee before speaking.

"Afternoon, Maeve," he says, turning toward me and ignoring Justin completely. "Mind if I step in for a second?"

"Who is this guy?" Justin raises his eyebrow and I want to tell him I'm right there with him in his anger. Before my brain can process what's happening Connor is speaking again and shaking Justin's hand.

"Connor, nice to meet you. I'm here to vet you for Maeve." He has the audacity to wink at me and my mouth falls open. "I need to make sure you're ready for her family."

"Um, what?" Justin sputters.

"Justin, he's not—"

"Maeve, we have to make sure Justin here is ready for the wedding," Connor interrupts me. "I know her family, they're dear family friends," he explains to Justin, resting his hand over his heart. "Are you prepared to suffer through the pranks of her cousins and talk to her dad with a shotgun pointed at you?"

Justin's eyes go wider the more Connor talks, and I can't tell if I want to scream or laugh. Instead, I focus on my gum so I don't do either.

"Actually," Justin sputters as he picks up his backpack and stands from the table, almost tripping over his seat. "I'm not interested anymore, good luck." Then he's off and out of the café. He wasn't kidding about the sprinting record he set.

"Why did you do that?" I yell, hitting Connor's arm in the process.

"Ow, that hurt." He rubs his arm and turns toward me.

"He was my last chance at finding a date to Charlie's wedding. Why do you have to make things in my life so hard?" I rub my face and fall back in my chair.

"That's what she said," he mumbles under his breath.

"I hate you, you know that, right?" I shake my head, biting my lip to hide my laugh. As much as I want to be mad at him right now, I'm grateful he came over and stopped me from picking Justin. I'd rather figure out another solution than pick any of the people I've talked to in the last two hours.

"Yeah I'm okay with that. I was bored and had some time to kill, so I thought I'd spend it with someone I know. I thought that poster on the board might have been yours," he shrugs and sips his coffee. "Why do you need a date for Charlie's wedding anyway?"

"Do you really care?" I cross my arms and look at him.

He pulls his phone out of his pocket and glances at it. "I've still got a few minutes, so yes, I do care."

"So glad you could pencil me in," I say.

"Of course, extra charity work always looks great on a resume." He winks at me.

"First of all, fix whatever is wrong with your eye. Second of all fuck you. Go find someone else to bother." I shove my notebook into my bag and stand up. Moving around him to leave, I'm not going to sit here and explain my problems to him if he's only going to be an asshole. I thought for a second maybe I could talk through the last two hours with someone, but it seems like he's only here to make fun of me.

I storm out of the café and leave him sitting at the table alone. He doesn't call after me or get up to follow me, which is probably best for his safety.

## SIX

## CONNOR

Ever since my run in with Maeve, I've been off. I planned to apologize to her in class the next day, but took the coward's way out and waited right until class started. I leaned forward and whispered how I was sorry for crashing her date search, only to be met with a shrug of her shoulders. She didn't turn around, and I wasn't sure if the dizziness in my head was from her dismissal or the sudden realization that she smelled like a mixture of cinnamon and a fruit I couldn't pinpoint.

On top of that, last week we had our first quiz and I spent half of the time staring at the questions. It was like they were written in another language. I'm sure I failed the quiz, and I went to the Learning Center after. Finally willing to admit defeat and figure out ways to improve whatever is making this so difficult. It turns out, the tutoring spots fill up during the first three weeks of classes, so I'm officially on my own and I have no one to blame but myself.

I've been dreading coming to class all weekend to get my quiz back. Professor Kader is old school and told us she wouldn't be posting our grades online until she physically gave the quiz back to us. My leg is bouncing out of control as she advances around the room and hands them out. At least she's handing them back face down, preventing everyone from seeing how badly I did.

Other students sigh in relief and high five each other when they get theirs back. It doesn't look like too many people are disappointed, and I bet I'm the only one who massively failed. She's making her way down the aisle toward me now, stopping and handing Maeve her quiz first.

Maeve nods and sets the paper down on her desk, but Professor Kader steps into my line of sight before I can see how she did. I look up at her and the disappointment in her eyes is front and center as she hands me my quiz.

I reluctantly take it from her before she walks away. Taking a deep breath I peek at the top corner of the quiz, lifting it up and seeing a red F across the top. I don't need to see more, and shove it in my backpack, I don't care if it gets ripped or torn.

Looking back toward the front of the room, I sit up straighter to peer over Maeve's shoulder. It's not hard to do with my height, and her quiz is still on her desk. The large A mocks me from a distance and I can't tell if I want to cry or scream. I'm so sick of not understanding what I'm learning, and she just gets an A?

I didn't think she was dumb, but I wasn't expecting an A. Maybe a B- or a B at the highest. But I guess the Barbie doll sorority girl has got some book smarts too.

I'm useless the rest of class, unable to pay attention or take notes, only able to think about how I can fix this. Listening to the lecture would have probably been the first step, but I didn't understand the last three so it seems like there's no point until I figure out a tutor solution.

I bet I could find another student willing to help me, but I still haven't met anyone yet. It's been three lonely weeks, and the club sign-up night proved useless when I found out there isn't a gaming club on this campus. Brad has managed to become a ghost. I only know he's alive because his food disappears from the fridge and towels appear in the bathroom. I ended up spending my birthday last week buying my first legal pack of beer and using a Frankenstein's monster pint glass my dad sent me as I watched horror movies alone. I should have taken my parents up on their suggestion to visit and celebrate with me, but I didn't. I'm starting to wonder why I even came to this school.

I scan the room and brainstorm potential people in here to ask, but I only know Maeve. Maeve who hates me. Maeve who got an A. Maeve who might still need a date to Charlie's wedding.

A pit forms in my stomach as my best worst idea comes together, and if it doesn't work I'm not sure what I'm going to do. What's the worst that could happen? She says no? It's not like she would say no by throwing a coffee on me, although I probably deserve it. My leg bounces faster the more I think about it now that I have a plan and the end of class is only a few minutes away. I rehearse what I want to say, sure I'll mess it up when it comes time to ask her.

After the longest class of my life, Professor Kader finally dismisses us. Maeve moves quickly, out of her chair and into the hallway faster than half the class. I have to rush to make sure I don't trip over any of the desks, my long legs prone to catch on at least one chair leg.

I finally make it out of the classroom and spot her down the hall. She isn't hard to miss with her pink crewneck and matching pink scrunchie, her hair bouncing back and forth as she walks.

"Maeve," I call. "Wait up!"

I see her stop abruptly and slowly turn my way, her gaze shoots daggers at me and I contemplate turning around and pretending it wasn't me who called for her. Running in the opposite direction and hoping she never brings it up again. But I need her right now as much as she might need me.

She crosses her arms and waits for me to catch up to her, making no move to meet me halfway, and I have to applaud her for that. I wouldn't move to meet me either.

"What do you want?" she asks when I stop in front of her.

"Can we talk over here for a second?" I gesture toward a small alcove with windows in the hallway, not wanting anyone to over hear what I'm about to ask her.

She sighs and rolls her eyes, popping her gum and following me over a few steps.

"I have a proposition for you," I say, not wasting any time. If she ends up saying no I want to get it over with as fast as possible.

"Explain." She waves her hand toward me.

"Are you still looking for a wedding date?" I ask, adjusting my backpack to my other shoulder.

"Yes." She narrows her eyes at me and I can see her gum sitting in the side of her mouth when she talks.

"I want to be your date." I lower my voice and look behind me to make sure no one can hear.

"No fucking way, not happening." She shakes her head and tries to move to go around me.

I step in front of her, nearly crashing into her before she can get far. "Please, Maeve. I need a favor."

"Fine." She steps back from me and tilts her head. "You have thirty seconds to explain why on earth I would want to spend any more time with you than I already have to." She pulls her phone from her pocket, unlocking it and starting a timer for thirty seconds, holding it up so I can see it counting down.

I panic and all the words come rushing out of me in a few breaths, "I need a tutor and you did well on the quiz. So I thought you could tutor me and I would go to the wedding with you. You said you needed to convince your mom you're in a relationship and I already know your family so it would be easier than explaining everything to some newbie." I finish, taking a deep breath as the timer counts down the final ten seconds.

She's staring at me with her mouth wide open, gum almost falling out, as the timer goes off. "You're serious?" she asks.

"Yes," is all I say. She must think I've lost my mind, but I've thought this out for the last eighty minutes. We both have something the other needs, and I'm willing to put aside my indifference toward her if she is. There will never be enough time in the world for me to get used to her loud personality. She's not the type of girl who would sit and play board games with me on a Friday night. She's got the same vibe as my ex and her friends—bubbly, probably fake, and will never see me as a serious romantic partner— but I can suffer through all that if it means I can make my dad proud.

"Oh, that's rich, you've lost your goddamn mind, O'Shea. Good luck with your grades, but I'm not helping you." She steps around me and I let her go, I'm not going to stand here and beg her.

I watch her walk away, and decide I have one last bit of desperation in me. "At least think about it!" I shout after her.

Her middle finger is the only reply I get.

## SEVEN

MAEVE

Hannah is on the couch watching *Schitt's Creek* with Greta asleep on her lap when I return home. Greta has adapted well to our apartment, but her favorite spot has to be on a warm lap while taking a nap. There have been several occasions where I've woken up from my own nap to find Greta curled up next to or on top of me.

"You will not believe what happened to me today," I shout, dropping my backpack and myself into the pink armchair next to the couch, knocking one of our decorative pillows to the floor in the process. Hannah and I have spent countless hours shopping online and browsing the local home stores to perfect our apartment's aesthetic. There's probably too much pink, but she doesn't seem to mind.

"One of your videos went viral and you got a brand deal so you're dropping out of college?" Her guess takes me off guard and I freeze as I stare at her. I should be used to this, she's always doing and saying the last thing you would expect. One time her and her brothers replaced all their nice Christmas cards with a less flattering family photo. Their dads were not pleased, but the rest of the family loved them. We had one turned into a magnet and it's currently on our fridge with a million other pictures. Honestly, with all the dances they do post on social media they would go viral for being triplets before any of my outfit of the day videos did.

"Fuck, I wish. But sadly no," I finally reply. "Connor asked me to tutor him in exchange for going to the wedding. Which sounds like the last thing I want to do." I recap the thirty second speech to her and Greta's little ears perk up as her eyes slowly open, clearly she loves drama as much as we do.

"Okay, so tell your mom you aren't bringing a date? Then this whole thing solves itself, and you can stop worrying about it," she suggests, probably sick of hearing me complain about it.

"No, I can't tell her that. I need to guarantee she will leave me alone. She's still sending me dates because she doesn't think I'll be able to find one." I show her my text message thread with my mom, full of photo after photo of random guys her friends know who would be 'good for me.'

"Damn, that's some persistence, Aunt Shan. Maybe you should have blocked her." Hannah shakes her head. "Don't you have enough to do this semester though? You have the fundraiser next month."

"Yeah, that's true," I agree, knowing my to-do list grows several more pages by the day. I'm going to end up needing a new planner by the end of this month if I keep it up. Between class work, the fundraiser, and researching internships I barely have time for myself. Flipping through the other photos my mom has sent me, I dread the upcoming weeks and how many more dates she's going to send my way. If I don't find someone to go to the wedding with me I'm going to have to deal with whoever she picks, including having to make small talk and explain the giant Murphy family. Which is not something I have the energy for. Connor's face from this morning flashes through my mind and a hint of guilt creeps in at brushing him off so quickly. He looked so broken down about his grade, worse than when we beat him in volleyball this summer. I gasp when I realize Connor was right. "Wait, if Connor comes to the wedding I wouldn't have to take the time to teach him as much about our family."

"No that's not—"

"Sure I have to take time to tutor him, but that's what? Two hours a week?"

"I mean—"

"And it'll be easy. Our cousins like him for some ungodly reason."

"What if—"

"Han, you're brilliant. Why didn't I process this before? I definitely should tell him yes."

"Maeve!"

"What?" I stop and look up at her.

"This isn't going to work, you can barely hold a conversation with him." I hear the disapproval in her tone, but I'm going to ignore it.

"Well, I guess I have to practice. I'll, ugh, spend time with him," I say through a full-body shudder.

"I think it's a bad idea. You're either going to kill him or fall in love with him." Hannah shakes her head and scratches Greta's head.

"I won't fall in love with him, that's some made up thing for books and movies. I don't even like him. How could I fall in love with him?" I retort.

"Well if you end up killing him I'll help you hide the body."

"Thank you, glad to have your full support on this."

"You don't," Hannah corrects as my phone starts to ring.

"I totally do." I wink at her. "But I have to answer this, it's Ry." Ryan—my older brother—is right on time for our weekly check-in call. He's got some boring finance job I can never remember the name of, and the least I can do is entertain him with some college drama once a week. He might act like he doesn't love me sometimes, but I bet he looks forward to this call as much as I do.

"See if he thinks it's a good idea," she shouts as I disappear down the hall.

"You really think this is a good idea?" Ry says for the millionth time in the last thirty minutes.

I filled him in on all the details of Situation Connor, since he was already familiar with my deal with our mom. Since he's been around Connor more during our summer vacations than I have, I was hoping he would have some helpful insight to the situation, but he's only got questions.

"I do. We both need something the other can provide," I state. "Unless you want me to put up some shady Craigslist ad for a date?"

I hear Ry sigh, and I can picture him running his hand over his face like he always does when I've bested him. "No, don't do that. I guess go with Connor. But can I tell you something?" He shifts to a more serious tone and I start to worry.

"What?"

"You know I can hear how stressed you are, right?" he asks.

"That's a question," I say, avoiding telling him the

answer. I'm aware I'm stressed, but I work best under pressure.

"Maeve, be serious." His voice holds a big brother scowl that silently says 'I know more than you.'

"Fine, I might be a tad stressed," I admit.

"You don't have to figure everything out on your own. You don't have to plan the fundraiser by yourself." He pauses, waiting for a response from me. I'm starting to get annoyed, so I only grunt before he continues. "I can help you with Mom, and your sorority sisters can help you with the event. If you agree to tutor Connor you aren't going to have enough time to do your own work or keep searching for the internship you need. Are you sure you want to do this? He can figure something else out."

"Yes, I'm sure. I'm not doing this to help him, I'm doing it to help me. Mom won't leave me alone, so I need to shut her up. You don't have to listen to her. You're a man, you don't have the same pressure from her to follow in her footsteps. Not bringing a date is only going to open the door for her to keep trying to set me up. I'll figure everything else out, don't worry about me," I tell him, well aware of the fact my internship goals are looking more like a summer goal instead of next semester with all the things I've been adding to my plate.

"I can't help it. One last question?" he asks.

"Shoot."

"You're not doing this because you secretly like Connor, are you?"

A burst of laughter explodes from my lips before I can stop it. Of all people, Ry having the audacity to ask me if I secretly like a lifeguard is so ironic, and I don't think he realizes it. He's had a crush on the head lifeguard, Cyrus, for years now and he's been too scared to do anything about it. "You're one to talk Mr. I've-Liked-Cy-For-Years-

But-I-Pretend-I-Don't," I shout into the phone. Ry sputters, but I don't let him get a word in. "For your information, I don't like Connor in any type of way, friendly or romantic. Which is why this situation is perfect. And if I do end up liking him—which I won't—I wouldn't be scared to say something. You're just mad I was able to snag a lifeguard before you were. Fuck you, Ryan. Love you and talk to you next week." I end the call and toss my phone onto my bed. My blood is boiling that he would accuse me of agreeing to the situation for a romantic benefit. I feel bad I yelled at him, but someone needed to call him on his bullshit. We're all sick of it, but no one is brave enough to say anything to his face.

I need to do this and prove him wrong. Prove Hannah wrong.

If I can't balance planning one tiny event, school, and dating—well, fake dating—then I have no right to open my own event business. Doing this will prove to everyone I'm capable of handling myself. I'm not just some stereotypical sorority girl in the movies who is obsessed with their looks and the cutest frat boy. If I can pull this off I'll show everyone I can do anything I want, and they can't stop me.

It looks like Connor just became my new boyfriend—*fake* boyfriend.

I should probably tell him.

# EIGHT

## CONNOR

I've had the worst sleep in my twenty-one years over these last two nights. The conversation with Maeve won't stop replaying when I close my eyes. I bet she went home and laughed about it with Hannah. By now I'm sure all of her cousins have heard about how I begged her to tutor me. The story has probably gotten so out of hand that it's being told with me on my knees and my hands clasped in front of me. Next summer I'm sure they'll all waste no time bringing it up and making fun of me. It was a stupid fucking idea, and I never should have asked her. But now she won't get out of my head.

Her stupid brown hair up and off of her round face, hazel eyes burning me alive. Her expression, the picture of annoyance with that damn timer mocking me. I can hear the beeping of it when I try to sleep, and her face torments me like her image is burned into the back of my eyelids. And her spicy but sweet scent lingers around me like it's attached to my clothes or hair.

Our next class is finally here and I have to see her again—I'm going to have to see her every week. I'm trapped in a horror movie of my own making where I've opened my own personal portal to Hell.

Kill. Me. Now.

She still isn't here and class is about to start. I wouldn't be surprised if she transferred schools to avoid having to see me again. Who wants to see that awkward kid twice a week? Not her.

My leg's bouncing fast enough to shake the desk and I have to hold it down to get it under control while my heart pounds so hard I swear I can hear it. I see her shoes before I see her, the pink sparkly sneakers scream Maeve, and I'm annoyed I recognize them.

She drops her backpack to the floor, narrowly avoiding my foot in the process. When she takes a seat and spins around to face me, she doesn't say anything about almost severing my foot. I lift my head to see she's got her arms resting on my desk, tapping her pink nails on the surface. The rhythmic beat echoes through the classroom, getting louder with each tap and matching the rhythm of my heartbeat. I can't read her expression, but the pit in my stomach says she's about to say something mean and it's fifty-fifty on if I'm going to throw up or scream.

"I'll do it. First study session tomorrow," is all she says, and I'm frozen in place. When I don't reply she continues. "I'll text you the details."

"You don't have my number," I finally say, confused and shocked, unable to process what's happening. I think it's a good thing? But I'm also scared.

"No, but my cousins do." She rolls her eyes.

"But I'm literally right here, I can give it to you now," I say, confused why she needs to involve anyone else when she doesn't need to. It's probably because she wants to talk to me as little as possible.

"Fine," she sighs, rolling her eyes again and reaching

into her backpack to retrieve her phone. Her nails clack at the screen before she hands it to me, open to a new contact.

I take the phone from her, careful to avoid touching her fingers, and enter my number. Saving my name as 'My Favorite Lifeguard' with the lifesaver emoji, I hand it back to her with a smirk.

She peers down at the screen and this time, her eye roll is so aggressive that they look like they do a full three-sixty. "You think highly of yourself, I'm definitely changing that," she grumbles, tapping to edit the contact but Professor Kader clears her throat before she gets the chance. Maeve shoots me one last glare before spinning back to the front of the room as class starts.

Maeve doesn't give me time to ask her questions after class, running out of the room again. I have no clue where she goes after this, but she doesn't waste any time getting there.

I need to talk to someone about this and make sure it's a good idea before I get too far. What if it ends badly? I'd have to quit my summer job so I wouldn't have to see her or her family again.

I pull out my phone and open up one of my pinned group chats, BAYWATCH BOIS, which is blessed with a photo of me passed out clutching a unicorn stuffed animal I randomly found at a party. The group chat consists of me and two of the other lifeguards from Sutter State Park. Cy, who has worked there longer than I have, but recently left to run his late parents' bookstore. And Zach, who only worked there one summer, and is now in culinary school. He was Cy's college roommate and moved to Black Willow

Bay after he dropped out, and quickly found a place in our small town.

They're my two best friends, and I trust their opinions more than they know. Earlier this year, when we were up drinking late one night around a campfire I opened up to them about my sexuality and how something always felt off. I never felt like I experienced attraction the way other people do, always faking comments to fit in. With Cy and Zach being gay and bisexual, respectively, I could talk to them about it without any judgment.

After a few hours—and Googling some terms—I understood my sexual attraction to people wasn't based on looks but was dependent on my bond with said person.

I said, "I'm demisexual," out loud and Cy cheered while Zach did a cartwheel and I rolled my eyes at them trying not to draw attention to how I was blushing fiercely. The support from them was something I didn't realize I needed until they gave it, and it gave me the courage to come out to my parents as well.

When I told them, they gave me confused looks until I explained what it meant. The whole time I was worried they were going to be mad, but my dad simply nodded after my explanation and said, "That's cool, I like all these new terms now. I'll have to learn more of them." While my mom said, "You can be whatever you want and I'll still love you." When I called my sister to tell her she simply said, "That makes sense, I'm sending you a pin." That demisexual flag pin now lives on my backpack.

Understanding my demisexuality helped explain why I was never really interested sexually in my first girlfriend. We never got further than hand stuff, but I never felt like I was fully into it. She was nice at the beginning of the relationship, but the lack of sexual chemistry quickly became an issue and ultimately ended our short lived relationship.

In addition to Cy and Zach being my best friends, they both know the Murphy family well. Cy has known them since he's worked at the campground, and Zach had a fling with Sidney, one of the Murphy cousins, two summers ago. They ended on a good note with him going to school in New York and her moving to California. I bet I will see her at Charlie's wedding—if I go.

I contemplate what I should text them, typing and deleting several messages, before finally deciding what to send:

CONNOR

If I was hypothetically in a situation where I found myself at school with Maeve Murphy and agreed to be her date to a Murphy wedding—how badly does that end for me?

ZACH

Sorry did I miss something this summer?? Do you like Maeve now??

CY

Who is texting us and what have you done with Connor?

CONNOR

No you didn't miss anything. And this IS Connor. Long story short, we are swapping skills. Her brains for my amazing dance moves. Bad idea or no?

CY

Yes

ZACH

No

CY

You can't dance

CONNOR

Great, this is helpful

CY

You two don't get along, I don't see this ending well

ZACH

This is a great opportunity for you to come out of your shell

CY

Wait yes, that is true

CONNOR

What? I'm plenty out of my shell

ZACH

It took you three months to say hi to me the first year

CONNOR

Semantics

ZACH

I say do it, she's a good match for you

CONNOR

To be clear, this is not an actual date. I am using her to get my grades up

CY

Sureeee, dude

ZACH

Yeah, you sure about that?

CONNOR

Hundred percent, plus she'd never be interested in me in any type of romantic way. There's no way we'd ever get feelings for each other

CY

Don't sell yourself short

ZACH

Hate is a feeling too. And anyone would be lucky to date you

CONNOR

Okay, I don't need a therapy session. That was not the point of this text. Thank you for the insight, goodbye

CY

Good luck!

ZACH

Give Maeve a hug for us!

I reply with the middle finger emoji and right before I put my phone in my pocket I get another message.

UNKNOWN NUMBER

Library study room 4 at 2 tomorrow

I send a thumbs up emoji back and save Maeve's number to my phone under 'Barbie.'

C onnor shows up to our first study session ten minutes early, which surprises me. I had bet Hannah he would be at least fifteen minutes late, so it looks like I'm buying us dinner tonight. I guess I shouldn't be too surprised, since this study session is for him and not me, but I've trained my brain to expect the worst from him. Stemming from the first time we met and instantly started fighting.

He looks less exhausted than he did yesterday, the bags under his eyes less visible. But his messy red hair and black hoodie and sweatpants combo tell me I might be wrong. I feel bad, but that disappears when he opens his mouth.

"Do you have to wear pink every day? Is that a sorority requirement or something?" He waves his hand toward my outfit. Little does he know this is toned down, I left my sparkly pink shoes at home today in favor of my favorite pair of white Keds. But my pink floral sundress and pink cardigan are a little loud—for him, not me.

"Why? Do you have something against the color?" I

cross my arms and straighten my back, proving his words can't hurt me.

"No, you just always look like a Barbie and I wasn't sure if it was on purpose," he says, pulling his notebook and textbook out of his bag.

"Barbie is an icon, so thank you for the compliment. Meanwhile you look like the Empire State Building at that height," I bite back. "Wait, do you run their social media accounts? Is that why they're so snappy?"

"Clever, but no." He rolls his eyes at me, pulling out his laptop from his backpack.

"Bummer, I would have had to get your autograph. Now let's discuss this whole thing." I gesture to the space between us, switching the subject before he can tease me more.

"What's there to discuss? Let's study." He furrows his eyebrows at me in confusion, and no wonder he needs help, he's probably one of those people who doesn't study until the night before.

"Connor, my tall ginger acquaintance, we need to plan. If you can handle that."

"Fine, what do we need to do?" He groans and leans back in his chair. His legs reach my side of the table, moving quickly when his foot accidentally hits mine.

"First, I was thinking about studying Tuesdays and Thursdays at this time, in this room. Does that work for your schedule?" I ask him, opening up my planner. I'll need to book this room online for the rest of the semester to make sure we don't have any issues.

"Yeah, that works. But I don't have classes on Friday, so I'd rather not stay on campus any later than I need to. Could we study at my apartment on Thursdays?"

"That works, I don't have classes on Friday either. Text me your address," I tell him, writing this change in my planner as my phone dings with a text from him. I might book the room for Thursdays anyway, because if his apartment is disgusting there's no way I'm spending an hour every week there. It's bad enough I have to spend my weekend at frat house parties. I don't know if I could handle another place where the bathroom hasn't been cleaned since the house was built.

"What else?" he asks, setting his phone down and crossing his arms.

"We need to lay out rules for the fake boyfriend thing," I pause, waiting to see if he has any objections. When he only stares at me, I continue. "We need to keep this deal quiet. If all my cousins find out about this my aunts will find out, then my mom will find out and we don't want that."

"Why not?"

"I need her to believe I'm on track for society's college-engagement-marriage path and leave me alone," I explain.

"Why?"

"Why do you care?" I snap back.

He shrugs and mumbles, "I dunno."

I stare at him, waiting for him to say more. To explain why he would possibly care about my motivations for wanting to get my mom off my back. But I also want to tell everyone about my plans, so I spill. "I want to open my own event planning business. If I get my mom off my back then I will have more time to focus on that."

"Neat," he says with a small nod.

"Anyway, I told Hannah and Ry but they will keep it a secret. If you tell the other lifeguards, please tell them to keep it a secret."

"Got it, I only told Cy and Zach. They won't tell. What do we have to do to convince your mom we're dating?" he asks, sitting up and leaning against the table.

"Considering we don't have the best track record, we need to practice."

"Practice like, doing *stuff*?" His face starts turning red, making his freckles stand out along his cheeks and nose. They're actually kind of cute, and I've never registered how much of him is covered in them before. I'm 90 percent sure they're all over his body, and my curiosity spikes at how high they go up his legs.

"Connor, no!" I shout, bringing my voice back down so somebody passing by doesn't think I'm in trouble. "The first rule is there is no kissing whatsoever. Or other *stuff*."

"Thank God," he sighs.

"Yeah, you're right, thank God. I meant practice dates. We need to be comfortable around each other," I explain. "A few dates off campus before the wedding would be enough. That way we don't want to kill each other at the wedding."

"Works for me, as long as I don't have to kiss you. Cause, no offense, I'd rather eat moldy leftovers."

"Same, glad we are on the same page," I agree. "We also need to start planting the seeds, maybe a soft launch?"

"A what?"

"A soft launch of our relationship—fake relationship—on social media," I clarify, continuing when the confusion still coats his face. "I'm going to post a picture of us, but I won't show either of our faces. You'll do the same."

"That's so dumb." He rolls his eyes.

"Yeah well, this whole thing is dumb, so come over here." I point to the empty chair next to me.

Connor does as I ask, but not without huffing and acting like I've asked him the worst thing.

Pulling up the camera on my Instagram story, I move closer to him.

"I'm going to grab your hand, okay?" I ask, holding up the hand not holding my phone.

"Sure, fine, whatever. Make it fast." He flips his hand palm up on the table, leaving it open for mine.

Interlocking our fingers, I take a quick picture making sure our hands fill most of the frame. I add a pink heart and an orange heart and post it, hoping it will be good enough to work.

I feel a squeeze around my fingers and I jump, realizing I never let go of Connor's hand.

"Sorry, that's it." I pull back, but he squeezes again and keeps our hands in place on the table.

"You're good. But I have to do the same, right? Can I see what you posted?" he asks, leaning closer to me.

His scent invades my space and it takes a second for me to pull up the photo and show him as I attempt to figure out what he smells like. It reminds me of the summer, but it's not sunscreen or the river. It's fresh and bright but salty with a splash of zest, like the ocean and citrus. He nods when he sees the photo, releasing my hand and pulling my chair closer to his. I'm not sure what's louder: the wood of the chairs hitting and echoing through the room, or my heartbeat suddenly racing. I must've had too much caffeine today.

"Put your legs over mine," he says, leaning back and gesturing down to his lap. My brain short circuits from trying not to look at his crotch while simultaneously remembering the last time we had this much physical contact. He was pulling me back from getting into a fight during vacation, and the warmth of his arm around my waist was nice, and that pissed me off. Before I can answer, Connor jumps in at my hesitation. "Or not, it was a dumb idea. I'll do the hands too," he says, shaking his head.

"No, no. It's a good idea," I jump in before he gets out

of position, leaning back and throwing my legs over his. My dress moves up my legs at the quick motion, and the feel of his sweatpants against my skin is soft, and I can feel the warmth of his body through them. Crossing my ankles, my legs look perfectly at home over his and it's unsettling. "Like this?" I ask, making sure this is what he wanted, smoothing my dress skirt over my legs so it looks effortlessly draped.

"Can I rest my hand on your knee?" he asks, stumbling over the second half of the sentence as he holds his hand in the air and his phone in the other.

"That's fine." I nod, and when his hands rests over the spot above my knee, I try not to react to the skin to skin contact. His fingers aren't rough, but soft and I wouldn't be surprised if he uses lotion or if it's simply because he's not the sporty type.

He doesn't move his hand at all, no brush of his thumb or squeezing of my leg like I would expect someone who has their hand on me to do. Instead he lifts his phone above us and takes a photo before releasing my leg and typing on his phone. "This good?" He turns his phone toward me for approval, and I see he added the same two hearts I did. The photo shows just enough where you can see the edge of my dress, with his hand on my leg being the center focus. It's a pretty good photo, but I'm not about to tell him that.

"That's good. We should also follow each other," I say, removing my legs from his lap and trying to forget what the feel of his touch is like against my skin, and why it had my stomach twisting.

"Great, now we study?" Connor stands, returning to his side of the table right as my phone gets multiple notifications in a row. I glance at it and see messages from my cousins and sorority sisters rolling in too fast to count. I knew I could count on this generation to be chronically online.

"It's working already." I smile and show him my phone screen, with more messages incoming.

"Wow, people really need to get their own lives," he huffs, shaking his head. His phone has started to go off, too, but he slips it into his backpack.

I'm glad to see he seems serious about studying, so I also put my phone away. Opening my textbook, I can't help but think this might work out after all.

## TEN

CONNOR

I've suffered through two more study sessions with Maeve since the first one. I'm finally starting to understand the material, but I can't shake the feeling there's something deeper about why I can't focus on the material. Studying on campus is harder than studying at my apartment. Even if Maeve thinks it's nerdy, she still comes over.

When she first came over she managed to point out all the board games in my dining room and the multiple video game consoles in the living room. At least she was nice enough to bring cookies, which eased the sting of the nerd jokes. I assume they were from the Pride Alliance, since they had rainbow flags all over them. She must have picked them up on campus. She's always stopping and talking to people, and everyone seems to know who she is.

There's always someone who wants to talk to her. Even though she booked us a private room, her sorority sisters don't care. We kept getting interrupted by various sisters asking about their upcoming talent show, the event she's in charge of. She's been attempting to fill the remaining spots and sometimes I feel like she should get help with the event, but I'd never bring that up to her. I learned more about her event compared to our actual class while studying on campus, so I can brush off her jokes easily if it means she teaches me something useful.

But I don't need to think about her now, it's the weekend. A perfectly Maeve free Saturday night. It's just me, *Doctor Who*, and my Switch. Brad is out somewhere again, so I don't have to worry about making small talk with him.

Right as I'm about to finally beat this level in my game, my phone goes off. The sound scares me and I send my phone flying across the room as I go to reach for it. I must have accidentally turned on the ringer, since I usually leave it on silent or vibrate. Pausing my game, I climb out of bed and retrieve it from the ground where it landed. Luckily there are no scratches or cracks. Unluckily, it looks like Maeve is FaceTiming me.

My stomach twists, I don't know why she'd call let alone FaceTime me. My curiosity gets the better of me and I swipe to answer the call after a few more rings.

The sound is so loud I almost drop my phone again, and I struggle to make sense of what I'm seeing on the screen. It's bright white, her phone must be on a counter near a light. I can hear the music and voices of a party, and Maeve yelling off the screen.

"We'll be right out, fuck off!"

"Maeve? Did you mean to call me?" I ask, moving my phone like I might get a better glimpse of what's going on.

"Is that Connor? Hi, Connor," Hannah shouts from the other side.

"He answered? Perfect. Han, sit down next to the toilet," Maeve says, picking up her phone and filling my screen.

There's a shower curtain behind her and I conclude she's in a bathroom with Hannah. Her makeup is smeared around her eyes, and her sweaty hair is sticking to her forehead. My eyes dip down to her chest, noticing the shine disappearing into her shirt from sweat. Her pink tank top is tight and leaves almost nothing to the imagination. I hope where my eyes are aren't obvious on the small screen, before redirecting them back on her face.

"Are you busy?" she asks. No pleasantries or questions of how my night is going.

"It depends, what's going on?" I ask skeptically.

She sighs and rolls her eyes. "Listen, just answer the question, Chewy."

"Chewy? Like Chewbacca? I'm not even hairy, and frankly—"

"Connor!" Maeve shouts at me, then at someone off screen. "Go away, you fuckers!"

"Right, okay, no I'm not busy," I say. I'm a little scared of her at this moment to push her any more than I already have.

"Can you come pick us up from this party? Our sober sister decided she didn't want to be sober and Hannah did too many shots. I'm too drunk to drive and I need to get her home," she pleads, and now I feel bad for not answering her on the first ring.

"Yeah of course," I say without hesitation. "Send me your location, I'll be there soon."

"Thank you, thank you, thank you," Maeve repeats, and I'm already halfway out the door when her location comes through.

Standing outside the party I reread the text from Maeve:

BARBIE

We are in the first floor bathroom, I need your help

The last thing I want to do is go to this party. Parties back home are fun because I know everyone, and people there actually like me. But here it's filled with people I don't know, and don't care to know. These open frat parties are all the same, too loud and too many freshmen trying to show off but not knowing their limits.

I slip my phone back into my pocket and suck it up, weaving my way through the crowd on the front porch to get into the house. It's loud, dark, and I have no idea where the bathroom is. The air smells like stale beer and sweat, and my feet stick to the floor with every step. I'm determined to get out of here as fast as possible.

Trusting my instincts I see a line of girls coming from one of the hallways and follow it to a closed door.

"Hey, no cutting!" the girl at the front of the line shouts.

"I'm not cutting," I tell her, knocking on the door. "Maeve, it's Connor."

I hear the door unlock before it flies open. As Maeve pulls me into the bathroom and locks the door, the girls in the hallway start yelling as my eyes travel to the ground where Hannah is slumped against the wall.

"I can't carry her," she says, pointing to her cousin.

"I can walk," Hannah mumbles, throwing her arm up in the arm and hitting the towel rack. "Ouch."

"Han, sweets, you can't walk. We're going to get you home. Is it okay if Connor carries you?" Maeve talks to her in the calmest voice I've ever heard from her, and it feels like a side of her I'm not supposed to be seeing.

Hannah gives her a thumbs up and hiccups.

"Okay, let's get you up," I say, stepping around Maeve and pulling Hannah up on her feet. Maeve helps me keep her balanced as I reach behind her knees, scooping her up in my arms. She's not too heavy, but I don't frequent the gym so I'm unsure how long I'll be able to hold her.

Maeve leads us out of the bathroom, yelling back at all the girls in the hallway who are mad she was locked in there so long.

Pushing people out of the way, she creates the perfect path for me to get through without bumping into anyone or dropping Hannah.

We're almost out the door before I hear a random guy call after me, "Dude you know you don't have to play savior. It won't make her want to fuck your nerdy ass."

The comment makes my blood boil, but I can't do much with Hannah in my arms. Even if she wasn't, it's not like fighting him would be worth it. I plan to ignore the comment, but Maeve doesn't.

She spins around and back toward the guy. "Fuck you, Austin," she yells.

"Maeve," I warn her.

"No, I'm not going to let him talk to you like that," she says, looking at me before turning back to Austin. "For your information he doesn't have to try at all. He's given me more orgasms in one night than you ever did in six months. I feel sorry for anyone who has to fuck you."

Austin stands there with his mouth wide open, and all his friends start laughing.

I'm also stuck where I'm standing staring at Maeve. I've seen her stand up for her cousins before, and I never thought she'd stand up for me. Especially not that vulgarly.

Before Austin can say anything back to her she's focused on our mission to get Hannah out the door and home. My feet follow her to my car out front, unlocking it as she pulls the back door open for me to deposit Hannah across the seat before we get into the car.

She points in the direction I need to go, telling me to

start driving as she makes sure Hannah doesn't barf in my Jeep before buckling up. I do as she says, unrolling the back windows a few inches for Hannah.

Maeve lets out a gasp when she finally sits correctly in her seat, causing me to slam on my breaks. Hannah rolls off the seat and there's a groan as my heart races and I look around for a deer or someone walking across the street.

"What the fuck was that for?" I grumble, taking several deep breaths as Hannah continues to struggle in the back.

"What. Are. These?" Maeve emphasizes every word as she plucks one of the six rubber ducks from my dashboard.

"They're rubber ducks. Have you never seen one before?" I tease, holding back from yelling at her for scaring me.

"They're back here too," Hannah calls from the backseat, stretching her arm between the front seats with a duck in hand.

"Connor," Maeve screeches. "Why do you have a box of ducks in your back seat?" She does her best to look to the back, where Hannah is attempting to climb back on the seat. "Do you have some kind of rubber duck fetish?"

"No. It's a Jeep ducking," I say, hoping she drops it as I continue driving toward their apartment.

"Which is…" Maeve's trails off, meaning she's not going to drop this.

"It's a Jeep thing," I say, rolling my eyes. "Jeep owners leave a duck on another Jeep's mirror whenever they see one. It's like a communal 'hello' and people can get pretty creative with the ducks. I just have regular ones though." I pause, pointing to the back seat where Hannah is playing with two ducks. "My dad loves finding a Jeep and leaving a duck behind. He's got accessories for them in his car, like hats and sunglasses."

"Wait, that's adorable," Maeve squeals, picking up a second duck from the dashboard.

"Don't make fun of me, everyone does it." I glance over at her, ready to defend myself for my ducks.

"I'm not. It's cute. Do they have names?" she asks.

"They need names!" Hannah shouts from the back.

"No, they don't," I say through a sigh, regretting picking them up.

"This one is Quackers," Maeve states, placing the blue duck back on the dashboard before inspecting the yellow one still in her hand. "This one is Sunny," she decides, placing it next to Quackers.

"Sunny! So cute," Hannah cheers, dropping her ducks in the process.

"Fine. But only those two," I argue just for argument's sake.

"Ugh, you're no fun," Maeve whines. "But fine, I'll name the rest later." She crosses her arm, sinking into her seat.

"You will not," I say with finality.

"We'll see," she mumbles back.

The car goes quiet, and guilt starts to settle in my stomach at cutting off their fun when it really didn't bother me. Thinking of a way to lighten the mood I say the first thing that comes to mind. "So what was with Austin?" I ask.

"Don't start," Maeve warns. "I was bored last year. He was a mistake."

"I didn't know you liked me enough to be picturing me in bed," I tease, hoping it lightens the mood.

"Shut up. I only said that because he's an ass *and* it's important we sell this," she uncrosses her arms to hit my shoulder as I'm driving, but not enough to mess me up.

"Whatever you have to tell yourself, Barbie," I say, my shoulders starting to shake with laughter.

"Shut up. It's not funny," she yells, covering her face with her hands.

"It's kind of funny," Hannah mumbles and hiccups before laughing.

Soon all three of us are filling the car with laughter as we pull up to their apartment building.

## ELEVEN

MAEVE

Getting Hannah upstairs was a whole ordeal because she suddenly decided she wanted to dance. Connor attempted to carry her, but she wiggled out of his arms. We ended up following behind her as she crawled up the stairs, thinking she was dancing and trying not to laugh because she stopped whenever we would.

She's finally in bed with Greta curled up in her arms. There's water and a garbage can next to her, and she's on her side so she doesn't die if she barfs in her sleep. She looks peaceful, and I let her sleep because I can give her shit in the morning. Last time I was this drunk she took a photo of me eating pizza in the street. That photo lives on our wall of shame collage in the living room, and I regret not getting one of her crawling up the stairs.

"She's all set," Connor whispers from behind me, causing me to jump.

"Right, we should leave her alone," I agree, plugging in her phone and leaving her room. Connor follows me down the hall when my head suddenly starts pounding. I must sway because his hands are on my hips as he pushes me into a standing position.

"Woah there, you might be drunker than you think," he says from right next to me. I can't tell if I'm dizzy from the drinks or from his close proximity, but it's probably the drinks.

I stand there for a minute, trying to make sense of what I need to not feel like death tomorrow.

"Food," I mumble, heading for the kitchen.

"Why don't you go to bed?" he suggests.

"No, no. I need food first," I say, opening up cabinets until I find the boxed mac and cheese. "You can go home," I tell him.

"Yeah, not happening," he argues, plucking the box from my hand. "Go sit down, I'll make it." He points to the kitchen stools and holds the box out of my reach. Damn his extra lengthy arms.

I want to argue with him. I don't want him making me mac and cheese, but I also don't want to do it myself. Huffing, I make my way over to the stool and sit down.

He gathers the ingredients and supplies, and I occasionally direct him to the right cabinet. Then he fills the pot with water and turns on the stove, turning around to face me as he waits for it to boil.

He's leaning against the counter with his arms crossed, dressed in his usual black hoodie and black sweats. He looks slightly out of place in this tiny kitchen, like he's too tall for it. If he stood in the middle and spread his arms out he would span the whole length.

"I'm sorry for ruining your night." The apology slips out and surprises me.

"You didn't," he says without elaborating, seemingly unaffected by my niceness.

"I'm also sorry about Austin, he's always been the worst," I say, filling the silence.

"Then why'd you date him?"

"One, I didn't date him. It was only sex," I clarify. "Two, I was bored last semester and it was only for a few months. I filled my weekends with meaningless hookups. He happened to be one of the lows."

Connor only nods in response, returning his attention to the mac and cheese. I'm glad he doesn't ask me to elaborate. Last semester, I treated my stress with sex and it wasn't a good idea. Each time I ended up regretting it after and guilt still creeps in about hurting some of the people who wanted more from me.

"Thanks for doing this," I say, breaking the silence again. I can't stand silence, especially not if he's only here because of me.

"Adding the fire department to tonight wouldn't have been a good call," he teases.

"But that's how I plan to meet a hot firefighter," I groan, throwing my hands up in the air.

"Sorry, Barbie. You're stuck with me," he says, shrugging and stirring the pasta.

"That's not a bad thing," I admit.

"Anything's better than Austin, right?" he jokes, and I don't like the self-deprecating tone.

"You know what I said is probably true," I say before my brain can stop me.

"Which part? The hot firefighters?"

"No, the orgasm part," I clarify, seeing his pale cheeks go red at the mention and finding satisfaction I put it there. "I bet you're better in bed than him, don't sell yourself short." I'm not lying either. Connor seems to care about people whereas Austin would never do anything for me without me asking first. I've seen Connor take care of Cy multiple times at past parties when he got too drunk. I have a feeling he's kind in bed, attentive to his partners needs. He'd probably take his time tracing all the dips and valleys of their body, teasing them until they were begging for more. Wait, what the fuck? Why am I thinking about Connor in bed?

"You're very blunt sometimes," he says after a few stirs, snapping me out of my wandering thoughts as I adjust on the stool to calm myself down, imagining how he would be in bed.

"Don't you love it?" I ask, putting my hands under my chin and tilting my head to the side.

This gets a small laugh out of him, and tonight is the most I've ever made him laugh. It's intriguing and I want to hear more of it.

"This is almost done, bowls or plates?" he asks me, pointing to the cabinets.

"How about I eat it out of the pot," I suggest, holding out my hand to retrieve the golden yellow creation.

"If you think I made mac and cheese to not have any, you're insane, and I'm not eating out of the same pot as you," Connor argues, pointing to the cabinets again.

"I don't have cooties," I whine, directing him to the bowls.

"You can never be too safe," he says, shrugging and serving me a bowl.

We eat our mac and cheese in silence. Me at the counter, him still across from me leaning against the counter.

It's so quiet in the apartment that I don't know where to look, so I watch him as he watches me. Neither of us back down from our silent staring contest as we eat, and when he picks up his scooping speed I do the same. Then, he starts to eat faster and there's no way I'll let him beat me in anything, so I don't break eye contact and pick up my speed again. I struggle to eat as fast as him, some of the mac and cheese falling back into my bowl as I scoop it. He must have some kind of boy vacuum mouth though, because he finishes and throws his hands up in the air before I'm halfway through my bowl.

"I win!" he shouts.

I can't be mad because the smile on his face is adorable, it makes his green eyes pop and his freckles stand out more. I should come up with more ways to make him smile. It would be helpful for convincing my family he's my real boyfriend.

"I didn't know we were racing," I defend myself.

"Yeah, yeah. Keep telling yourself that." He smirks and my stomach feels like it's in knots. Maybe eating fast wasn't a great idea when I've been drinking. I don't want to barf in front of him, and if I stay up any later that might end up happening.

"I should probably go to bed," I say, tossing my bowl into the sink and standing up.

"Go, I'll clean this up." He gestures to the pots and bowls around the kitchen.

"You don't have to do that. I'll do them in the morning."

"Nonsense, go to bed. I've got this."

I almost argue more, but he glares at me so I do as I'm told. I go through a quick version of my nighttime skin care routine so he doesn't judge me for all the things I have to do. After my makeup is off, I change into my pajamas at record speed so there's no chance of Connor running in on me. Removing the nipple cakes from my boobs feels so freeing at the end of this long night, and they don't stick to my nipple piercings like other ones do.

Right as I'm crawling into bed and plugging my phone in, Connor appears in the doorway.

"Kitchen is all set. Here's a glass of water for you," he says, holding it up and bringing it over to me.

"Thanks," I say, taking a sip. It tastes like the best water I've ever had; I didn't realize how badly I needed it. There's a warm feeling in my stomach and I'm not sure if it's from the water or the fact that Connor is taking care of me.

"No problem. Have a good night, Maeve," he says, retreating from my room.

"Hey, Connor," I whisper from my bed. He stops in the doorway to turn my way. The hallway light backlights him, making his red hair look blond. "Why'd you answer?"

I see the corner of his mouth turn up before his mouth goes back to a thin line. He taps the side of the door frame, glancing down at the floor then back at me. "Why'd you call?" is all he says before disappearing.

Then I'm left alone, staring at a Connor-less doorway until the hallway light turns off and I hear the front door shut, wondering what the fuck just happened.

## TWELVE

MAEVE

I woke up this morning thinking about last night. Connor's question lingered with me as Hannah bounced around the apartment making breakfast. Luckily, neither of us were hurting too much.

Why did I call him? What is it because I saw how he has taken care of Cy in the past?

I know plenty of people on campus who weren't at the party, but I called him.

Part of me didn't expect him to answer, but he did.

When he agreed to come get us, Hannah had managed to mumble, "Told you he's nice."

I hate to admit she was right. What he did last night wasn't something he'd do for someone he hated. Maybe we were starting to grow into friends.

Am I getting excited about that? I'm not sure, but I have time to figure it out. Tonight I told him we need to go on a date. If we can't be alone together for a meal we'll never be able to convince my family we're dating.

He's picking me up after my weekly sorority chapter meeting ends, and no meeting has ever gone so slow in my entire life. I've been staring at the clock for the last hour and it feels like it hasn't moved an inch.

I usually enjoy these meetings, hearing about all the updates and things to come in the next week. But this time my stomach feels like it's upside down and twisted like a bad horror movie. I'm anxious and nervous about the date. It's dumb. It's a fake date. It will be no different from sitting with him and studying. I can't even find the strength to be annoyed about the couples costume ideas my mom is sending me for the wedding welcome dinner on Halloween now that she knows I have a date.

Mary, our president, finally adjourns the meeting and all the sisters filter out. I check my phone to see if Connor texted me he's here—but he didn't.

The sisters slow down in the hallway, and I'm annoyed they're getting in my way. I want to get outside and see if he's here.

Hannah stops in front of me and I run into her.

"What the fuck?" I groan, almost dropping my phone.

She spins around, with the scariest evil smile spread across her face. "You're going to love this," she tells me, stepping away as the other sisters step to the side and make a path toward what was causing everyone to slow down.

Connor is standing at the end of the hall near the doors. He's dressed in black jeans, a gray Henley, and holding a single pink rose.

I stand there, staring at him and trying to make sense of what I'm seeing. I didn't expect to see him in anything other than sweatpants, and I especially didn't expect to see him with a rose.

I'm glad I ended up wearing a dress to the meeting, so I don't feel underdressed.

Hannah nudges me, pulling me back to the present. All

the sisters' eyes are on me, staring and watching me act like I've never been picked up for a date before.

"Stop staring, and go mind your business," I quip at them, causing them to scatter down the hall and out of the building. Hannah guides me down the hall to Connor, giving my hand a squeeze before leaving and mouthing *"Have fun."*

"I didn't know you knew how to dress up," I tease when we're finally standing alone.

He shrugs, handing me the rose. "This is for you."

"Thanks," I say, taking it from his hand and noticing all the thorns have been cut off.

"You look nice," he says, a hint of red on his cheeks.

"Thanks, but you really don't have to be this nice to me," I tell him.

"I'm practicing," he clarifies. "You are going to have to get used to me complimenting you if we are going to convince your family we're dating."

That makes more sense, he doesn't actually think I'm nice. He's not dressed up for me. He didn't bring me a rose because he wanted to. He's practicing, because this is all fake. I can't let myself get caught up in this when it's nothing but a ruse.

"Good point," I agree. "You look nice too. Ready to go? I'm starving."

"Yup, lead the way," he says, holding the door open for me.

"One thing first," I say, stepping next to him and pulling out my phone. Connor freezes in the doorway, but puts his arm around my waist when he sees me open my camera. The warmth of his hand makes my stomach twist more. I ignore it as I lean my head into his shoulder and take a photo, quickly posting it to my stories so I don't over analyze how we look cute together.

Connor leads us to his car and I can't help the laugh that slips from my mouth when he unlocks it and the Jeep Wrangler's lights shine on the pavement.

"What?" he asks, eyebrows furrowed as he turns back at me.

"Nothing, it's just—" I hesitate, wondering if this is worth saying out loud. A slight raise of an intrigued eyebrow is the only thing that makes me continue. "You match your car, it's cute," I say, pointing from his red hair to the bright red of the car. I didn't register the color of it when he picked me and Hannah up, too focused on getting her home safe. "I also didn't take you for a Jeep person, which I forgot to say last night."

For a moment, I see only the whites of Connor's eyes as he rolls them and sighs. "It's my dad's favorite car brand. He got this for me when I got my drivers license," he explains, continuing our walk to his car.

When I climb into the front seat, I'm greeted by the ducks from last night. "Hello duckies," I say, picking up the blue one. "Hello Quackers and hello Sunny." I place Quackers back and give Sunny's head a light tap.

Connor buckles up, ignoring the backup camera, choosing to back out of the parking space by resting his arm on my seat and turning around to look out the rear window. He's not the most muscular person I know, actually far from it, but there's something about the way he effortlessly backs out of the space while wearing a Henley that makes him suddenly attractive. I'm not sure if it's still lingering feelings from my thoughts about him last night, or if it's the way the Henley hugs his chest and arms in all the right spots, but when I inhale and the smell of whatever deodorant he uses, a shiver runs down my spine and I have to shake it off before he notices.

"Did you hear me?" he asks, putting the car in drive and his hands back on the wheel.

"Sorry what?" I stumble over my words, too flustered from him backing out to form a full sentence.

"I asked if you were going to name the rest." He points to the ducks on the dashboard.

"Right." I nod along, pretending that maybe I heard him the first time. "This black one should be Toothless," I say, tapping its head.

"That's a good name. *How To Train Your Dragon*, I assume?" Connor asks, pointing to me like he's on the same wavelength as me.

"Yeah, I love that movie," I admit, not as annoyed as I thought I would be at how quickly he understood what I meant.

"Me too. So what about the rest?"

"I'll think about it, for now let's leave it at Quackers, Sunny, and Toothless. Also you need more variety in the ducks you give out," I say, reaching back and picking up one of the yellow ducks from the box.

"Maybe when those get lower I'll get different ones. But let's go eat," he says, pulling into the parking lot of the diner and to a spot right up front. Putting the car in park, he plucks the duck from my hand and drops it back into the box before getting out of the car.

A few minutes later we're sitting in a booth at the best local diner. Bud & Honey's, named after the cute elderly couple that owns it, is appropriately decorated with bees and flowers and every time I eat here I feel more at home. Bud and Honey remind me of my grandparents and the burger and fries Connor and I each order are my favorite things on the menu.

Connor's across from me bouncing his leg and looking anywhere but at me.

I reach across the table and grab his hands, wrapping them in mine. "Connor, breathe."

His eyes dart to mine, and he looks so scared. "What do we do?"

"What do you mean? Have you never been on a date?"

He moves his hands from under mine, before bringing them to his face to rub his eyes. "Maybe once? But not really, no."

I bite my lip, suppressing my smile. It's kind of cute he's nervous about this. I'm glad I'm not the only one.

"We talk. That's it. We have to get to know each other," I tell him, grabbing a French fry.

"Got it, okay." He nods like a bobble head. "Well, um, what's your favorite conspiracy theory?" The question catches me so off guard I choke on my fry. He pushes my water toward me and mumbles, "Sorry."

"Jeez, I meant favorite color and movie, but I guess we can start there." I shake my head at him. "My favorite would have to be about the lizard people living under New York City because it's so ridiculous."

"Same," he shouts, throwing his hands up in the air.

The reaction surprises me, making me laugh. And we end up talking about conspiracy theories until our food is gone.

The conversation comes to a lull, but I don't want it to stop. He seems to share the same sentiment when he beats me to speaking.

"Time for the check? It's getting late," he says, checking his phone for the first time since we sat down.

"Sounds good, I didn't realize how long we were sitting here. I should probably do some planning for the talent show," I tell him, throwing my bag over my shoulder and ignoring the disappointment gathering in the pit of my stomach.

Connor has already started heading to the counter to pay, and I pick up speed to reach him.

"You don't have to pay. Payment in food was a part of the original deal," I whisper to him so the cashier won't hear us.

"Nonsense," he says, handing his card over to her. "I'm obviously paying because our deal changed from your original idea."

I don't fight him even though it kills me. I was the one who wanted to do these fake dates, I should at least pay half. But letting him pay makes this ruse not feel so silly, and I bet if I Venmoed him he would send it back. Overall, this has been one of the best dates I've ever been on. I know I said I didn't want any kissing in this arrangement, but if he leaned in to kiss me tonight, I might let him. And the realization of that equally scares and delights me.

## THIRTEEN

## CONNOR

Ever since our date over a week ago I've noticed a shift in the way Maeve acts around me.

In class yesterday she smiled at me when she got there, and gave me a tiny wave as I sat behind her. Which I wouldn't think anything of if it was anyone else. But she has never smiled or waved at me intentionally without it following a joke. This smile was different, too, less smirk and softer at the corners. Her eyebrows didn't raise in challenge and her eyes felt more welcoming.

Has she noticed a shift in me? From being alone with her in her apartment to our date, I've had more casual me-and-Maeve time than I've ever had in the five years I've known her. I'm less nervous around her now that it's possible for us to have a conversation without it ending in us both being annoyed with each other.

It's starting to feel like she's becoming more of my friend with each passing day, but I'm still waiting for the rug to be pulled out from under me when all this ends and we no longer have an excuse to be nice to each other. I'm sure by the time she comes to the Thousand Islands next summer we'll be back to not talking unless it's in a group setting.

Today we're studying for the midterm and she brought me a muffin from one of the cafés. I've gotten them a few times before our study sessions, and I can't help but wonder if she noticed or if this was a lucky purchase. I also don't know if it's poison or a peace offering, and I'm too scared to ask her. If she was pretending to be nice until I was comfortable, now would be the perfect opportunity to strike and mess with me. Or she's also starting to feel like we are becoming actual friends and this is her only way to show it.

It's like she can read the confusion on my face because she breaks the silence first as I stare down the muffin like it's going to tell me if it's been injected with something that's going to make me run for the bathroom after one bite.

"I didn't do anything to it. Don't overthink it. Eat it," she demands, pushing the muffin closer to me.

"Why?" I ask, inspecting it. The paper is still intact, and no chocolate chips seem out of place. I smell it, and I don't detect anything dangerous. It must be a peace offering.

"Are you for real right now?" she grumbles, reaching across the table for the muffin.

I pull it up and out of her reach before she can take it from me. "No, I want it. Thank you."

"Yup, don't expect another one after this whole overre-action." She rolls her eyes and pulls out her notebook, but this eye roll is more playful than previous ones. The small tilt of the corner of her mouth trying to hide a smile gives her away, but I don't point it out. "How are you feeling about the midterm tomorrow?"

How am I feeling? I'm terrified. I'm going to fail and I

haven't learned anything since we started, matter of fact, I've learned less if that's possible. I've researched a million different learning disorders from dyslexia to dyscalculia, and I'm now convinced I have every single one. I should seriously consider dropping out and joining a circus. Are circuses still a thing? I'll have to Google it later.

"Good," I tell her instead.

I guess studying with her has helped and I'm being dramatic, but I don't feel confident in my test taking abilities. I've never been able to take a test calmly. My heart rate picks up and my palms get clammy. As long as I can remember, I've never been a good test taker. There was one time in high school where I sweated through my shirt and I had to go to the nurse's office and get one from the lost and found.

"I made some flashcards for us to go through. You can take them home to study more too," she says, pulling a stack of white note cards from her bag.

I'm about to thank her, but we're interrupted by a girl popping her head in the door. I assume she's a sorority sister based on the Greek letters on her shirt.

"I wanted to know if you could squeeze my band in for the talent show?" she asks, not glancing my way or noticing we are clearly in the middle of something.

"Hi, Georgia, can I talk to you about this in an hour? I'm in the middle of something right now," Maeve tells the girl, getting up and starting to shut the door. Part of me wants to say something snappy to the girl, but another part of me is happy Maeve didn't stop our study session to work this out like she did when we started this.

"Right, that works. Text me," the girl chimes and disappears from the doorway.

"Sorry. We should probably lock this door when we study," Maeve grumbles, locking the door behind her. Her sorority sisters never leave her alone, either someone is stopping her in the halls or her phone is constantly lighting up. She doesn't have the ring or vibrate on, and now I'm starting to understand why. I don't know how she gets anything done and I feel guilty for roping her into tutoring me when she could be spending her time doing something more important.

"Don't people only lock it if they're hooking up?" I ask her, attempting to lighten the mood by repeating a rumor I heard and avoiding thinking about my test anxiety and potential learning disorders.

"Do you care if they think that?" She sits and stares at me, challenging me to say more.

"No. Do you?" I stare back, not willing to admit it makes my stomach twist a bit as I beg my cheeks to not turn red and give me away.

"No," she replies swiftly.

"Glad that's settled then, let's see those flashcards," I say, taking a bite of the muffin. Chewing, the chocolate chips melt on my tongue satisfying the emptiness in my stomach. Probably since this is the first thing I've eaten all day. I've been too anxious to eat, but this muffin tastes amazing. Even if she was lying and did something to it, I don't care.

For the next forty-five minutes Maeve goes over the flashcards with me, splitting them into ones I get right and wrong. The wrong pile is embarrassingly higher than the right pile and I struggle not to fixate on it.

I'm starting to get frustrated and I want to give up. Or I want to scream. Maybe cry? Actually, all of the above.

"Do you want to stop?" she asks, and I can hear the pity in her voice.

I drop my head to the table, burying it in my arms. Rubbing my eyes in the process to make sure I'm not crying. When I'm met with nothing but dry skin I nod into my arms and peek up at her, slightly visible through the red of my hair but blurry as my eyes struggle to refocus.

"Don't stress. I know it feels like you don't know anything, but that's not true. You're already doing a lot better from our first session." She pushes the notecards my way. "Take these and study more, you've got this."

It's nice she has faith in me, I don't have faith in me. Not stressing is easier said than done. "Thanks, you didn't have to make all of these for me," I say, picking up the stack and adjusting them into a neat pile, trying not to think how long she spent making these when she has so much going on.

"It's not a big deal, it helped me learn everything by writing them all down," she says, shrugging and putting the rest of her things in her backpack. She stands and moves toward the door, stopping and turning around before unlocking it. "Also, make sure you try to sleep tonight. If you stay up playing video games, you won't be able to focus tomorrow morning," she warns.

"I'm well aware of how sleep works, and you're not my mom," I remind her, rolling my eyes at how she thinks I don't know how to take care of myself. Now I'll definitely never tell her the muffin was the first thing I've had to eat all day.

"Don't make me call her, red," she threatens, another nickname slipping from her full lips. I like red better than Chewy, though, so I don't point it out.

"How would you call my mom?" I counter, knowing there's no way she has my mom's phone number.

"I have my ways," she says, smirking as she unlocks the door and leaves me sitting in the study room with nothing but her note cards.

# FOURTEEN

## MAEVE

Thankfully the midterm was a breeze this morning. Making all those flashcards for Connor was a huge help in remembering the things I wasn't fully confident on. I managed to be one of the first to finish and get out of class early.

Which was beneficial since I need to set up a table in the lobby outside of the Veva Café. With the talent show a week away, tickets are now on sale. All around campus there are always clubs and organizations promoting their events or fundraisers, and I'm hopeful the talent show will bring a good crowd with the promise of potentially watching some interesting acts. Most of the acts are student bands, but there is one guy who has a puppet that roasts people who I'm hoping attracts a lot of attention. Last year he performed at an open mic night and became an instant campus favorite. People are constantly asking him where his puppet is.

To sell tickets, sisters usually sit in shifts at the table throughout the week with a max of three at a time. Although, that doesn't always happen and we either have not enough people or too many sisters lingering around and making the table seem unapproachable. I signed up for every time slot I had free to monitor how well sales are doing, so I'll be living at this table for the foreseeable future. I'm glad I was able to snag the spot by the café, in case I need caffeine or something to eat. This spot always gets the most foot traffic, and I'm convinced people are more likely to stop after they've gotten their coffee.

To capture the attention of anyone passing by I bought a sparkly bright pink table cloth to go over the one the college gives us. If I can get people looking my way I can strike up a conversation and hopefully convince them to buy tickets. If I don't, the audience is going to be full of Mu sisters and that would be embarrassing for my first solo planned event.

"Maeve, it looks great," Hannah's cheery voice comes from behind me. "So sparkly, I love it."

I turn around to see her with a new backpack. Taking a closer look as she moves to the back of the table with me, Greta's golden eyes peer at me through the circular window of the backpack. We've only had her for a month, but I would do anything for this sweet cat. Whenever we come stumbling back from the bars with pizza and French fries she's always bouncing around and trying to steal food from us. One morning, I found her sleeping on top of a pizza box we had left out, luckily the pizza was all gone which I'm sure Greta was bummed about.

"Stop! You got her a backpack?" I shout, overwhelmed by the cuteness.

"I did, and a harness." Hannah sets the bag on the table, unzipping it and pulling Greta out. She's wearing a light purple harness with a matching leash attached, and I pull my phone out of my pocket to get a picture of her. "I thought we would hang out for a bit, and she would bring people over. I didn't sign up for this time slot, but I don't have anything else to do. I also want to get her used to being outside and around people, so it's a win-win."

"Han, you're brilliant," I shout, hugging her as Greta gets distracted by the texture of the table cloth, her nails getting stuck in the sequins.

"Thanks," she laughs, standing up straighter and puffing her chest out. "I can be sometimes."

More sisters file in after that, some stopping by to say hi, and a few others who signed up for the next hour. Chatty Casey makes her usual appearance, and when she lingers for too long I have to remind her we can't crowd the table and send her into the café where there's a table of sisters hanging out.

Every time the door opens my eyes are drawn to it, since Connor should be done with the midterm by now. But every time someone who isn't him walks through, I'm disappointed. He was still taking the midterm when I left and I caught one last glance at him. He looked exhausted and I hope he listened to me and didn't stay up all night playing video games. I was planning to talk to him before class and give him encouragement and reassurance, but he barely made it in time. I don't know if he comes through here every day, but the first day he came to the café after class. He doesn't owe me anything, though, so I could easily wait until I see him again or text him. But waiting feels like too long and texting him might not get me an honest answer.

After what feels like the entire school coming through the doors, I finally see a tall figure dressed in black pass by. His head is down, but the red hair peeking out from his hood is how I'm sure it's Connor. I also recognize his black high top sneakers, since they're worn down and he's got the black laces, but I refuse to acknowledge I pay that much attention to him to be able to identify him by his shoes alone. It was bad enough that yesterday I didn't second guess myself when buying him a chocolate chip muffin. It's strange navigating from our usual bitterness to semi-friends, and I've unintentionally learned more about him than I ever expected to, and I'm starting to care about how things make him feel.

"I'll be right back," I tell my sisters, pushing out of my chair so fast that it makes a loud scraping noise along the floor as I hurry to catch up to him. "Connor, slow down," I call after him, hoping to stop him before he gets into the café.

He stops in his tracks, keeping his head down and not turning my way. He doesn't look up when I reach him, and I get the sense something is wrong.

"I wanted to check in with you. How'd it go?" I ask him, bending my head to meet his eyes as I move in front of him. They're puffy and red, and I can see tear stains over his freckled face. "Oh, Connor," I whisper, grabbing his arm and pulling him into a small alcove right before the entrance of the café.

He doesn't struggle, following me out of view of others so we can talk more privately.

"It didn't go well," he says through a sniffle, and my heart breaks for him.

"I'm going to hug you, okay?" I warn him.

"Um, why?" His eyes finally meet mine and the confusion and sorrow in them would make me poke at him if I didn't have this overwhelming need to comfort him.

"Trust me?"

He sighs and nods, stepping closer to me. I wrap one of my arms between his backpack and hoodie, while the other pulls his head closer to my level. He doesn't move for the first second, then his arms wrap around my waist and pull me closer as his body relaxes around mine. His head drops to my shoulder and my toes start to come off the floor.

"I'm sorry," I whisper, rubbing my hand over his hair as his hoodie falls and he cries into my shoulder.

I focus on comforting with light touches and whispering words like my mom always does for me when I'm crying. If he wasn't wearing a hoodie I would scratch his skin too since that always relaxes me. But part of me is too focused on the citrus scent of him and how this is the first time we've touched each other this much. I can feel the warmth of him wrapped around my waist as he holds me to him, with my feet barely on the ground. If he was to stand up fully he would be picking me up, similar to two summers ago when he pulled me away from a fight. Instead this time, I'm facing him with my arms around him and I'm not trying to wiggle my way out of his hold. We stay wrapped up in each other for a few beats before he lowers me as my feet flatten on the ground and he lifts his head up.

"Sorry," he apologizes, wiping his face with his sleeve.

"Don't apologize. You're allowed to have human emotions. I bet you still passed," I tell him, adding some cheer in my voice and not overanalyzing how I miss the loss of his warmth. I don't know if he passed, but I hope he did.

"Let's hope, or else I might have to fire you as my tutor." He tries to smile, but it quickly falls from his face.

"It's a good thing you aren't paying me," I tease. "But really, you'll be okay. Trust me."

"Okay, Barbie, I'll trust you," he says, wiping the last stray tear from the corner of his eye.

# FIFTEEN

## CONNOR

I'm confident I answered at least a third of the questions correctly. Maeve's face kept popping into my head during the midterm. Her sitting across from me and correcting me on wrong answers. It turns out her correcting me stuck, and helped me remember some of the things I was struggling with.

Last night I went to bed confident I definitely passed, choosing to trust Maeve, but this morning I woke up with the gut feeling I failed miserably. I've been carrying around the flashcards all day struggling to figure out which things I answered right or wrong, and it's all I've been able to focus on.

I've been so focused on it that I must've missed Maeve arriving at my apartment to study. I smell her perfume before I see her, and when she clears her throat I almost jump out of the dining room table chair. The flashcard in my hand goes flying to the floor as I tell my heart to calm down.

"What are you doing?" she asks, popping her gum and

crossing her arms with absolutely no signs of remorse for the fact she scared the soul out of my body.

I look down to the table where all the note cards are scattered since I've been throwing them all over without caring where they land.

"I'm reviewing your cards to figure out what I got wrong on the midterm," I admit, gathering up the cards to go through them again and picking up the one off the floor.

She sighs, walking over to me and takes the cards from my hands. "That won't be helpful. It's only going to drive you crazy."

"But I need to study more, I don't know this stuff," I argue.

"Taking a break is also good," she says, shoving the cards in her backpack. "When's the last time you took a break?"

"Ummm…" I start, coming up with nothing when all my past memories have me always sneaking in another flashcard.

She sighs again and moves around the table to the corner of the room where there's a built-in bookcase that's home to my board games. She made a comment about how many there were the first time she was here, but I was quick to change the subject since I didn't need to hear her make fun of me.

"What about playing one of these?" She gestures to the shelf, and I'm starting to get concerned there might be something wrong with her.

"You're serious?" I ask skeptically.

"Yeah, I could use a break too," she says, lifting her phone and tossing it in her bag. "There's not much for us to study anyway. How about you teach me how to play a game? I bet I could beat you." She raises one eyebrow at me in challenge.

"That's not the kind of game we would play," I say, standing up and moving over to meet her in front of the shelves. Pulling the *Eldritch Horror* box off the top of the stack, she eyes me as I hold it up in front of her. "This is more my style."

"What is it?" she asks, taking the box from my hands and inspecting it.

"It's a cooperative game where we have to fight monsters and save the world," I tell her. "It's my favorite one, I play it with my dad all the time. We're both into horror and I hope one day I'll be able to continue to play with my kids," I continue, not sure why I'm telling her this extra information, but I can't seem to stop it because no one ever lets me talk about this. "We don't win a lot; I can count on one hand how many times we've won. But I like the game and the monsters, so I don't mind it. Actually we don't have to play this one, I can pick something easier." I move to take the box from her, now that I'm talking about it more there's no way she would last a whole game since it usually takes a few hours. Once people hear that and see the rule book they always ask to play something else.

"Who says I need something easier?" she asks, moving the box out of my reach and setting it down on the table. "What kind of monsters are these?" she asks in a lower voice, pointing out the one on the cover. I can tell she's embarrassed she doesn't know more, but right now, I'm grateful I'm the smarter one in the room.

"A variety of different ones from your basic zombies to the more complicated Nightgaunt. I can tell you more about their lore as we go if you want?" I offer, sitting down adjacent to where she's now opening the box and pulling items out.

"Sounds good. Oh, do we get characters?" her voice rises with each word as she pulls out the character cards and starts flipping through all of them. "Why are these people so hot?" she asks, laughing and showing me the shirtless sailor character. "I want to be him," she says, slapping the card down on the table with finality.

I do my best not to roll my eyes at her as I grab the stack from her hand. "We need to be two other characters. Playing with two people is hard, so me and my dad have figured out the best pairing. Which, unfortunately, does not include him," I tell her, holding up the sailor's card and slipping him back into the pile.

"Fine, just know I object," she says, crossing her arms and pouting. I can't help but focus on the way her lip sticks out, and part of me wants to reach up and stroke it with my thumb. Would it be soft beneath my touch? Would she gasp or sigh? Would I be able to pull her close enough to smell her gum?

"Your objection is noted. Let me set up the board and how about you pick dice for each of us? Then, I'll explain the rules," I tell her pointing to the shelf with multiple containers of dice of varying colors. I shake off the lingering feeling of desire for her that won't seem to dissipate, and Zach's "hate is a feeling too" is in the back of my mind to explain why I'm feeling so frazzled around her recently. But it doesn't feel like there is much hate left between us, slowly being replaced by our friendship.

"Like we each get our own set?" she asks, getting up and moving to inspect the dice.

"Yeah, that way if one of the dice keeps rolling one we can put it aside and swap it for a different one. Since all the containers have twelve to thirty-six dice we'll have plenty to pick from. It's more of a superstitious thing, but it works," I explain when the furrow between her eyebrows becomes more pronounced.

"Whatever you say, Jack," she says, running her hand over the containers and stopping at my favorite set, a set of thirty-six smaller clear dice that give the appearance of deep red, unless you hold them up to the light and see it's the red pips making them that color.

"Jack?" I ask, knowing I'm going to regret asking.

"And the beanstalk, duh," she says, rolling her eyes and turning away from me as she tries to hide her smile. I shouldn't be surprised it's another tall nickname.

"Wouldn't that make you Jack if I'm the beanstalk?" I pause shuffling a deck of cards to look at her and stop myself from making a dirty joke about her climbing me.

Her hand freezes over a different set of dice as she spins to face me. "Hm, guess you're right. I'll have to come up with something better." She shrugs, popping another bubble and grabbing a container of dice off the shelf. "I want this set." She holds up my second favorite set, twelve purple dice with gold pips. I bet if I had a pink set she would pick them, but purple is a close second it seems.

"Okay, which one is for me?" I ask, nodding toward the remaining sets and leaving the potential fate of this game to her.

"This one," she says, confidently picking up the red set in her other hand and sitting down.

"Perfect, now I can tell you the rules. They're going to be confusing at first, but you'll get them better as we play," I tell her, setting the rulebook on the table and trying not to laugh when her eyes widen at how thick it is. "This is also going to take a few hours," I admit, hoping it doesn't scare her off.

"Oh jeez, okay, let me text Hannah," she says, pulling

out her phone, her nails clicking on the screen as she types a message before putting it back. "Okay, I'm all yours. Teach me"—she pauses, glancing at the game box—"*Eldritch Horror.*"

She listens attentively to rules as I start to show her examples of the various steps. I'm expecting her to stop me and bail when I pull out a second instruction packet, but she doesn't. Her genuine interest makes something in my gut tighten and I could get used to her not making fun of me. My cheeks are starting to hurt from smiling, and I'm hoping she doesn't point it out. But her zero hesitation about playing with me when she saw the rule book isn't something I'm used to, and I'm grateful for the distraction from school.

Suddenly my phone starts vibrating in my pocket. "One second," I pause my instructions, pulling out my phone to see who is calling me. My dad's face lights up my screen, his contact picture one from a few summers back with a bouquet from the farmer's market. "It's my dad. Do you mind if I answer it?" I ask Maeve, not wanting to be rude.

"Go ahead," she agrees, grabbing her phone as I answer the call.

"Hey, Dad, what's up? Aren't you at work?" I ask, starting to worry that he's calling me during the middle of the day.

"Yeah. But there's a sale on games right now; your mom sent me the link. Did you have any interest in playing *Wingspan?*" he asks.

"Is that the bird one? Yeah that sounded cool, I say get it," I tell him, excited to learn a new game with him. "I'm actually about to play *Eldritch* right now."

"And there's no pink dice!" Maeve shouts, looking up from her phone. I knew she was mad about that.

"Who's with you? Is that a girl?" Dad inquires as my face heats and I have no doubt that I'm as red as my hair right now. I haven't told him about Maeve tutoring me or the fact that I've been hanging out with her.

"Uh…" I sputter, not sure what to say to him.

"Put me on speaker," he demands, and I listen.

"Hi, Mr. O'Shea," Maeve says cheerily, putting her phone away and leaning toward mine.

"Hi, darling, you're playing *Eldritch*? First time?" he asks.

"Yeah. Dad, this is Maeve. She's one of my class-mates," I tell him before she has the chance to say anything else that I'll have to explain.

She raises one eyebrow at me, popping her gum as my dad says hi to her and asks why she needs pink dice. "Pink is my favorite color, and Connor only has purple dice," she informs him, shaking the set she picked.

"Maybe if we win this I'll get you pink dice," I say, raising my eyebrow back at her.

"I agree with Connor," Dad chimes in. "You've got to earn a set by winning." I lean back in my chair and cross my arms, glad I could count on my dad to back me up.

"I guess that's fair. Just means I have to win this now," she challenges.

"Have you two started playing yet?" Dad asks.

"No, I was about to finish telling her the rules," I say, tapping the last page of the instruction booklet like he can see me.

"Think you can handle it, Maeve?" Dad challenges her.

"Yes, sir. I'm ready to defeat some monsters." She rubs her hands together before cracking her knuckles as my dad chuckles on the other end.

"Well, I'll leave you kids to it then. I'll buy *Wingspan*

and we can play the next time you're home. I think your mom and Morgan would like this one too," he tells me. He asks me about a few more games and expansion packs before hanging up.

Between talking to my dad and teaching Maeve, I've forgotten all about class and the midterm.

Two hours later and we're almost done with the game. I wasn't sure about playing at first with how long he said it was going to take, but I learned all the rules quickly and I've gotten really into it. All I have to do is roll a five or a six to pass, but the amount of dice always changes depending on what we're doing and I'm still having trouble figuring that out.

The two characters we ended up playing as are Diana, a redeemed cultist, and Leo, an expedition leader. Leo isn't as hot as the sailor guy, and gives more Clayton from *Tarzan* vibes. While Diana looks like a girl I'd either love to ask out or cosplay as, so obviously I made Connor let me be her. He rolled his eyes at me when I called her hot, but I heard him mumble an agreement under his breath.

During the whole game he's been practically bouncing out of his chair with excitement any time we've successfully completed a task or defeated a monster. He kept his word of telling me about each one and the lore behind it. They're kind of scary, but it's fascinating to hear him talk about them. I've never seen him this animated before. I've known him for five years and this is the most I've heard him talk. And I think I like it? It's accompanied by a smile that doesn't feel fake or forced, just happy.

We're one roll away from winning the whole game, and it's my turn. My heart is racing and I'm wishing I wasn't the one this was riding on. I don't want to add another loss to his game stats; he's too happy right now to bring the mood down. After yesterday he needs a win, while I'm simply competitive and want to win.

"Are you going to roll?" Connor's voice pulls me out of my thoughts.

"I'm nervous." I look at the purple dice on the table in front of me, then at him.

"Don't be," he reassures me. "It's just a game. I don't care if we win or lose, I'm glad you stuck around this long."

His words sound calm and unbothered, but I can feel the bounce of his leg under the table. I pick up the dice, making sure to grab the handful that has given me good rolls the last few times, and shake them quickly before scattering them across the board.

I scan the dice struggling to make sense of what the outcome is. Not wanting to react wrong, I check with him for confirmation. His mouth is wide open and a smile starts to spread across his face. At the same time, we both jump out of our chairs and cheer.

I clap my hands and jump around while he hoots and hollers. Then, I feel his arms wrap around my waist and lift me in the air. His ocean and citrus scent fills my nostrils as he spins me around, and I can't help but giggle at how different this hug is from the one yesterday. My arms come together behind his neck to keep myself steady as he sets me on the ground.

My head is spinning and my adrenaline is pumping,

and before I can think about what I'm doing my mouth is on his. The second our lips touch my brain jumps in as I register what I've done.

I pull my mouth away from his and lean back to study him, trying to figure out if he's going to yell at me. He should—I can't believe I kissed him without consent. My arms are still around his neck and his arms are wrapped around my waist, both of us frozen in this moment. The heat of them is different from yesterday, like someone turned his temperature to the max setting.

His expression might seem unreadable to most people. But I've gotten to know him well over these last three weeks. His freckles are standing out against his flushed skin, and his pupils are blown so much that his green eyes appear black. Then, there's the slight uprise of the corner of his mouth that tells me he enjoyed what I just did.

I don't have time to process or say anything before he is pulling me back to him, fusing his mouth to mine. The heat from his arms radiates through my whole body as I open for him.

The kiss is fast and frantic as my fingers wrap around his red curls and my nails scrape his scalp. He moans into my mouth as our tongues fight for control, both of us refusing to let the other lead.

I feel my body being moved backward, my feet doing whatever he wants them to. My legs hit the back of the table and his hands grip my waist. A jolt of need pulses between my legs as his fingers brush the skin above my sweatpants. Then, I'm being lifted up to the table.

I hear board game pieces and dice clatter to the floor as Connor's hands leave my body. I'm mad they're gone, but our mouths are still locked together. I bring my legs up to connect behind his back and pull his body closer to mine, seeking any kind of friction I can get.

Setting me on this table was a brilliant idea on his part, when our centers line up perfectly and I can feel the hardness of him behind his sweatpants. I can't help myself when I move my hips against him. There are so many layers between us, but it already feels so good.

I grip his hair harder, not wanting this kiss to end and refusing to overanalyze what's happening right now. Every time I scrape my nails against his scalp he moans, and I get the greatest feeling of satisfaction that craves *more*. I probably look desperate clinging to him like a koala, but the instinct to be touching every part of him is too overwhelming. His arms finally wrap back around me to help keep me upright as my back arches into his touch.

We kiss for what feels like forever, not coming up for air unless it's to nip at each other's lips. He's kept my hips still by holding me tight to him, and I can't take it after a while. I need more to satisfy the ache building up inside of me. I need him to fuck me on this dining room table, and I need it right now.

Taking my hands out of his hair, I grab the collar of his hoodie and pull him with me as I lower myself to the table. There are still some pieces on the table, and one pokes me in the back but I don't care. I'm too focused on how the movement causes our mouths to break apart right as I grind myself against his erection, and how this feels like the most exciting thing to happen to me all year.

"Fuck, Barbie. Keep going," he hisses, following me to the table. His hands fall to either side of my head, caging me in.

I smile, pulling his mouth back to mine and not breaking the movement of my hips. I didn't think about whether this table is secure enough to hold both of us, but I don't have time to wonder about it. Right as Connor brings one of his knees to the top of the table we hear the front door open.

The heat of him on top of me is gone as quickly as it was there. His eyes are wide as they bounce from the doorway to me, sprawled out over his board game and panting like a cat in heat.

I can see his erection through his sweatpants and I decide I'm going to sue whoever came into his apartment. As the footsteps come closer, Connor pulls me off the table and returns to his chair in one motion.

I follow his lead and take a seat, attempting to hide the blush on my face with my hand, hot intensity burning my palm. Our breathing manages to return to a non suspicious level as Connor's roommate passes by with nothing but a grunt our way before going into his room.

I look over at Connor who looks like he isn't sure what just happened. I'm not sure what happened either. Was I really about to let him have his way with me on his dining room table? I wasn't supposed to be wanting him to do that. This wasn't a part of the plan, and it's against the set of rules we established.

Before he can say anything, I grab my backpack from the floor and pop out of my chair. "I should be going. I told Hannah I would be able to feed Greta and she'll scratch the couch if she doesn't eat on time," I lie and run out of the dining room as fast as I can. I don't bother to put my shoes on fully before I'm out the door and in my car.

## CONNOR

Cold water pours over my head and down my body to where I grip my cock. Rubbing my thumb over the tip, I attempt to suppress the name escaping from my lips.

I haven't been able to stop thinking about Maeve since she ran out of my apartment like her ass was on fire. I thought taking a cold shower would help subdue my erection and give me time to process what happened. But once I was naked and I saw how hard our make out session had gotten me, I needed to do something about it.

I've never experienced this strong of a desire for anyone before, the entire scene replaying in my mind on a tortuous loop. The way she ran her nails along my scalp and how it sent a tingle down my entire body. The sounds she made when I would bite down on her lip echoes inside, and the taste of her fruity gum still lingers in my mouth even though she had thrown it away midway through the board game. An overwhelming *need* keeps building inside me because of one person, and my mind is racing at the meaning of it. But as the tightness in my balls grows with each stroke of my hand, I refuse to focus on it and only on the relief a second out of reach.

As soon as I picture her underneath me, spread out across my board game and arching into me like I'm the only one that can satisfy the ache between her legs, I'm spilling all over my hand. A moan slips from my lips at the release, and I pray the shower is loud enough to muffle the noise so my roommate doesn't know what I've just done. I catch my breath as my release washes down the drain and the expected sense of relief never comes.

I'm confused and frustrated. One second we were playing a game and the next we were dry humping on the table. I thought she didn't want any kind of romantic entanglements in our arrangement. I don't understand why she would kiss me, and I don't know why I can't stop thinking about it. This isn't supposed to be happening.

Could she be warming up to me? These past few weeks something has been growing between us, but I thought it was simply friendship. But maybe she likes me. It's one of the only explanations as to why she would sit through a two hour board game with me and not complain once. I never thought I would find a girl who wanted to play games with me, let alone get excited and kiss me when we won.

And do I want her to like me? Do I want to be more than friends with her?

Getting out of the shower, I put on my sweatpants and head back to my room. I need to talk this through with someone who knows her before my racing thoughts send me into a spiraling mess. Flopping back on my bed I open the BAYWATCH BOIS group chat.

CONNOR

I need Maeve help

I stare at the screen, waiting for a reply and hoping someone is available to talk. It's still pretty early in the day, so they could both be busy with their lives. They don't owe me their time right now, but if I'm lucky they'll both at least reply and I can set up a time to talk to them later. An eternity passes before multiple texts come in at once.

CY

Wait what happened

ZACH

Tutoring not going well?

CY

Don't tell me you fucked something up

ZACH

Dude if you hurt her the murphys are going to kill us

I roll my eyes at their dramatics as my fingers fly over the keyboard on the screen before they draw any more conclusions.

CONNOR

Can the two of you shut the fuck up and listen? I didn't do anything, she did

She kissed me

Half an hour later and I've explained the whole situation to Cy and Zach, minus the solo shower session which I'm too embarrassed to admit happened. Their faces light up my phone, since they roped me into FaceTiming after my 'she kissed me' message, barely giving me time to put a shirt on.

"Dude, you like her," Zach says, his grin so wide that his eyes wrinkle at the corners.

"I do not like her," I correct.

"But you did kiss her back." Cy raises his eyebrows at me.

"A lot," Zach adds on. "How is this all feeling for you?"

"I'm confused, bro," I admit. "I had everything figured out this summer when I came out to you guys, but now I don't know?"

"Can I be blunt with you?" Cy asks, and Zach moves closer to the screen like this is going to be good. Cy is usually the one to call me on my shit when I'm being dumb, so I'm not surprised he's taking charge now.

"Do I have a choice?" I wince, afraid of what he might say.

"No. Anyway, nowhere does it say demisexuality is defined by any one type of connection or bond. And while Maeve might not be your favorite person in the world, you have known her for almost five years. Granted most of that was only one week at a time over the summer. But now, you're seeing her at least four times a week with your classes and studying, not to mention the time you saved her from that party and the diner date. Spending so much time with her is definitely making a difference in your relationship, and whether you like it or not, you are forming a relationship with her. I know you said it wasn't romantic to start, but would it be such a bad thing if it started to lead you that way?"

We all go silent after that as they wait for me to process what Cy said. I always thought my first real sexual attraction would come after I had started dating someone because I wanted to date them. Not because I was fake dating them. I thought I was safe from developing any feelings for her that might lead to more. But now? Thoughts of her on my table and how she pulled me on top of her won't leave, like someone is sitting on the repeat button inside my head and I have no way to turn it off. I already feel my dick reacting to those thoughts and I have to find a way to control myself.

"No," I finally say, admitting the scariest thing I've had to admit since asking Maeve for help. "It wouldn't be a bad thing. But what if she doesn't want that in return? What if this goes badly? I'll never be able to work at the campground again. There's no way I could face her family after. I'd have to switch schools and move across the country probably."

"Connor, stop," Zach cuts off my spiraling thoughts. "You need to talk to her about it. From what it sounds like, she was into it so I don't see why she would defame you in any way. But you'll never know how she feels until you ask."

"I agree, you need to ask her." Cy nods.

"Could you ask her?" I direct my question at Cy, who keeps in contact with her throughout the year through social media. If he could find out so I didn't have to hear rejection from her that would be my ideal situation. While they're not wrong about me needing to ask her, they are both underestimating how much confidence I lack. There's a reason the two of them do most of the talking when we're together, and talking to Maeve about this is going to be harder than it sounds.

"No, you're not in middle school," Cy chastises. "Be a grown up and talk about your feelings."

"Fine I'll try, but if this goes poorly I'm blaming both of you. I'm going to go now," I say, not wanting to talk about this anymore than we already have. Before I hang up I pause. "One last thing, can you text me tips on how to talk to her? I've never done that before." I'm embarrassed to ask, but it seems like this is the semester of facing my fears, so if I'm going to attempt this I might as well get some tips. I probably should have figured out how to talk to a potential romantic interest before the age of twenty-one, but my one bad experience in high school left me feeling like I was only friend material and not boyfriend material.

"Yeah we will." Zach nods, hiding the smile creeping up at the corners of his mouth.

"Of course, we want this to go well for you. Good luck," Cy says, as his hand blocks the screen before his picture disappears, followed by Zach's. Then I'm left staring at a dark screen and my reflection wondering what the fuck I got myself into.

## EIGHTEEN

MAEVE

The second I got in my car I tracked Hannah on the FindMy app to see where she was. Luckily, she was at our apartment so I drove as fast as I could back to the Mu Mansion and prayed I didn't get pulled over or no one stopped me before I got into our apartment.

"Hannah! Crisis!" I yell, slamming the door and locking it so no other sisters decide to come in unannounced. It's happened plenty of times before, and now I'll always knock after finding Brittany ass up and bent over her couch with her boyfriend naked behind her. I shudder at the thought, and curse my brain for making me think of it again.

"In here," she calls from her bedroom. Dropping all my stuff on the couch, I rush into her room where she's laying under the covers on her phone with Greta asleep on her lap, practically crashing into her door frame as my socks glide on the hardwood floor. Normally, I would walk over and give Greta head a scratch, probably waking her up a bit. But I'm too stressed out trying to figure out what just happened at Connor's apartment.

"So something happened," I start. I pace back and forth on her carpet, making sure to stay on it so I don't step on the hardwood and lose my balance because I don't need to add injury to the events of today.

"Okay, I'm listening," she says, setting her phone down and sitting up.

"You can't say 'I told you so,'" I warn her, stopping pacing to point at her.

She clasps her hands over her mouth, gasping, "Did you kill Connor?"

"No. It's worse." I throw my hands up in the air and start pacing again. "It's so much worse."

"What's worse than killing him?"

"I kissed him. Not he kissed me. I. Kissed. Him!" I get louder with each word as Hannah gasps. "Then I left. And now I'm here."

"Ohmygod tell me the whole story right now," she demands. So I do. I tell her about how he needed a break, about the game, and how I was having fun playing it. How he rarely wins, so when I rolled the winning roll I must have gotten caught up in the excitement and kissed him. How I pulled away, and he pulled me back. And I'm not sure how far we would have gone if his roommate hadn't come home.

"Ohmygod I felt his dick, Han. Like right up against me!" I yell at the end of the story. Leaving out all the details about how much my body truly enjoyed the makeout session and subsequent dry humping. How satisfying it was to have him follow my lead as I pulled him over me, and to hear his moans each time my nails raked over his scalp. I definitely don't tell her how I'm still worked up, and my heart is pounding faster than ever. If I were to excuse myself and slip my hands down my pants it wouldn't take me long to reach an orgasm that would surely piss me off.

"Did you like that?" she asks, as I bite my lip and try to not think about his dick.

I hesitate for one second before quickly saying, "No."

"You hesitated," she shouts, pointing an accusatory finger at me.

"I did not." I poorly defend.

"You did, you like him," she yells, throwing a pillow my way.

I catch it in the air as I fall on her bed, bouncing when I hit the soft cushion of the duvet and bring the pillow over my face. "I don't know what's happening," I mumble into the pillow. Maybe if I keep it over my face long enough I'll suffocate and not have to deal with any of these feelings. But that would leave a mess for her to clean up, so I don't press the pillow into my face.

I feel her move closer, the bed sinking on one side of me and the sound of Greta's tiny thump on the floor as she jumps off the bed. Hannah slowly removes the pillow from my face and looks down at me. "You might be developing a crush on your fake boyfriend. I told you this was a bad idea. I mean, I thought you were going to kill him and we'd have to call the uncles. But this…"

"Is a disaster," I finish before she can. "I can't deal with this on top of tutoring him, planning the talent show, getting all my work done, and finding an internship. It's too much," I groan to her ceiling.

"Do you want help? I don't have much going on this weekend. The show is only a few days away so at least that's off your plate soon," she says.

I should accept the help, but I don't want to. If I can't handle one tiny event how am I going to be able to run a business where there are multiple events in a weekend or month? I need to prove to myself I can do this before I sink all my time into a pipe dream that will only end up crashing and burning if I can't handle it.

"No, I can do this. I'll tell Connor I got caught up and it won't happen again," I decide, sitting up on my elbows. "Everything will be fine. It's going to be fine. Just fine."

"How many times are you going to say that before you believe it?" she asks, and I can hear the doubt in her tone.

"Fuck off, it's going to be fine," I repeat it again since I'm now in an endless loop of reassuring myself everything is going to work out like I planned it.

"Well if it isn't *fine*—"

"Which it will be," I cut her off as she glares at me and sighs before continuing.

"If it isn't, you know I'm here. I won't judge you if you develop a crush on your fake boyfriend and want to explore things. And if it ends poorly, I'll help you cover at the wedding. If you like him and ignore it it's only going to stress you out more. Harboring feelings for someone like that doesn't help you sleep at night, trust me," she finishes, a blushing creeping up her cheeks.

"But what will everyone else think? I mean, it's *me and Connor*," I emphasize our names like they're the last two things that should go together.

"Who the fuck cares," Hannah shouts, throwing her arms up in the air and startling me. "Sorry, but also not. Because who cares what people think? If you're happy and he makes you happy then fuck what anyone has to say."

"Are you okay, Han?" I ask cautiously, not being able to let what she said go since it seems like she might be talking about something else with the way her blush deepens. I have an inkling which specific person she might be talking about, but I don't want to ask and be wrong. None of my advice would be helpful right now when I'm so distracted.

"Yes, I'm fine. Everything's fine," she snaps, and we both stare at each other for a second before we both scream, "We're fine," and dissolve into laughter.

"Do you want to go out tonight?" I ask her after our laughing has ceased. I stand up, determined to take my mind off everything tonight.

"Obviously, let's get tacos and margaritas for dinner. I'll text the Mu Mansion chat and see if anyone wants to join," she says, picking her phone back up and typing away before she finishes her sentence.

This will be perfect. I'll hang out with my sisters. Get caught up on their drama. Between Brittany, who seems to know everything about everyone, and Georgia, who keeps screenshots of everything, there should be plenty to talk about. Hell, I'd be happy if Chatty Casey came, too, anything to distract myself.

Overall, avoiding thinking about Connor is key. I can't recall how his lips felt soft and right against mine. How I wanted nothing more than to have him make me come on his dining room table. I bet he's attentive in bed, and he would take his time while I told him what to do. Maybe a solo session with my vibrator wasn't a bad idea before dinner, not like I would need long. And as much as I'm annoyed at the thought of him being the reason for needing a release, it would be fine once I dealt with it and moved on. One quick Connor induced orgasm and no more ever again in my entire life. It'll be fine, just fine.

## NINETEEN

CONNOR

This past weekend was torture. I couldn't get Maeve out of my head no matter how hard I tried. My body finally seemed to be so excited at the potential of getting laid that I couldn't stop it when she invaded my dreams like some horny version of *A Nightmare on Elm Street*.

Now it was time to face the music and see her again. My leg won't stop bouncing and my heart is racing as I sit in a desk chair too small for my frame. I got to class early in case she did, too, so I could talk to her and get this over with quickly. But the minutes came and went and there's no sign of her as class is about to start.

I'm watching the clock on the wall and right when the second hand turns the clock to 8:00 a.m. Maeve finally comes rushing in. She's in her usual pink outfit and it's *tight*. All those years I thought she might try to kill me, but this is what's going to end my life. A tight pink bodysuit disappearing beneath her high waist jeans. I can see every curve she has and I want to grab her hand and pull her into an empty classroom and set her on another table to pick up where we left off. But I have to talk to her like Cy and Zach said and not let my hormones take over.

Before I can lean close to her and say anything, class starts and I'm torn between paying attention to the lecture or paying attention to the way Maeve's shoulders are tenser than usual, pinching her back. How she's leaning forward in her chair instead of against it and getting her hair all over my desk like she usually does. There's something wrong, and I'm wishing I would have texted her over the weekend instead of waiting until today to talk to her.

I barely register when our midterms get passed back; I don't care about my grades right now. Maeve was right, I passed, but not with a high enough grade for my liking. I should be satisfied and relieved, but school seems so unimportant compared to her. When class ends she springs out of her seat but her speed is no match for my long legs as I weave through people to catch up to her.

"Barbie, hang on!" I yell behind her hoping to get her attention.

She stops suddenly, spinning around to face me. I barely have time to stop myself before I run straight into her.

"What?" she snaps, and I'm positive she's either going to kick me or yell at me so I have to choose my next words carefully.

"I was hoping I could buy you a coffee, since I see you don't have one yet." I glance down to her empty hands that have a grip so tight on her backpack straps, turning her knuckles white. "And maybe we could sit down and talk?" I ask, making sure my voice is soothing and not confrontational.

She contemplates my offer, and this feels strangely like the time earlier this semester when I asked for her help in the first place. I don't break eye contact with her as we both stand silently for an eternity and I'm grateful she isn't telling me to fuck off like the first time.

Finally she says, "Fine." Then spins and starts heading toward the café.

Our walk, ordering, and waiting for our coffees is silent. There's tension in the air around us that feels different from all the tension we've had before. Neither of us is willing to admit we liked what happened at my house for the sake of pride.

Once we get our coffees, I lead us to a table tucked away in the corner to reduce the amount of people that could potentially hear this conversation. She sits down and readjusts in her chair several times before finally settling for crossing her legs on the chair and resting her head in one of her hands, looking at me expectantly. My eyes are glued to her mouth as she takes a long sip out of her coffee, her full lips wrapped around the edge. And when her tongue peeks out of the corner of her mouth to catch a drop I have to bite my tongue to keep from groaning.

"Well are you going to start?" she clips, snapping me out of my thoughts about her mouth.

"Right, I wanted to talk to you about the other day," I say, struggling to remember everything Cy and Zach texted me about communication. Make eye contact with her, be direct, and don't push her if she doesn't want to talk about it.

"I'm sorry I did it without asking," she sighs into her cup before taking another sip.

"Thank you, but you really don't have to apologize. As much as it might surprise you, I enjoyed it," I tell her and resist the urge to touch my cheeks to cool them down.

"Oh I could tell," she says smugly, letting some of her guard down and I'm certain my face is now the same color as my hair. "It wasn't bad, but we did say no kissing."

"Right, which is why I wanted to talk about that since you created the rule and then broke it," I tell her, keeping my tone non-accusatory even though that's exactly what I'm doing.

"Yeah, my bad. I got too excited about winning the game. I guess I can get a bit competitive," she says, shrugging and taking another sip of her coffee. "Although, when you think about it, it's a good thing we kissed." She's avoiding eye contact with me, and I can't tell if she's being serious or making fun of me for pulling her back after she pulled away.

"Explain," is all I say.

"Well," she draws out the word, twirling her hair in her finger. "Since we are 'dating'"—she puts air quotes over the word dating— "we should at least know what it's like to kiss each other. So in the overall scheme of things it's probably good we got it over with and didn't kiss for the first time in front of my family."

"I agree." I nod, glad we seem to be on the same page. "What about other—" I'm cut off when one of her sisters comes running up to the table. Of course we're being interrupted again when I finally have the courage to talk to her about this. Maybe I should have waited until we were back at my apartment to talk about this, but waiting a week would have only made it more awkward.

"Hi, sorry to interrupt but I have a crisis," she says, holding her phone out to Maeve where I can see a picture of some guy holding up his fully casted arm. "Aaron from Alpha Pi broke his arm this weekend trying to jump from their roof to the pool so his band can't play at the talent show," she speeds through the news like it's her fault this guy was a dumbass. I have to hold back my laugh and subsequent eye roll because that entire sentence sounds like something from a 2000's romcom.

"Motherfuckers," Maeve growls, which makes it harder to hold back my laugh. But when I process that this means more work and stress for her the urge to laugh disappears. Every time she opens her planner I expect to see her to-do list with things crossed off, but more things get added to it faster than she can do them. She's always mumbling to herself about what's next and I don't understand how she can juggle so many things when I can barely focus on my classes. With the show two days away I can only imagine how stressful it's going to be to find a replacement act. "They couldn't have waited a few more days to be total morons? Fucking hell."

"Maybe we could see if they can find a replacement?" her sorority sister offers, and I'm pretty sure if this was a cartoon, steam would be coming out of Maeve's ears. If this Aaron guy crosses her path he better hope she doesn't break his other arm, she's definitely the type of person I wouldn't want to cross right now.

"No, it's fine," Maeve sighs, standing up and taking her coffee. "Sorry, I have to deal with this. I'll see you tomorrow?" She gives me an apologetic look and I want to ask her to sit back down and finish our conversation, but I don't want to give her any more stress.

"Sounds good," I say with a thumbs up, slumping back into the chair and taking a sip of my coffee as she sprints out of the café with her sorority sister. At least we're on the same page about the kiss not being a mistake, but now I'm worried I'm the only one who wanted it to mean more. I need to find another time to talk to her when we won't be interrupted, but that's not going to happen before the talent show is over. I'm going to have to not overthink until then, which is easier said than done.

TWENTY

CONNOR

BARBIE

Can we move the study session to my place?

CONNOR

Sure thing

I look down at my phone and back up at Maeve's place. I've done my best to avoid the Mu Mansion since my first visit, and I'm unsure if I should buzz her apartment or text her since she let us in last time while I held Hannah upright. The building is tall and has a small lobby with mailboxes for all of the apartments. The mailboxes and buzzers are all decorated in different themes, with the different occupants' names on them. Looking them over it's easy to find Maeve and Hannah's, even without their names, the pink sparkles and cat stickers give them away. I don't have time to make a decision before the entrance door is thrown open.

Maeve is standing there, laundry basket propped on

her hip and gum in full bubble, popping when she nods for me to come in.

"Sorry about the last minute location switch. I'm squeezing laundry in and with the talent show tomorrow this is the only time I could do it," she says, letting go of the door and heading up the stairs.

"No problem. Did you find someone to fill the empty spot yet? We can skip today if you're too busy," I suggest, following her inside. I don't want to add any more pressure to her this week than needed. Climbing the stairs, I try to keep my eyes averted from her ass, but I can't help it when it's right in my line of sight.

Her claw clip is barely hanging on with each step, and she's wearing a light pink lounge set with shorts that look soft to the touch. I'm annoyed I notice how it hugs her curves in all the right places. The high waisted shorts are not high enough to hide the sliver of skin showing before a crop top covers her torso. It would be so easy to reach out and slide my hand up them to cup her ass. This whole thing is so confusing, and I wish we would have had time yesterday to talk more about whether kissing or other *stuff* was officially on the table.

"We don't need to reschedule, I just need to put these away and then I'll be all set to study." She opens her door and slides into her apartment. "We only have two dryers for the whole Mansion, and Brittany will put your clothes in the donation box if you leave them in there for too long. Plus I want to not think about the show for an hour."

I grunt so she knows I heard her and follow her into the apartment. I'm surprised by how clean it is, and not at all surprised by how pink it is. With Maeve always being on the move, I was certain her place would be a mess during the weekday. I didn't take a good look around last time I was here since I was too focused on making sure neither Hannah or Maeve got sick. It's small, with the kitchen and living room all in one space, but there are cat toys everywhere and empty alcohol bottles line the tops of her kitchen cabinets that give it a lived in feel. Overall, the space is pretty clean and there aren't any dishes piling up in the sink; I bet Hannah is the one doing most of the cleaning.

Greta prances over to me and meows, rubbing against my legs. I drop my backpack and give her a quick head scratch before following Maeve down the hall. I pass Hannah's room, complete with one of the largest cat trees I've ever seen. There's a small bathroom and decorations with the Mu Eta Psi Greek letters fill the walls of the entire apartment. Obviously crafted by either Maeve or one of her sorority sisters, and I want to know which ones are hers and which ones aren't.

When I finally get to Maeve's room I see the mess I must have missed last time since it was dark. Her desk is full of books and papers, there's a chair full of clothes, and her shoes go far past the shoe rack against the wall.

She runs around the room folding laundry and putting it away at the same time. Her hair flops from one side to the other and she almost trips over multiple pairs of shoes. I could stand here for hours and watch her, but we should study since my midterm grade wasn't as high as I wanted it to be.

I step further into the room when she whips open her top drawer and starts shoving clothes into it. I'm about to offer to help her when I see the clothes she's stuffing into the drawer are all her underwear.

I've seen girls underwear before—well, once before. But there's something about seeing all the lacy pairs and thongs that has my face heating, and thinking about how they would look sliding over her perfect round ass as I pulled them down her legs has blood rushing to my dick.

I avert my gaze and try to look anywhere else, but her voice pulls me back to her.

"Sorry, almost done. I'm moving as fast as I can so we can study." She shoves more underwear in the drawer and glances over her shoulder at me with an apologetic look. Her fast movements cause something to come flying out of the drawer and onto the floor between us. Without thinking, I reach down to pick it up, my longer arms beating her to it. "No, don't—" she shouts and lunges forward for it, but I pull it up and away from her.

Looking up to where she can't reach I register the softness of the U-shaped vibrator in my hand and whatever blood was left in my body shoots straight to my cock. I swallow, attempting to remain calm as my heartbeat fills my ears, imagining Maeve using this on herself. The way she would run it over her pussy before slipping it into herself, the sounds she would make as she got closer to her climax. The flush of her skin after she comes.

"What's this?" I ask, pulling myself away from the picture of her masturbating, and smiling at the way she's got her arms crossed, pushing her breasts up and I can see the faint outline of her nipples.

"What? Don't act like you've never seen a vibrator before," she snaps and tries to act like she doesn't care, but the blush on her cheeks gives her away.

"You use this a lot?" I try to hide the desire in my voice, but I can't help the roughness behind it.

"Wouldn't you like to know." She doesn't back down from her stance.

"You seem pretty stressed," I say, stepping closer to her, my feet moving before I can stop them. "I could help you relax if you wanted." I wave the vibrator around in my hand and point it toward her. She backs up, stopping when she reaches the dresser. Her blush deepens and I hold my breath waiting for her to say something. I don't know what I'm doing, only that I can't get the thought of the other night out of my mind and how I want to taste her lips again.

"I don't need your help relaxing, I can do that on my own."

"I know." I take another step closer. "But aren't you the one who said we have to get to know each other better? After all, I know what kissing you is like but not what you look like when you come? Shouldn't I have the most accurate data so we can be convincing?" I'm right in front of her now, vibrator still in my hand and between us. I have no idea where this confidence came from, but it might be desperation for her. She could take it away from me if she wanted to, tell me to leave and I would be gone in a second. But I can't help myself with how badly I crave this information. It feels like years before she finally answers.

"You're right, I guess we have to do it"—she uncrosses her arms and rests her hands on the top of the dresser—"for the data, of course."

"Of course." I set the vibrator on the dresser and wrap my hands around her waist, lifting her up on it, making sure she doesn't hit the mirror attached to the back. Doing this for the data is purely scientific, to find out if she moans when she comes or if she's quiet. I can feel her skin burning through her shorts, and I can't help my thumbs when they reach up and slide across her skin at the top.

She gasps at the contact and arches into my touch, her gum sits at the side of her mouth and it makes me want to find out what flavor she picked today. I want to know if I can taste the flavor like last time. She's perfectly lined up in front of me and if there was less clothing between us I would contemplate losing my virginity to her right here. My cock pushes painfully against the zipper of my jeans thinking about the possibility of sliding into her, being surrounded by her heat as she rode my cock to completion. I push open her legs with mine, crowding into her space.

The rise and fall of her chest quickens and she's looking up at me like she isn't sure what's supposed to happen next. I feel the same way. I don't know what I'm doing; this is all new for me. All my other goals for the day are out the window, replaced with the sole task of seeing what Maeve looks like when she comes.

I rake my hands higher up her sides, slipping them under her top and brushing the bottom of her breasts. I groan as my fingers meet the soft skin there, the lack of a bra evident as I rub my thumb over the curve. I drop my forehead to hers, needing a moment to collect myself. It's been a minute since I've come, and this won't last long if I get my dick involved. I want to pull her top off and find out what sounds she makes when I pull her nipple into my mouth. To drop to my knees and find out what she tastes like between her legs. I've never gone down on someone, but the thought of doing it to her is only going to lead to me giving into my desire to grind against her until this ache in my balls is gone. But right now isn't about me, it's about her.

"You okay?" she asks between breaths, her breasts rubbing along my fingers with each inhale.

"Yeah, this is new for me." I close my eyes and shake my head against hers, prepared for her to laugh at me like everyone always does.

"Me too." She laughs, not at me, but with me. "We can figure this one out together." She reaches up for my hand and brings it down to the vibrator next to her, wrapping my fingers around it. I've seen this type in porn before when I was struggling to figure out what I liked, one part designed to slip into her while the other half sucks on her clit.

"Do we need lube?" I ask her. The goal here is to help her relax, and not hurt her, I know that much from all my research.

She drops her head back with a groan, almost connecting with the mirror. The movement causes her breasts to peek out from under her top and my other hand has a mind of its own as it cups one of them. She gasps, and arches into the touch as my thumb rubs over the soft skin, creeping up to her nipple when I feel something cold and hard. I quickly take my eyes off her and lift my hand more to move her top and reveal her nipple to the air. Her *pierced* nipple.

"You have your nipples pierced?" I ask and it sounds like I've lost my voice. I recall all the times I noticed how her nipples were hard under her shirt, about what was really making them hard and my dick cries out for me to do something about it.

Rolling her head back up to look at me she takes a deep breath before speaking. "Yeah, you like them?" she asks, tone sultry as she pulls her lip between her teeth.

"Very much," I say, running my thumb over the metal balls on either side, lightly grazing the peak of her nipple as she moans at the touch. "But lube?"

"We don't need it," she says in an exasperated sigh, moving my hand from her breast down her body and into her shorts.

I understand what she means when my fingers easily glide along her pussy, already soaked. "Barbie, are you not wearing underwear?" I'm barely able to get out the question, feeling like I've completed a 5K with no water.

"Laundry day, remember?" she laughs and guides my

fingers further down, finding her entrance and pushing one in. "Oh fuck," she groans and removes her hand from mine as I take over and slip a second finger into her. She's warm and wet and I'm about to lose my mind watching how she starts to move her hips, seeking more.

I pull my fingers out of her, and she whines at the loss of contact, but when I lift them to my mouth her eyes darken. The desire to know what she tastes like taking over as I slip them between my lips. It's sweet and musky, and I don't break eye contact as I pull each finger out of my mouth with a pop.

Maeve's hand flies to the back of my neck and she pulls me down to her, crashing our mouths together. The kiss has the same intensity and urgency from the other night. She demands access to my mouth, running her tongue across my lips and I open for her. At this moment I'd do anything she asked me to. She devours me, sucking my tongue and tasting herself.

My hand moves to her head and I take her claw clip out, letting her hair fall down around her face and shoulders. Tossing it behind me, it clinks against something as my fingers intertwine through the strands at the back of her head, my grip tightening as she kisses me harder.

I nip at her lip quickly before looking down at the vibrator and realizing I have no idea how to turn it on. "How does this work?" I ask, holding it closer to her.

She bites down on her tongue in concentration as her fingers come around the vibrator, holding down a button until a light starts flashing. She clicks a few more buttons and the vibrator comes to life in my hand. I run my finger over the suction end, and can feel the way my skin tightens.

She whimpers, like I'm taking too long exploring the vibrator and not her. Smirking at her, I move it under her shorts to run it along her pussy, getting it ready to slip inside her. She moans when it makes contact with her clit and I can't help but smile as I bring my mouth back to hers.

After a few strokes I line it up with her entrance and slowly push it into her. She gasps, breaking our fevered kisses and arching into it. When I have it fully in her I remove my finger from the suction part and let it connect with her clit.

Her other hand flies into my hair and she drops her head back as she moans, and I welcome the pain of her pulling it. I release her hair and pull her to the edge of the dresser.

"Fuck, I need more, harder," she says and I pick up my pace of moving the vibrator in and out of her. She's so close to me now that the movement causes my hand to brush my dick. It feels like this is the hardest I've ever been, and my balls tighten as she connects her ankles around my back, pulling me closer.

"Like this?" I ask, making sure I'm still keeping up a good pace for her.

"Yes, I'm so close. Don't stop," she gasps between breaths and picks her pace, grinding against the vibrator and my cock.

"Do it, let me see it," I growl and lean back to look down as her mouth opens in the loveliest moan and her body flushes across her chest and up her neck. She comes around the vibrator and I'm lucky it didn't take her long, because a few more seconds of her grinding against me would have ended in an embarrassing walk home.

Her breathing slows and I pull the vibrator out of her, finding the button to turn it off and dropping it on the dresser next to her. Her legs are still wrapped around me and I can't help but cup her face in my hands and pull her to me in one last quick kiss before I'm pulling away.

"Fuck, Barbie, how am I supposed to walk around now knowing you look like that when you come?" I groan and step back from her, committing this moment to a memory box locked deep in my brain.

"Look like what?" she asks.

I shake my head and rake my hands through my hair, blowing a bubble with the fruity gum now in my mouth. "Like a fucking goddess."

## TWENTY-ONE

MAEVE

After months of planning this talent show to help fundraise for the sorority, the day is finally here and I couldn't care less. My mind completely forgot about finding an act to fill in Alpha Pi's band spot after Connor grabbed my favorite vibrator, made me come, then left. Who does that? His confidence mixed with his uncertainty of what to do was a new turn on for me that I never saw coming. I was up all night trying to recreate the best orgasm of my life to date, but nothing worked. I couldn't get the burning desire that he brought out in me to rise on my own. Ignoring my only one Connor induced masturbation session rule, I finally let myself picture him as I pretended that he was still in my room with me as I came.

I must have worked my pelvic floor too hard last night, because I woke up this morning with some pain, but I took some aspirin and tried to focus on today. The event starts in thirty minutes and I still need to fill the spot. I've texted every group chat on campus that I have, including a random group project chat from last semester. They all owe me a favor after I did the majority of the work for them and they only showed up to present.

Luckily the show is all set up and enough tickets were sold to make it not embarrassing thanks to the work of the other sisters. Several are calling around to find another act but either people are leaving early for fall break or they simply don't want to. They've been an amazing help with selling tickets and searching for a fill in, but I'm ready to get this event over and focus back on finding an internship since I've still had no luck. Definitely not so I can focus on how Connor makes my vagina feel.

Pacing outside of the performance hall I'm about to give up and call it quits on filling the last spot when the tall ginger who has been stuck in my head strides through the doors dressed in his usual black hoodie, this time sans sweatpants in favor of jeans. A pair of jeans that hug his legs nicely and I wish he would turn around so I could see how well they outline the curve of his ass. My heart races and I instantly feel calmer when he looks at me, and that freaks me out. I shouldn't be this excited to see Connor, when his presence has only annoyed me the past five years. There's too many mixed emotions fighting for a spot in my brain and no time for me to analyze them. I wipe away the smile starting to spread across my face before he can tell as I wave at him and end the call that's been ringing for too long. No one answers calls anymore, fucking college students.

"Hey, Barbie, fill the spot yet?" he asks, stopping in front of me. I have to look up to meet his eyes, and I'm annoyed further when I notice how green they appear in this light. I shouldn't be staring into his eyes, I have shit to do.

"No, the show will end up being shorter than we originally planned." I shrug, accepting my fate. I'm sure no one will care, but I will know I didn't pull this off flawlessly.

"I had a feeling," he says, reaching into his pocket and pulling out a card. "Would a magician work?" he asks, doing something with the card to make it disappear and reappear in his other hand.

I stand there with my mouth open. This was the last thing I had on my bingo card for the semester—well Connor was the last thing I had, but Connor performing magic was *certainly* not on there.

"Is that a no?" he laughs nervously, putting the card back into his pocket.

I reach out and grab his hand before he can grab the strap of his backpack. "No, that's perfect," I tell him. "Come with me." I start pulling him toward the room with the rest of the acts before he can back out or my sudden burst of adrenaline fades.

Running into the room, I find Hannah and fill her in on Connor's act which was only me saying "magic" because I don't actually know what he's planning to do, but it doesn't matter if he's willing to get on stage. He could play solitaire for all I care. Checking my phone, I see I only have a few minutes to finish my make up and head to the stage to introduce the show.

I go to step away from Hannah and Connor, but he reaches out and grabs my hand before I get too far. "Where are you going?" he asks, eyebrows furrowed.

"Someone has to host this thing," I say, slipping out of his grip as I skip toward the stage and tell myself the twisting of my stomach is from nerves and not his touch.

The show runs as smoothly as one would expect a student talent show to go. Most people only cheer on their friends performing and some of the acts could have used more practice. But really, I don't mind as long as they're willing to perform.

Finally we get to Connor's act and I'm intrigued to see what he has up his sleeve—literally and figuratively. Everyone claps as the previous act leaves the stage, one of the college's many dance troops. They danced to a mashup of Taylor Swift songs and I loved every minute of it.

Standing at the bottom of the stairs I tell them how great they did before I climb up to the stage, microphone in hand.

"And now, for our last act of the night," I start, catching sight of Connor out of the corner of my eyes. He's changed from his hoodie into the shirt from our first date and my heart skips a beat. Did he plan this? No, not for me, he probably would have done this if Hannah was the one planning the event. "The magic styling of Connor O'Shea," I say into the microphone, raising my hand in his direction and welcoming him to the stage before I let my thoughts run away.

He jogs up the stairs with ease, joining me and taking the microphone. "Thank you, Maeve," he says to me before I leave the stage. "But I do need a volunteer if you're up for it," he says, stopping me in my tracks and grinning at me, and I can't back down from a challenge. Especially not when this new confident side of him is emerging and I want to see how far it goes.

I return to center stage, getting closer to him again. "I'm definitely up for it."

"Perfect," he says into the microphone and I hear his voice fill the room. "We'll start easy, but if you don't mind I need you to position the mic for me." He places the mic in a stand then grabs one of the leftover music stands from the musical acts, placing both between us and tilting the stand to face the audience as I position the mic between us.

He pulls out a deck of cards from his pocket and offers it to me with his palm up, slightly leaning over the music stand with his other hand behind his back. "Do me a favor and give the deck a shuffle, ma'am."

I bite my lip, hiding my laugh at how polite he's being as I take the deck from his hands. I shuffle it, examining the face of the cards and messing them up to the best of my ability before handing them back to him.

"Thank you, ma'am," he says with a slight smirk that has me biting my tongue to keep from smiling too much. "We are going to use four of a kind for this one, so which one would you like to pick?" he asks, placing the deck face down on the music stand so the audience can clearly see it.

"How about threes?" I say, thinking of the first number to come to my head, which happens to be my birth month.

"Now in particular, which three of the four would you like to be your card?" he asks, picking the deck up and running his thumb over the corner of them.

"Diamonds, please," I say with confidence.

"Perfect, now I'm going to take out the four threes and place them on the stand here." He taps the music stand and then starts searching the deck for the cards. Pulling each card out, he places it face down on the stand and keeps the rest of the deck in his hand. When he's got all four out he says, "Now keep them face down so you don't know which is which and give them a shuffle for me, please. Then when you're happy with the shuffle, deal them face down on the stand."

I do as he says, shuffling the four cards in my hands and placing them down one at a time on the stand next to where he placed the rest of the deck. This trick must be pretty easy since he's got a 25 percent chance of getting it right compared to using the entire deck, but maybe he's starting small.

"Now, one of these is the three of diamonds, right?" he asks, and I nod. "And you picked the threes, you shuffled the cards, and you mixed these four up." I nod. "And you agree I couldn't possibly know which one of these is your card?" I nod again. "But how about I cover my eyes and you mix them up one more time."

I can't help the instinctual eye roll when he covers his eyes with his hand and I move the cards around one more time on the stand, uncovering them when I tell him to.

"Now, hold a finger up on each hand," he instructs, and when I raise both of my middle fingers the audience laughs and he rolls his eyes at me while shaking his head. "Lovely, now push two cards toward me," he says, leveling the stand so the cards don't fall when I push them.

Taking my middle fingers, I push the two middle cards toward him and he picks one up in each hand still facing down.

"Lastly, pick one of these two cards for me to drop," he says, holding them out to me. I tap the left one, and he drops it to join the discarded ones on the stand. "That leaves us with this card. And I want you to think about this. You decided on the threes, you picked the three of diamonds, you shuffled them, and you shuffled them when I wasn't looking. Right?"

"Right," I nod, getting suspicion with how he's going to pull this off.

"Let's see if this is your card," he says, flipping the card over in his hand and revealing the three of diamonds, lifting it up to the audience who all gasp and I have to say I'm impressed. "But here's the thing, you didn't have a choice."

"What do you mean?" I ask, crossing my arms and tilting my head, wondering where he's going with this since the trick is over. I'm sure he's going to pull out some physiological reasons for why I picked the three of diamonds like he's secretly wearing three diamonds somewhere.

"It was inevitable you were going to pick the three of diamonds because the rest of this deck is blank," he reveals, flipping over the discard cards to show blank faces. Then, picking up the rest of the deck and flipping them over one by one to reveal the same blank white face. My brain tries to catch up as he reveals card by card, tilting the stand again to show the audience the blank cards as they gasp.

"What the fuck?" I ask through a disbelieving laugh as I pick up the cards and inspect each one. Only to see the generic red side and the blank white face, while the three of diamonds sits on the stand not changing. "How did you do that?"

"A magician never reveals his secrets," he teases, snapping and pointing at me as the audience breaks out into a round of applause.

Before I know it, Connor has performed multiple tricks and bested me in each one. He was a hit with the audience and had them on the edge of their seats the entire time. It seemed like they were bummed when he finished and I ended the show. I'm willing to bet they enjoyed him more than the puppet guy. He could be his own fundraiser next semester, and people could bet if they could best him.

After I left the stage, I helped the sisters clean up and set everything back up the way we found it. By the time I was done, Connor was gone and I attempted to shake off the disappointment of his absence as something painful tightened in my gut.

"We are going to pregame at Casey's, you in?" Brittany comes up beside me, and I jump at the abruptness of it.

"I'm going to head home, I'm starting to get really bad cramps and I think I need to lie down with a heating pad,"

I tell her, unable to ignore the cramps and unsure if it's something lingering from this morning. I normally don't get them with my IUD in, but sometimes they creep up— or maybe I have to poop. Either way, my abdomen hurts. The show was a success and now I can go home and relax the rest of the night alone since Hannah left for break with another sister ten minutes ago. As I head out I finally glance down at my phone and see a text.

CONNOR MY FAVORITE LIFEGUARD

Had to run, you did a great job. I might swing by later

I think I left my notebook at your place

I bite my lip, suppressing the smile threatening to break free as I tap back a thumbs up on the message. Maybe I won't be alone tonight after all.

# CONNOR

I'm itching to get back to Maeve's apartment. After I got off the stage I had so much electricity running through me, I was bouncing off the walls. I never would have been able to do it without her by my side, her presence a calming source for my anxiety. Being able to banter and play off her reactions made the whole thing a breeze. I wasn't sure if she would need me, but with all the stress she's been putting on herself I wanted to make sure I came with a back up plan in case she did.

When I walked into the performance hall, she was on the phone, and I saw her attempt to hide her excitement to see me, but I didn't take my eyes off her for a second so I saw the way her eyes lit up and her mouth started to turn into a smile.

I wanted to stay around and talk to her, but Brad had texted me that he locked himself out of the apartment. I almost told him to fuck off, but I don't want to be the worst roommate in this relationship. I told Maeve I might stop by her apartment to get a notebook I left behind, but there wasn't a notebook. And the "might swing by later" was definitely a for sure, but I didn't want to give away how desperate I was to see her and hear what she thought of my act. Plus maybe I could talk to her about us. We completely skipped the conversation of expanding our fake relationship past kissing, motivated by a horny haze. I don't know where that leaves us, but I need to find out.

Arriving at the Mu Mansion, I'm able to slip into the building when one of the sisters walks in as I get to the door. She greets me and tells me how much she loved the card tricks, which only puts more of a bounce in my step as I climb the stairs to Maeve's apartment.

I knock on her door when I get there, checking my phone to see if she ever sent back a message, but she didn't. After a few knocks my excitement starts to diminish, thinking maybe she didn't want me to come over? Maybe she hated the whole act? Maybe I'm making up how she was excited to see me?

I knock again, and when she doesn't answer I start to worry. My gut is telling me something is wrong. She normally answers me. Even if it was to tell me to fuck off. She wouldn't just ignore me. Trusting my instinct, I twist the door knob to find it unlocked.

Letting myself in, I pray she's not naked somewhere fresh out of a shower. I'd probably lose all function and forget about talking to her, opting for giving her another orgasm instead. But it's too quiet and a bit eerie until Greta prances out from the hallway and meows at me. Her meow is less friendly and more forceful as she turns and runs off back down the hall.

I follow her all the way to Maeve's room and turn the corner to see Maeve on her floor in the fetal position. She's clutching her stomach and trying to reach for her phone on the bed with no luck.

"What the fuck? Why are you on the ground?" I shriek, my voice cracking.

"It's fine, I'm fine, it's just some bad cramps," she says, groaning and clutching tighter.

"I don't think so. You can't stand up to get your phone," I argue when she reaches for it again and doesn't move an inch.

"I can stand," she counters.

"Okay, so stand up," I challenge.

"No, I don't want to." Her eyes shoot daggers at me and if she was able to stand up I would be getting hit right now.

"Where's Hannah? We need Hannah." I pat my pockets, searching for my phone to call her.

"She went home for the break already," she groans from the floor.

"You're clearly in pain. You need to go to urgent care," I argue, stepping closer to her to help her get up.

"I'm fine, Connor, you can go," she says, waving her hand in the air.

"I can't go. You can't move," I shout, my heartbeat pounding and not for a good reason. What if I leave her here and she dies? I'd never be able to live with myself.

"I'll be fine!" she screams back at me.

"Nope. I'm taking you to urgent care," I say, bending down and sliding one arm under her bent legs and another around her back.

"Fucking hell," she shouts as I scoop her up in my arms. "Put me down," she yells, trying to wiggle out of my grasp, groaning and leaning into my chest as what I'm sure are not cramps hits her again. "Don't forget my purse," she mumbles into my chest before I step out the door.

I carry her down the stairs and to my car; she doesn't weigh any different from Hannah's drunken dead-weight so it's not too bad. But by the time I'm setting her in the front seat I'm glad I got a close spot in the parking lot.

The drive to urgent care is silent besides the groans of pain coming from Maeve every so often. Meanwhile, I'm internally thinking of all the things that could be wrong with her. What if her appendix burst? Can she die from that? How long would I have to get her help if that's the case?

Before I can spiral too much we're checking in and in a back room faster than I thought. Luckily there was no one else in the waiting room when we got there and Maeve's pain seems to have subsided for now. When they called her name she was able to stand on her own, but struggled. I stood up to help her and her hand grabbed mine tight as she peered at me with pleading eyes. She asked the nurse if I could come back with her, which I was surprised by.

The nurse showed us the room and left, telling Maeve to put on a gown and keep her underwear on, which left my face heated and my gaze averted. I kept my eyes on a poster about flu season as she changed before a doctor came in.

Now I'm in the corner chair as the doctor asks Maeve about why she's here and remembering how much I don't like being here. Normally, I only go to the doctors if my mom yells at me for avoiding it. If they pull out a needle I might have to leave so I don't pass out.

"When did the pain start?" the doctor asks. I've already forgotten his name.

"A few hours ago, some this morning, but worse over the last few hours. I thought it was bad cramps, then all of the sudden I was on the floor and I couldn't move. It was in this area," she explains pointing to her abdomen.

"Are you expecting your period soon? Or could you be pregnant?" he asks.

"I'm not pregnant. I"—she glances at me as a flush colors her cheeks before she continues—"have an IUD in, so I'm not sure when my period was supposed to be here."

The doctor nods in understanding, and I'm confused as to how she wouldn't know when her period was coming if she gets one every month. But my period knowledge is limited to simply knowing what types of tampons and pads my mom and sister prefer if I ever need to pick them up.

"There isn't much we can do for you here," he starts to explain. "I suspect either your IUD has moved or you could have had an ovarian cyst burst. Both of those things would need an ultrasound to check, so you're going to have to go to the emergency room since we don't have one here. I can give you some aspirin for the pain in the meantime, but I really would recommend going to the emergency room."

Maeve nods and I can tell by the flare of her nostrils she's stopping herself from yelling at this doctor right now.

"Before I go to grab that, did you want anything else done while you're here?" he asks, glancing over at me then back to Maeve with a raise of his eyebrow. "Any testing for STIs?"

"No," Maeve clips. I'm starting to worry for this man's safety if he stays here longer than necessary when he glances back at me like he doesn't believe her when she says she doesn't need any testing. "I've had those recently. Just the *aspirin* will do," she says, and I can hear the disdain in her voice when she emphasizes aspirin. Hell, I'm about to hit him for the tone he's using.

The second the doctor leaves the room Maeve sticks her hand out to me and gestures for her pants. I'm quick to toss them her way and step aside as she slips them on under the gown. She snaps when she's done and I toss her shirt toward her, averting my gaze when she drops the gown to put it on. The doctor is back soon after that, and she takes the aspirin from his hand with a quick "thanks" and is out the door before I can stand up.

I jog after her to catch up as she makes a beeline for the exit, stopping at the desk to make sure she's good. They tell her they'll send her a bill if needed and she nods, starting up again before making her way through the automatic doors and into the parking lot.

I pull my keys out and unlock the car before she can get there so she doesn't rip the door off its hinges. Once we're both in the car I hesitate before pulling out.

"To the emergency room then?" I ask, not sure if she only wants me to take her home.

She sighs. "This is such fucking bullshit. But yes, to the emergency room. I have to make sure this IUD isn't going rogue on me." She turns her head toward the window, bringing a hand up to her eyes. No doubt trying to hide the fact she's starting to cry.

I reach over and grab her other hand in mine, rubbing the back of it with my thumb. "It's going to be okay, I'll get you there in one piece. And hopefully the IUD isn't on vacation." I reassure her and feel relieved when she chuckles at my IUD joke. When I start to pull my hand away, she squeezes tighter and it feels like she's squeezing my heart. I don't let go of her hand, maneuvering the gear shift and pulling out with my other hand to get her to the emergency room as fast as possible.

## TWENTY-THREE

## MAEVE

The emergency room wait takes longer than urgent care since I'm no longer actively screaming in pain. I must not be as much of a priority as other people. I should have said I was having chest pains, that would have gotten me back there sooner. I saw that on some medical drama show, so I'm not sure if it would have worked since those shows are rarely accurate. The exam room is cold and it smells clean, which I guess is good, but it's also overwhelming with how strong it is. There's a continuous beep going off somewhere I can't identify and people keep yelling in the hall, and I just want to go home.

"Do you have any gum?" I ask Connor as we wait for the doctor to join us and bite my nails trying to distract myself that I'm in a second exam room and gown for the night with another small cloth draped over my lap. The small pieces of nail polish flake off on my tongue and I need to stop before I get some stuck in my teeth.

"No. Is there any in your purse?" he asks, picking up my purse off the ground.

"No, I'm out," I tell him, annoyed that I didn't pick up

another pack earlier today. It helps me not bite my nails but I guess I've already done enough damage to them where I'll need to repaint them soon. I'm still pissed off that the urgent care trip was essentially useless. What's the point of them if they're going to be staffed with the most incompetent doctors who only give me aspirin and tell me to go somewhere else while guessing what's wrong with me?

There's a knock on the door and a tall brunette woman enters the room, "Hi, I'm Doctor Gray, you're Maeve?" she introduces herself, shaking my hand, and I'm relieved to have a female doctor this time, hopefully she understands better than Dr. What's-His-Face. "I see you're here concerned about your IUD. Could you tell me what's been happening?" Her calm tone is soothing and I already feel more relaxed.

Taking my nails out of my mouth, I fill her in on all the details of tonight from the crippling pain to what the doctor at urgent care said. She nods as she takes notes.

"And how are you feeling now?" she asks.

"Still some pain, but I can walk and breathe," I tell her.

"Got it. Do you know if you previously had any doctors tell you to watch for any ovarian cysts?"

"No." I shake my head, as my pulse picks up because that sounds like something I don't want to have.

"Okay, so because I don't know if you previously had one, there's no way for me to tell if one burst and caused your pain. They don't leave anything behind, so there's nothing I can look for. Unfortunately, a lot of the time women are misdiagnosed with ovarian cysts because doctors don't know what else could be wrong with them. It's also rarer that you would get one in the first place with the IUD, but it's not impossible. What I can do is check to make sure your IUD is still in place and hasn't moved through an internal ultrasound. If everything is all set there, I can't do much else besides send you home with pain medicine and tell you to rest and come back if the pain returns," she tells me, standing up and pulling a machine with wires and a wand from the corner of the room. "Would you like to do this alone or have him stay?" She gestures over to Connor who is sitting in the corner looking like he can disappear into the chair if he sits still enough. But with his tall frame and lengthy legs there's nowhere for him to hide. His skin is whiter than usual, and part of me feels guilty for dragging him along.

"Can he hold my hand?" I ask, and I know this won't hurt, but I need someone with me. Usually my mom would be here but she's hours away, and Connor has been so great tonight. As much as I would have scowled at the idea of him being the one to find me earlier this semester, I'm glad he's here with me now.

"Yes, he can stand on the other side there," Dr. Gray says, pointing to the space opposite of where she is.

Connor nods a few times like he's hyping himself up before pushing off the chair and coming to stand at my head. Taking my hand between his, he rubs my fingers since he must feel how cold they are. The warmth of his hands is soothing and I close my eyes to focus on the feel of his fingertips instead of the fact that I'm being exposed to this room while my fake boyfriend is doing very real boyfriend-like things. His grip is soft and tight around my fingers. His nails aren't long, but they're not short either.

The doctor takes her place at my feet where she slowly lifts the cloth, moving the wand of the ultrasound between my legs. I brace myself for pain or discomfort, but there isn't any as she works. I must tense at some point, because Connor's hand squeezes mine in encouragement, but when

I look over at him he's got his eyes glued to the wall behind him.

The ultrasound is over quickly, and Dr. Gray ensures my IUD is still where it needs to be and apologizes for not being able to do more for me. She sends me home with pain medicine and we leave the emergency room. This visit was objectively better than the urgent care one, but I still feel like it was almost useless since pain meds seem to be the only solution. The only benefit of this is knowing my IUD didn't try to vacate my uterus prematurely. I still don't know what caused the pain in the first place and I'm frustrated, upset, and scared it's going to happen again.

Heading outside I'm greeted by the cool October air and a moon that isn't quite full yet. Crickets chirp in the bushes and an ambulance siren gets louder as it approaches the hospital. Connor follows close behind me as the tears threaten to break free with every step I take. When he steps closer, his hand brushes mine and that's all it takes for me to grab it and pull him to me. I spin as I step in front of him and bury my head in his warm chest. I hear an "oof" from him as I drop his hand to hold him closer as the tears come flooding out of my eyes like a bursting dam.

He relaxes as his arms come around my back. One cups the back of my head as I sob and the other strokes my back. It's the opposite of when I comforted him after the midterm, and I would normally examine why we suddenly seem to be so comfortable around each other but the tears are too much right now. He doesn't say anything as I cry and cry. I don't know how long we stand there in the parking lot next to his car, but I'm grateful he doesn't rush me along.

When the tears have finally subsided I pull away and wipe my eyes, seeing I left a wet spot on his chest. He sees it and chuckles, which fills my heart with warmth that he's not mad about any of this.

"Will you stay at my apartment tonight?" I ask, not wanting to be alone in case the pain comes back. I don't want to ruin Hannah's break by calling her back and worrying her when the possibility I'm going to be okay is greater than not. Plus, if Connor doesn't mind it I wouldn't hate having him there just in case. He never mentioned any plans for the break, so I'm hoping this ask isn't too much.

"Of course. I'm not going to leave you alone after that. What kind of fake boyfriend would I be if I did? We can swing by my place and I'll grab some stuff. If you're hungry I can also swing through a drive-thru and get us dinner. Then I'll take you home?" he asks, making sure I'm okay with that plan.

"No drive-thru, I want to be home," I tell him, craving the comfort of my apartment. He nods and he opens the passenger side door for me, taking my hand and helping me climb in. Once he's seated and buckled up, his hand finds its way back to mine as he drives us away from the hospital. He doesn't let go of my hand all the way to his apartment. He returns five minutes later with a small duffle bag, and when he grabs my hand again I'm surprised with the realization I missed the warmth of it wrapped around mine. And instead of thinking about it too hard, I let myself enjoy the comfort as he drives us back to my apartment.

## TWENTY-FOUR

"Is the couch going to be good for you? I also have an air mattress," Maeve says when we get back to her apartment as I pull out several board games and my Switch from my duffle bag. "Are you planning on moving in?" She laughs, pointing at the games stacked on her coffee table.

"Well if I'm going to be here for four days I want to make sure I have entertainment," I tell her, setting my Switch on top of the games.

"Who says you're staying here the whole break?" she challenges, crossing her arms and furrowing her eyebrows.

"You said Hannah was gone, right?" I ask, recalling what she said earlier tonight.

"Yeah. Her brothers and their best friend, Will, are also home so she wanted to see all of them," she tells me.

"Right, so there's no way I'm leaving you alone at all until she gets back. I wouldn't be able to live with myself if something happened to you," I admit. I don't care if she makes fun of me. The last few hours have been scary for me, I can only imagine how scary they were for her. I would have broken down and called my mom the second I was at urgent care. When she wanted me to go back in the room with her I wasn't going to say no and tell her I was scared shitless, so I sucked it up instead.

She seems to be running through her replies in her head as she stares at me in silence. Her face relaxes and her eyebrows return to normal, her arms dropping to her sides before she replies. "Okay, I'll get you the air mattress and sheets," she says, spinning on her heels and leaving the room.

By the time she returns, I've moved the coffee table out of the way and she helps me get everything settled. The double air mattress has one of those built-in pumps and I wonder if it's one she brings camping each summer. I've never been up to see her campsite before, but I've heard enough stories to know her and her cousins all sleep in tents so they don't wake their parents up when they go to bed.

"I'm going to make some mac and cheese, do you want some?" she asks through a yawn and heads toward the kitchen.

Dropping the pillow in my hand onto the air mattress, my long legs give me an advantage and I'm in front of her before she can register I've moved, blocking her entrance into the kitchen. "No, I'll make it. I remember where everything is," I tell her.

"I'm capable of making my own food," she argues, trying to push around me. I ignore the rush of energy surging through my body when she touches my arm, and I wish I had an excuse to grab her hand again like in the car.

"I'm aware. But you're clearly exhausted. You put on this massively successful event, pretty much by yourself, and spent the night running around from doctor to doctor without getting any clear answers. So, no, you won't make your own food. You're going to go to your room, put on your fuzziest pajamas, and I'm going to bring you mac and cheese. Then you're going to go to bed and rest. Sound like a plan?"

"Fine," she huffs, sitting at the stool behind the kitchen counter instead of listening to me and going to her room to relax. "But before I go change, we need to talk," she says firmly, and I'm worried I missed some sort of signal and did something wrong. Either that or the hand holding was too much and she knows I want to talk to her about our whole arrangement.

"About what?" I ask cautiously, starting to gather the dishes to make dinner.

"When the fuck were you going to tell me you can do magic?" she asks in a voice just a level below a yell as my worry evaporates.

"Oh that? I'm a man of many talents," I say, glad she asked about something I can easily talk about. "I went to magic camps for a few summers and picked up on it fairly easily," I tell her, thinking of the multiple summers I spent learning card tricks and how to make things disappear.

"What else do you know how to do?" she asks, tilting her head in curiosity and resting her chin on her palm.

"You'll have to wait and see," I tease. "There's a funny story from the fall after my third time going," I start, continuing to make dinner and hoping if she doesn't want to hear this she'll stop me. When she doesn't interrupt, I continue, "It was one night my parents went out for a date night. I was either nine or ten, anyway, my babysitter Carrie was watching me. I wanted to play hide and seek, so I used my special skills to pick the best place to hide. She couldn't find me and started to panic so she called 911. I could hear her on the phone, but I wasn't sure if she was tricking me or not, so I stayed hidden. Right when she said something about my parents pulling in, I jumped out and scared her," I say, laughing through the last sentence because I still think it's hilarious to this day even if Carrie doesn't.

Maeve is laughing along, too, so I don't feel bad about it. "Wait, so where were you hiding?" she asks.

"The freezer," I say proudly, knowing I could never do it now unless it was a giant freezer.

"How the fuck did you pull that off?" she asks once she's stopped laughing.

"I told you a magician never reveals his secrets," I answer, pointing at her with a wink that's met with a familiar roll of her eyes. "Now go get comfy, I'll bring you dinner," I tell her, satisfied she must be feeling better and redirecting my finger down the hall. I raise my eyebrows at her to encourage an answer before she huffs, hopping off the stool and heading toward her bedroom.

Satisfied I don't have to talk about my feelings yet, I recall the last time I was here making mac and cheese with a drunk Maeve as I move around the kitchen. I can hear her drawers opening and closing as she moves around her room. I go on autopilot as I cook, listening for any sounds indicating she needs help—a sudden thump or a scream for help since I can't see her. Soon, the mac and cheese is done and I bring it to her room.

She's sitting in her bed with Greta on her lap, and I make a mental note to check to see if she has food too. She's in a pink hoodie that swallows her whole and says 'Black Willow Bay, NY' on the front. My heart warms at the sight of my hometown's name across her chest. A chest I now know has pierced nipples.

She sets her phone down, as I hand her the bowl. "Thanks, beanstalk," she says, and she must already be feeling better if she's back to calling me random tall names, and getting it right this time. "I appreciate all your help today. You didn't have to do that." She takes a bite of her food and it takes everything in me to not touch her when she moans at the taste.

"Well I need you to pass our class, so I had no choice," I tease back, not wanting to admit to her how much I'm starting to enjoy taking care of her. "I'm going to eat then head to bed, do you need anything?" I ask, ending the conversation before we start talking more and I say something stupid.

"No, I'm all set. Thank you again," she says with a more serious tone in her voice.

"Of course," I say, leaving her room and returning to the living room.

I eat, clean up, and finally relax on the air mattress for some much needed rest. But as I stare at the ceiling trying to fall asleep several things prevent my mind from relaxing. There's a group of people outside yelling, the clock on the wall gets louder with every tick of the second hand, and the glow of LED light on the Wi-Fi router is blinding. My heart feels like it hasn't slowed down since earlier tonight and all the only thought running through my head is if Maeve is still breathing in the other room. She's only down the hall, and I hope if she needed me she would yell. But I also don't know if she would.

I check my phone again to see how long has passed since I've tried to fall asleep and it's been half an hour. There's no way I'm going to be able to forgive myself if something happens to her and I'm not right there. After several more ticks of the clock, I grab my pillow and blanket to head for Maeve's room, determined to make sure she's still okay and hoping she's already asleep.

## TWENTY-FIVE

MAEVE

The sound of a door slamming jolts me awake. That's one thing I've always hated about apartment buildings: no one ever does anything quietly. No one has any decency to remain quiet when people could be sleeping. I wish I could get away with enforcing quiet hours for the mornings, but that might be a bit much.

Rubbing my eyes, I reach for my phone to check the time. There's no way it's earlier than seven. My eyes adjust and I ignore all the notifications on my phone to see it's actually 10:00 a.m., I must have slept more than I thought. Which makes sense after how long of a night I had—I'm not sure what time I ended up going to bed after eating the mac and cheese Connor made. I stretch and wince when I feel there's still some soreness in my stomach, I'm definitely going to need to take the pain medicine that Dr. Gray gave me. Taking a deep breath, my gaze roams over my room when something out of place on my floor stops me.

Laying there on my fluffy white rug is a patch of red and pink. Connor's wrapped up in a blanket, with his feet sticking out one end and his head on the other. It's shocking to find that I don't mind that he's on my floor, and my first thought is that I'm going to have to find him a bigger blanket. He's still asleep and he looks peaceful lying there, mouth slightly open and breathing steady.

My heart tugs at the guilt that he must have slept on the floor all night. Until I see a small bundle of fur tucked between his arms, snuggled against his chest. Greta lays there asleep, and their matching red hair pulls at my heart strings for a completely different reason from a second ago.

Making sure not to make any noise, I open my camera and take a picture of the two of them asleep on the floor. I open it and zoom in on the photo, smiling like an idiot at my phone and almost send it to Hannah before I stop myself. I haven't told her about last night yet, and explaining this whole thing sounds exhausting right now. Instead, I open up DoorDash and order some iced coffee and breakfast sandwiches so neither of us has to cook. I can fill Hannah in on the whole thing when she gets back in a few days.

Connor is still asleep so I take the time to check all my social media notifications. Sharing, liking, and commenting on posts from the talent show, I remind myself I'll have to make my own post once my brain is functioning. My DMs are full of tags from stories for my cousin Abby's birthday featuring photos of us. Opening up my calendar app, I double check my notes to see how old she's turning before finding our cousins group chat. The name is constantly rotating based on what we're talking about, so I keep the group pinned to the top of my messages. No one has started the birthday texts yet, so I take the liberty of changing the group name myself.

**Maeve** named the conversation "Abby's Feeling 22".

MAEVE

Happy birthday Abby! Hope those hockey boys treat you right today!

Abby recently moved about an hour from home after she got her dream job working as the social media manager for the hockey team in Buffalo. Part of me is sad everyone has started to move away from home, but I'm happy they're all happy.

Everyone is quick to chime in after my message, with similar birthday wishes and I love you's. It doesn't take long for her to send a message back.

ABBY

Thank you fam! Love you all so so so much and can't wait to party with you at Charlie's wedding!

The team surprised me with a cake and crown!

She follows up with a selfie of her wearing a silver crown with gems on it and an oval that says 'It's my birthday!'

I tapback a heart to the message, saving the photo and posting it to my stories to wish her a happy birthday on social media so people don't think I hate her. I wish I didn't always have to post about everyone's birthday, but one year I missed one cousin's birthday and my mom called me the next day to find out what was wrong. Posting a birthday story is easier than having to have that conversation several times a year.

Finally satisfied that no one online needs me and there are no fires to put out, I slowly get out of bed and tiptoe around Connor and Greta to brush my teeth and freshen up. As I'm brushing my teeth, this annoying look of happiness reflects back at me. Quickly shifting my face back to a neutral state I continue brushing, unwilling to admit I'm smiling because of a certain ginger giant on my floor.

After brushing my teeth, I check to see Connor is still asleep, so I run downstairs to grab our breakfast. The Mu Mansion is quieter than usual this morning, since most people went home for fall break or out drinking last night. I thought about going back home with Hannah, but I wanted a relaxing weekend after the talent show and midterms so I told her to go without me.

Slipping back into the apartment so as to not wake Connor, I lock the door and shriek when I turn around and see his tall frame holding Greta filling up the hallway that was empty a second ago.

"Morning, Barbie," he says through a yawn as he scratches his head. The movement of his arm causes his T-shirt to rise up and my eyes instantly glance down to the slice of skin that's now visible above his sweatpants hanging low on his thin hips. There's a dusting of equally red hair disappearing into them and I tell myself my heart is pounding because he scared me. "Did you get us break-fast?" he asks, snapping me out of my staring and my eyes return to his face. I can tell he knows I was staring because his cheeks are flushed the lightest shade of pink and his lips turn up in one corner. His hair is disheveled and needs to be brushed, but I appreciate getting to see him relaxed. Greta moves in his hand and he sets her down on the floor before approaching me.

"Coffee and breakfast sandwiches," I say, holding out the drinks to him and grateful I didn't drop them when he scared me.

"Thanks," he says, taking the drinks and heading to the

couch, setting them on the end table before jumping over the back of the couch.

I follow him with the sandwiches, sitting on the opposite end and passing him one. "You didn't have to sleep on my floor. You could have at least brought the air mattress in there," I tell him, hoping he doesn't hear the joy in my voice as I take a bite of my sandwich.

"I know, but I got worried. Better safe than sorry. I'll move the mattress in there tonight," he says, shrugging. I want to fight him about sleeping in my room again, but having him close will help me sleep in case anything happens. Plus, it's not like he'd be sleeping *with* me, just relatively close to me. "How are you feeling?"

"Sore, but it's manageable," I tell him.

"This wasn't my fault, right? I was thinking about it last night and you don't think our activities the other night caused this?" he asks, tripping over his words and not making eye contact with me.

"No, red, you giving me one orgasm did not cause a cyst to burst. If that's what it was," I say, and I do my best to not be mean, but the sarcasm spills from my tongue.

He throws his hands up in the air for defense. "I had to ask, you never know."

"You're an idiot," I laugh, throwing one of the couch's throw pillows at him as he bats it out of the air in time before it hits his face.

"Yeah, that's been established," he sighs, quickly changing the subject. "What's the plan for today? I did bring my Switch with me, which includes *Mario Kart* and *Mario Party* if you're feeling competitive."

"Hm, I would love the opportunity to beat you, but maybe later? I want to start by being nothing but lazy and watch old rom coms, if you're up for that?" I challenge, sure he's going to want to go home after hearing my plans. Instead his freckled face lights up with the dorkiest smile and I'm worried I might've had Connor wrong all along.

## TWENTY-SIX

MAEVE

Hours later, Connor and I have watched several movies and he ordered a grocery delivery because he wanted snacks for the weekend but didn't want to leave me.

We're currently watching the beginning of *Legally Blonde* and I'm starting to fade fast. It feels weird to go take a nap while he's here, like I should be entertaining him since he's my guest. My head keeps bobbing like I'm in class trying not to fall asleep.

"You can sleep, Barbie. You don't have to stay awake." Connor's voice wakes me up from my current state.

"I'm fine," I lie.

"You're not, lay down. Come here," he says, moving all the way against the far side of the couch and putting a pillow on his lap. My face must give away my confusion and hesitation because he says, "Trust me, lay down."

Not wanting to move much, I listen and readjust myself on the couch to lay down on his lap. Slowly lowering myself, his arm comes up around the back of the couch to give me plenty of room. Laying down makes me more tired and it won't take me long until I'm asleep. Then Connor's hand comes to my hair and starts to stroke it slowly. The pressure is perfect and his nails gently scrape my scalp. I have to bite my tongue so I don't moan on his lap.

"You can change the movie," I tell him as my eyes struggle to stay open through the slow pace of his fingers through my hair.

"I'm okay, you just worry about sleeping," he says as I allow the drowsiness to take over while on the screen Elle's studying montage starts.

Connor's voice wakes me from sleep as I struggle to make sense of what I'm hearing. Is he on the phone? His voice is quiet like he doesn't want to wake me up. The movie is still playing and it takes me a minute to process him reciting the lines before they're said on the screen.

I wait a few more lines to confirm I'm hearing this right and not in some weird dream scenario. He's getting every line right and I turn my head to look up at him, but his gaze stays glued to the TV.

"How are you doing that?" I ask right as Elle finishes up her epic courtroom monologue.

Connor jumps, and my head rolls closer to his stom-ach. Before things can get too dangerous I push up on the couch and sit up next to him. "Shit you scared me," he says, covering his heart with his hand.

"Now we're even from this morning. But that was impressive," I say, pointing back to the TV.

"My babysitter used to put it on all the time. She would make me watch it while I braided her hair and painted her nails," he explains and the mental image of a little Connor painting his babysitter's nails warms my heart. If it was the same one as his magic trick they sure went through a lot together.

"Do you want to paint my nails?" I tease, holding up bare fingernails. Before I went to bed last night I removed all the nail polish I had destroyed from biting my nails while in urgent care and the emergency room.

"Are you sure? Don't you usually get them done?" he asks, and I'm surprised he seems to care about the state of my nails.

"Sometimes. It can get expensive if you go a lot, so I alternate between getting them done and doing them myself. But I always get them done for special occasions," I explain.

"Got it, that makes sense. I can take a crack at it if you want," he says, reaching up to pick at a pimple forming on his face.

"Don't pick at that," I yell, slapping his hand away from his face. "Hold on, I'll get you something for it." I hop off the couch and head toward the bathroom. Finding my nail polish, I grab a hot pink and top coat. Next, I find my pimple patches and find the one that will best suit his needs. Returning to the couch, Connor has put on another rom com and moved closer to the center of the couch. Sitting down next to him I watch as he eyes me cautiously. I peel the back off the yellow star in my hand and hold it up to his face.

"You're joking," he says, glaring at me.

"I'm not, come here," I tell him as he reluctantly leans closer to me. Grabbing his face in my other hand, I ignore the spark of electricity running through my body when I feel his skin on mine. Focusing, I place the star over the pimple on his face and lean back to take in my masterpiece. "You look great," I tell him, and he must think I'm joking because he rolls his eyes at me.

"Give me the nail polish," he says, holding his hand out.

I do as he says, and we readjust on the couch so my hands are on the pillow in his lap for him to do my nails. "You better not spill it," I warn.

"Excuse me?" he feigns shock, placing his hand over his heart. "I would never spill. I think you're underestimating how often I did this."

"I'm definitely underestimating you." I shake my head, laughing as he unscrews the cap of the bottle. "I'm learning so much about you, what else have you got hidden up your sleeve?" I tease.

"You want to learn something really personal?" he asks in an almost whisper, and my heart picks up its pace because his tone has shifted from joking to serious.

"You don't have to tell me anything you don't want to," I tell him, wanting to make sure he knows he doesn't have to.

"I know, but I've learned a lot of personal things about you this week, and our friendship isn't like it was at the beginning of the semester. I consider you one of my actual friends and I want my friends to know this about me. So I'm going to tell you."

"Okay, go ahead," I say, focusing on keeping my fingers still as he starts to paint.

"I'm not sure where to start with this, so I'm going to start talking and hope it makes sense," he starts, taking a deep breath before continuing. "I'm demisexual, and it's a new label for me. You know what that means, right?" He pauses, looking up briefly for confirmation.

"Yeah, I do. Most of us—me and my cousins—are some type of queer. I'm bi, so I'm pretty well versed in all things queerness. Liam is like our token heterosexual. But tell me about what it means for you. It's different for everyone," I say as he laughs at my joke about Liam before returning to my nails. Is it easier for him to tell me this without looking directly at me?

"Basically I don't experience sexual attraction like other people. I need a bond with a person first before feeling attraction to them. It's always been something I've been confused about. In high school, I had my one and only girlfriend. With her, I only asked her out because my friends said I should, I didn't really like her romantically. When it came time to take the next step, I had a hard time performing. Now I understand it's because I didn't feel anything for her. But she didn't see it that way, and told her friends about it. The next day, everyone at school seemed to know about it and her friends laughed and pointed at me as I passed by. You reminded me of them when we first met, which was the summer after it happened. That's probably why I was so mean to you, then you were mean back and it started a whole cycle for us. Anyway, not the point, but I'm sorry about being mean to you," he says, taking a deep breath and shaking his head.

The first time we met flashes into my head, we were both sixteen and awkward. I had braces and he had a face full of zits combined with a lifeguard uniform that looked too big on him. I could tell he had his defenses up before Cy introduced us, and when he made fun of my braces I made fun of his too tall height and his baggy swim trunks. From there, our guards were always up no matter what we were doing. But now those walls are slowly coming down.

"I'm sorry too," I whisper, not wanting to break his train of thought but wanting him to understand I also feel guilty about how we used to interact.

"Thanks, but the point of me telling you this is to

explain the other night—and the time before that too. It's kind of a big deal for me. To be doing those things and to actually like doing those things has surprised me. I'm sure you, uh, felt that I liked it?" His eyes finally meet mine again, and his face is the brightest shade of red I've ever seen.

"Yeah, I did," I confirm, remembering how much I liked the feeling of him against me. "Are you trying to tell me you like me?" I was following along with him until the last part, like he didn't finish his thought before checking in with me.

He sighs, putting the cap back on the top coat bottle. I didn't register that he finished painting my nails. "What I'm saying is, despite my greatest efforts to avoid this, you have become one of my closest friends. And because of that, your objective attractiveness, and our unique situation, I'm finding myself experiencing new things for the first time."

"Ohmygod, we're actual friends," I gasp, coming to the realization he's come to, giggling like a child who just got told someone said she was cute.

"Tragic, isn't it?" he sighs again with a shake of his head, which only makes me laugh.

"This backfired on us, didn't it?" I joke, blowing on my nails to help them dry faster.

"Maybe not, because if you wanted to keep doing things I don't think it's a bad idea," he shrugs and averts his gaze again.

"You're a virgin, right? I assume so based on what you've said, but I want to check." The question is out of my mouth before I can stop it, but I want our communication to be clear.

"Yes. I am," he confirms, blush deepening.

"And you want to have sex with me?" I clarify.

"Not necessarily, but maybe with some time I might not be opposed to it," he says.

"I'm not opposed either. I'm a fan of orgasms." I ponder the opportunity.

"Lovely. That way once we end our arrangement and I date someone else I'll know what I'm doing."

That's when it hits me. He sees our arrangement for what it is, only that. Two new friends helping each other out and nothing more. These feelings of excitement and potential romantic sparks are one sided. But the idea of doing this and getting to spend more time with him, even if it's limited, is appealing.

"Okay, I would be down to do that," I tell him. "But not this weekend, I'm still not back to one hundred percent."

"Of course, that's not why I'm here. I don't want you to think I'm staying here for that. I really was worried about you," he explains, and my stupid heart strings tug again. I'm going to need to get them under control if we're going to do this.

"Perfect, then you have yourself a deal. Kissing and other *stuff* is now on the table," I say, amending our initial agreement. Sticking my hand out toward him, he shakes it and my stomach knots at the anticipation of all the possibilities this unlocks for us.

## TWENTY-SEVEN

CONNOR

I t's been over a week since Maeve and I talked about adding more to our agreement. Since then, we haven't brought the topic back up or acted on it. I chickened out when she asked if I liked her, worried it would scare her off if I said maybe I was starting to. I'm not ready to admit that to her yet, because once it's out there I can't take it back.

The rest of fall break we continued to watch movies and TV shows. We snuck in a few board games and several games of *Mario Kart*. To no one's surprise, she picked Princess Peach while I went with Dry Bones. We were pretty evenly matched, and I lost track of who was beating who after the tenth game. She told me about how she used to play with her brother when they were kids, and she was always determined to beat him. Then about how one summer she would sneak downstairs after her bed time and practice, muting the TV so she wouldn't get caught.

It was like we were in our own bubble, away from the world. But fall break had to end, and I was back in my apartment before Hannah returned. I'm not sure if Maeve told her I was staying there, but it didn't seem like it so I didn't want to stay and stand there awkwardly while Maeve explained the entire weekend to her.

With her cousin's wedding two weeks away she wanted to do one more fake date to make sure we were comfortable in public and not only in her apartment. She mentioned it the other day during our study session and my stomach has been twisted since. The only information I have consists of me picking her up and being required to wear a plaid flannel. I hope it's something easy and not too far out of my comfort zone. I've already done so many new things this semester. I don't know how much I have left in me, but that might just be the nerves of being with her one-on-one again. What if it's a disaster? What if it's awkward and we have nothing to talk about? I need it to be like it was in her apartment so I know I'm not making all these feelings up.

Sitting outside her apartment, I text her I'm here and wait. My heart is pounding. Should I have gone to her door? Do I need to roll my sleeves up? Is my car clean enough? Before I can answer any of those questions, Maeve is hopping in the passenger seat with a quick, "Hi, ginger."

She looks fancier than my brown plaid flannel and jeans, in a cream floral dress with a dark pink sweater over it and knee high boots. She's perfectly autumn and I'm wondering if it would be appropriate to lean over and kiss her right now. We did agree to do it more, and a boyfriend would kiss his girlfriend hello. It would purely be for practice, not because I crave the feel of her lips against mine.

"Hi, Barbie," I say, my mouth breaking out into an unauthorized smile as I grab her hand, rubbing my thumb along her skin and realizing how much I missed her hand in mine this past week. "You look nice today, can I kiss you?" I ask, pulling her closer by our joined hands.

A blush creeps up her cheeks and she bites her bottom lip. "Sure," she whispers, leaning closer to me as my free hand moves to cup the side of her face.

My fingers weave into her hair as I pull her to me. Our mouths come together slowly and I revel in the softness of her lip. I was going to leave this at a quick kiss, but when her tongue pushes against my lips I grant her access. Her hand squeezes mine as the taste of her fruity gum makes me lose all control and follow her lead.

But she's pulling away a second later, and the kiss is over before I can suggest blowing off our date to keep kissing her. "That was a good idea. We should get used to greeting each other with a kiss," she suggests, leaning back in her seat and letting go of my hand to buckle up. My mouth instantly misses the warmth of her, but now I'm eager to get to the next time I get to greet her. Maybe we can go on another date tomorrow, even if it's only lunch or dinner. Basically any excuse will do.

When her buckle clicks into place she gasps, and I worry that she pinched herself.

"What? Are you okay?" I say through a panic, grabbing her hand again to check for any blood or signs that we need to return to the hospital.

"I'm great, you worrywart," she teases, pulling her hand out of mine and pointing to the back seat. "When did you get pink ducks?" she asks, grabbing one of the small rubber ducks from the box on the floorboard.

A million things to say run through my head as she holds the duck between us, waiting for an answer. Telling her I ordered them a week ago because I thought they would cheer her up might be stepping too close to admitting that I'm starting to like her. I had every intention of hiding the box, but I forgot about it until right this second. At least she's smiling like she's ready to tell me she was right, and that's exactly why I bought these, even though her smirk is taunting.

"You were right. I needed more variety," I admit, knowing that will distract her from further analyzing the situation.

"I told you," she shouts in satisfaction, tossing the duck in the air and catching it.

"Yeah, yeah. Can we please go now?" I ask, raising my eyebrows at her and hoping she doesn't ask when I got the ducks.

"Take a left," she sighs, dropping the duck back in its box and pointing in the direction we need to go. I quickly glance at my hands on the steering wheel, making small L's with my hands to make sure I'm going the right direction. For some reason, I always go the wrong way when people tell me where to go, and I don't want to mess up in front of her. She doesn't seem to notice my hesitancy in turning, and I let out a sigh of relief that this is going to be okay.

She doesn't tell me where we're going, simply directing me when to turn. The drive isn't far, but it takes us far enough away from campus where we might not end up seeing anyone from school. I listen as Maeve talks about her night last night and some drama going on with her sorority sisters. I think I know who she's talking about, but keeping track of all of them is too hard so I only nod along. It's not long until we're pulling down a dirt road and parking in the grass in front of a barn that says 'Wicker Family Farm' on the front.

"This place has the best donuts," Maeve says, linking her fingers with mine and pulling me toward the entrance where we pay for tickets and get orange wristbands with the farm's logo.

The air smells distinctly fall, like pumpkins and spice, and when we walk through the doors, I'm overwhelmed with the sounds of children running around. I'm not sure where to go first, so I let Maeve guide me through the stands of fall foods to a counter with a wall of donuts behind it and a menu featuring every type of pumpkin drink I can think of.

"We'll take two cider slushies please," Maeve orders and my attention snaps to her.

"What's in a cider slushie?" I ask cautiously, because she's grinning at me like a mad villain as I pull out my wallet to pay.

"You'll see, they're delicious. I had one last year, but I couldn't finish it. Do you like apple cider? Or ice cream? Shit, I probably should have asked, sorry," she rambles as the employee behind the counter places two plastic mason jars cups with handles in front of us. The drink has an apple cider slushie mix on the bottom, vanilla ice cream in the center, and apple cider slushie again on the top. To top it all off, there's an apple cider donut sitting on top with a big straw sticking out of the middle. It looks delicious.

"I do like apple cider and ice cream," I tell her, picking up the drinks and handing her one as we move out of the line and head toward the open barn doors leading to more activities.

Maeve finds an open bench for us to sit at and eat what I assume will be the sweetest thing I've had in months. She points out all the different activities as we both go for our donuts first. There's an area with farm animals that lets you feed goats, photo op areas set up all over, and there's apple picking if you walk far enough back. But what she wants to do, and what her sorority sisters said no to last year, is pumpkin carving.

It's set up next to a large pumpkin patch and there's a sign with simple instructions:

*1. Pay 2. Pick 3. Carve*

She's pointing out the pumpkins she might want to pick while I'm focused on not bowing out of this drink before she does. I was right that it was sweet, but it's also surprisingly filling, and I don't want to be the first to give up.

When she gets a third of the way through, she finally says, "That's all I can manage. Are you all done with yours?" And I'm grateful, but I take one last sip before taking both of ours to the nearest trash can.

I follow her over to the pumpkin carving as I pull my wallet out before she can find hers. She glares at me as she zips her purse back up, but takes my hand as she leads us into the pumpkin patch. Heading to the ones she has already decided on, she picks one out for both of us before we return to the carving area.

Sitting down, she passes tools to me and my heartbeat starts to get louder in my ears. "Hey, Barbie?" I whisper so the kids around us don't hear me.

"What?" she whispers back.

"I don't know how to do this," I admit. My family has never carved pumpkins before; my mom has always bought fake ones from the store. Plus I'm not artistic and carving one would only end in a traumatic looking pumpkin.

She smiles at me, but I can tell by the way half her bottom lip is in her mouth that she's trying not to laugh. "It's okay, I can teach you," she finally says, moving closer to me. I love the idea of her teaching me anything and everything, but I can't tell her that. Not yet.

## TWENTY-EIGHT

## MAEVE

"It's really not that bad," I say, holding in a laugh.

"You're being nice," Connor says, keeping his eyes on the road.

Looking at the picture of us both holding our pumpkins, I smile because mine is like something someone would want to put on the front porch while Connor's screams to be put out of its misery. The eyes are two different sizes and shapes, while the mouth turns down like it's screaming instead of smiling like a Jack-o'-lantern. The plus side is this photo looks cute, and everyone on Instagram is loving the contrast of how they look together.

Part of me is reading into it too much, and making it a metaphor on how we must look together. With his muted wardrobe and red hair compared to my sparkles and pink, something about it doesn't sound like it should work but it does. I never expected to like him this much, but the more time I spend with him the more I'm proven wrong. The fall break weekend with him was surprisingly comforting, and the way he's always taking care of me isn't something I'm used to. But I have to remind myself that it's only an arrangement between us.

With our busy week we haven't had a chance to make good on our amendment to the rules, but the way he kissed me earlier has me thinking about changing that soon. A shiver runs through my body in anticipation of all the ideas in my head. The entire time at the farm our hands kept finding their way to each other, mostly from me pulling him around and showing him how to use the pumpkin carving tools. And each time we pulled apart, I was sad when the warmth of his hands left mine.

"Park in the corner, over there," I tell him as he pulls into the parking lot next to the Mu Mansion.

"Why? Aren't I dropping you off?" he asks, and I'm not sure he would pick up on a hint if it was labeled with a large neon sign.

"Yeah, but Hannah is home and I was thinking we could end our date the 'classic' way," I say, putting air quotes over the word classic as he parks where I told him to. The parking lot is surrounded by trees and this spot is out of the view of the building's windows, so while it's not completely private it's the best I can manage right now.

"Oh like, kissing?" he asks, struggling to get the word out as his face flushes crimson.

"That, but also," I start slowly, turning to face him and tucking my legs under me to get closer. I run my nails over his arm as his knuckles turn white around the steering wheel before I continue. "Maybe I could climb onto your lap and spread my legs over you, you could see the underwear I picked out in case something like this happened. Then, I'd lean down and kiss your neck." I lean closer and lower my voice as my nails reach his neck, dragging from his shoulder to his ear and I see his whole body shudder. Is he going to like the black lacy underwear I'm wearing?

Talking about what I could do to him and seeing his reaction already has them damp. Moving closer to his ear I whisper, "Then I might reach down and undo your belt, finally getting to take your cock in my hands. I've thought about it ever since I felt it through your pants."

His head drops back to the seat with a muttered, "*Fuck.*"

"Sounds like something you'd be interested in?" I tease, running my nails along his ear and back down his neck, over the goosebumps all over his skin.

"Fuck, yes," he doesn't hesitate answering, releasing his grip on the steering wheel and turning to lift me up over the center console and on to his lap. His hands gripping my waist reminds me of when he lifted me on my dresser, and I could get used to him tossing me around.

With his height, there's plenty of room for me to miss hitting the steering wheel, but Connor settles me right over him as close as I can get to his torso. My legs fall open and land on either side of him as he pulls me down and we both moan when our centers finally connect. I can feel him already hard beneath me, and I can't help the rock of my hips as I make good on my promise and bring my lips to the side of his neck kissing each freckle.

His hands grip tighter on my waist and my teeth scrape his skin with a small bite above his pulse point before he pushes me further down his lap and off his cock.

"Hold on," he gasps, taking a deep breath. "I want this to last longer than a minute. Can I?" he asks, moving his grip to the edge of my dress where it's risen up on my thigh. His fingers brush my bare skin, sending a shockwave straight to my core.

I nod, helping him move my dress to my waist and exposing the underwear I told him about. He tilts his head to get a better look, his eyes darkening as his hand moves further up my thigh. When his thumb brushes over the lace above my clit I can't help the moan that slips past my lips and the slight rise of my hips seeking more friction from his touch.

"Fuck, Barbie. You're already soaked," he says, lifting his head to meet my eyes.

"Tragic, isn't it?" I tease.

"Truly." He laughs, smiling wide as he refocuses his attention to the bottom of my sweater. "Can I take this off?"

I nod again, lifting my arms as he lifts the sweater up and over my head, discarding it on the passenger seat. A shiver runs down my spine as my bare arms are met with the cool air and one of the small straps falls down my shoulder.

"I knew this was a dress," he says, smiling again and running his hands up my arms to the straps. "Are you not wearing a bra?" he asks, inspecting the straps with his fingers.

"I'm not." My answer is barely audible, like I've forgotten how to speak, instead too focused on the antici-pation of what might come next.

"Fuck, I haven't been able to stop thinking about these piercings since the last time. I've been wanting to take your sweater off all day," he admits, cupping one of my breasts in his hand and rubbing his thumb over the hard outline of my nipple through my dress. The sensation is too much with the fabric and I whimper as he presses harder against the spot.

"Want to taste them?" I ask, smirking and toying with the tie at the front of the dress that keeps my breasts in.

Connor takes over where my hand is, undoing the tie and freeing one of my breasts in the process. Wasting no time, he takes my breast in one hand and places the other on my ass to silently direct me as he lowers his mouth to my nipple. My head drops back with a moan at the contrast of the cold air and the warmth of his mouth. He squeezes my ass and guides me closer to him, but I'm up too far on my knees to get the friction I'm craving.

His tongue explores my nipple and the piercing coming out of each side of it. My hands tangle in his hair, keeping his mouth to my chest as I let the pleasure take over. He hums against my nipple as his teeth scrape over the tip and I wonder how quickly you can come from only nipple stimulation.

When I peer down, we lock eyes and he smirks when he licks around the piercing. The sight is filthy and I tuck it away for later. I tighten my grip around his hair and pull him off me, pushing him against the seat as I bring my mouth to his. My bare breast rubs against the fabric of his flannel and my tongue enters his mouth and I finally settle over his cock again. Rocking against him, I can't help the speed and raw instinct seeking more, more, *more*.

"Can I touch you?" I gasp into his mouth.

"Please, do it quick," he gasps, pushing me back to make room for me to reach between us.

I quickly undo his belt, lowering his zipper as he bunches my dress in his fists. Reaching into his boxer briefs, I lower them as I wrap my hand around his hard cock between us.

"Fucking hell, oh my god," he gasps as my thumb rubs over the head of his cock, spreading the precum that's collected there. His hips lift and I take the opportunity to bring my other hand to cup his balls. He tries to watch, biting his lip as his breathing becomes more frantic. But when I move one finger to stroke the space behind his balls his head falls back as I make him lose control.

"That's it, Connor. Let me take care of you," I hum,

keeping my pace steady and running my thumb over the head of his cock again as he curses under his breath.

"I'm going to come. Maeve, I'm—" he tries to finish, but he's coming before he can get the sentence out. His cum coats my hand and drips down his shaft as his chest heaves and his breathing starts to slow down. Lifting his head, he takes in the sight of me still holding his cock and the most obnoxious grin breaks out across his face.

I roll my eyes at him, trying not to laugh at how stupidly happy he is right now. "Napkins?" I ask, before I can over analyze how fun it was to watch him be the one to come apart at my touch.

He reaches across to the glove box, popping it open and pulling out a stack of napkins and handing me some. I clean up my hand and his cock, tucking it back into his boxers and pulling my dress back to cover my breast.

"Wait, what about you?" He grabs my wrist when I reach for my sweater.

"I'm okay, you got off and that's all I was aiming for," I tell him, thinking back to all the times I've hooked up with guys before. They've always been done the second they finish, so I never expect anything more.

"What about what I'm aiming for?" he asks, running his hands over my thighs again. "What if I want to feel you again? I never really got to the first time, since we used the vibrator."

I think back to when his fingers were in me briefly to start, and how his touch had me on the edge. I don't know why I thought I could make him come and leave like he wouldn't want the same thing from me. With the way he was so adamant about taking care of me, I'm not surprised he wants to do the same now.

"Okay, you can make me come," I agree, grabbing his hand and guiding it to my pussy like the first time. His fingers slip beneath the lace and glide easily through me as I gasp at his touch.

"Barbie, shit. You're more soaked than last time. And only from giving a hand job?" he teases, and I don't have time to be annoyed how wet he gets me when the need to come is turned up to the max.

"Connor, please," I beg, rocking into his hand as he dips one finger inside me.

He pulls me closer, sitting up and holding me in his arms so I don't hit the car's horn. Getting a better angle, a second finger joins the first as he kisses my neck. "Tell me what to do," he whispers into my ear.

"My clit, your palm, stay still," is all I can manage as I reach down and position his hand where I need it. Moving my underwear fully to the side, I moan when his palm covers my clit. Wrapping my arms around his neck, I rock into the touch. He listens, staying still as I ride his hand to get myself off. He whispers in my ear as I keep my pace steady, the orgasm quickly building at the base of my spine. Things like "you're doing so well," and "that's it, just like that." But when he whispers how good I feel around his fingers, that's when the orgasm crashes into me as I come. The ache I've felt for too long finally subsided at the hand of the last person I would have suspected.

"This is my favorite date," he says through a laugh as he brings his lips to mine, and I'm surprised that I might have to agree with him.

## TWENTY-NINE

## CONNOR

I t's finally Halloween, which means today I spent hours driving Maeve and Hannah back home for their cousin Charlie's wedding. The last two weeks have been filled with non-stop working between classes and preparing me for this wedding. Maeve and Hannah even set up a Power-Point quiz for me on who everyone in the family was.

I was able to name all the cousins easily, since I see them the most during their annual summer vacation. But when it came time to remembering all the aunts and uncles, I got countless pillows thrown at me for mixing them up.

Standing in the bathroom of the hotel room that Maeve booked for us, I convince myself my anxiety is from meeting her family as her boyfriend—*fake* boyfriend, I remind myself—and not sharing a room with her. The second we got in the room she handed me my costume for the welcome dinner and immediately called Hannah, who I could barely hear through Maeve's phone.

"Han, there's only one bed," Maeve whisper-shouts into the phone.

"So? Build a pillow wall or something," Hannah replies.

"Still, isn't it weird? Should I go ask them for a different room?" Maeve asks, and my chest tightens at the thought of switching rooms. I want to sleep in the same bed as her. If this is the last weekend we're going to be spending together, I want as much of her as I can get before this is over.

"Don't be dramatic, you'll be fine," Hannah says, clearer now and I assume Maeve put the phone on speaker.

"You're right, you're right. I don't know why I'm freaking out," Maeve says, and I'm willing to bet she's picking at her nails even though she just got them done.

"I could think of a few reasons—"

"Okay, thank you for the chat," Maeve yells, cutting Hannah off. "I'll see you at the welcome dinner?"

"Yeah. I'll meet you on the shuttle," Hannah says before hanging up.

"Are you coming out of there?" Maeve asks, her voice closer than it was a second ago.

"Me? Yeah one second," I scramble to make sure the costume she got me is all set. I wanted to give her plenty of time to change and talk to Hannah without hovering. When I put the costume on, it took me a minute to recognize what it was. And I didn't bring anything for myself since I didn't know this was going to be a costume party, so there's no turning back. Stepping out of the bathroom, I see Maeve in a matching themed costume. "You couldn't make me Ken?" I ask, putting my hands on my hips over the striped Allan shirt.

She crosses her arms over her pink outfit, the white cowboy hat on her head slightly falling to the side when she tips her head to the side. "Have some self awareness,

Big Bird, you're not a Ken. You're an Allan, so own it," she yells, throwing her hands up in the air.

"Fine, but why did you pick Barbie costumes?" I ask, regretting the question because I realize the answer when I ask it.

"If you're going to call me Barbie, we might as well lean into it," she says, spinning and showing off her costume, the flared pants getting wider as she spins.

"Fair. Also why are we in a hotel if your parents' house is only twenty minutes away?" I ask her.

"Are you going to ask questions all weekend?" she glares at me, and I return it with a shrug before she continues. "The afterparty, duh. My parents are staying here, too, they already checked in and went to help set up the welcome dinner. You're about to see a whole lot of the Murphy family. I hope you remember the PowerPoint," she teases.

"Are there family member flashcards in the welcome bag?" I joke, grabbing the bag from the dresser that we got when we checked in and dumping it on the bed.

"Unfortunately, you're going to have to rely on your memory for that. But there is some aspirin if you want to be proactive and take it now," she says, rifling through the pile of stuff and pulling up a small packet.

"Maybe not a bad idea," I agree, taking the packet from her and grabbing the small water bottle from the bag to wash down the pills. "This bag really has everything in it, doesn't it?"

"Oh yeah, it's such a cute addition. These snacks are my favorite," she says, holding up three bags with labels on the front. "These pretzels are Charlie's favorite, the goldfish are Logan's favorite, and then the gummi bears are their favorite. It's so cute, and the little details like this are *my* favorite parts of weddings," she explains. "I have so many ideas for couples when I get to plan them. I want to create a whole presentation for personalization options and—"

She pauses when she glances my way, and I'm waiting for her to continue but she doesn't.

"You can keep going, I'm listening," I tell her, gesturing toward her with the water bottle that is now almost empty.

"Sorry, I didn't mean to ramble on about that. It's not even a thing yet, there's still a lot of time before I actually have my own business." She turns away from me, dropping the snacks and picking up her purse.

"I like your ramblings. I can tell you're really passionate about this, and even if I don't totally understand all of it, it's cool to hear about your plans," I reassure her, stepping closer and taking her hand in mine, hoping that helps comfort her.

"Thanks, Allan," she teases, her smiling reappearing on her face as she leads me out of the room. I follow without any hesitation. After all, I'm getting used to doing what she tells me to.

The shuttle to dinner was right on time, and Hannah met us there like she said. Her brothers were also on it, along with some of the other aunts and uncles. Everyone is dressed up to fit the Halloween theme, with Hannah and her brothers in Alvin and the Chipmunks costumes. It doesn't surprise me that Hannah is Simon, since she's definitely the smartest of the three of them. Finn as Alvin makes sense since he's the loudest, which leaves Jordan as Theordore and green suits him well.

Pulling into the welcome dinner, I see it's at a farm like the one Maeve and I had our date at. Trying not to think about how that date ended with her grinding on my hand I focus on everything happening around us. People are constantly coming up to Maeve to say hi and I'm struggling to recall who is who. I keep expecting one of them to be her mom, but Maeve said she might be too busy helping tonight to say hi. Luckily, the welcome dinner is mostly for close family and out of town guests, so there aren't as many people as there will be tomorrow.

"I'm going to go get us drinks." I lean into Maeve, resting my hand on the small of her back. She's still twenty, and I don't want to test if the bartenders are asking for IDs, so I assume I'll be getting drinks for us all weekend.

She turns her head toward me, kissing my cheek and whispering, "Okay, but don't be long." I don't overanalyze her response, not willing to admit that it probably doesn't mean she'll miss me like I want it to.

Heading to the bar, I see Maeve's cousin, Sidney, dressed like Sidney Prescott from *Scream*. The matching of their names makes me laugh to myself, and I think back to two summers ago when I heard her name more than any other year. Zach never stopped talking about her, and after she left to move across the country I saw a small spark in him go out that hasn't been restored since. She must have flown back from Los Angeles for Charlie's wedding.

She turns around as I'm approaching, and I see her eyes go wide for a second before she pastes a smile on her face, "Hi, Connor."

"Hey, Sidney. Good to see you," I reply, taking a moment to order a vodka cranberry for Maeve and a gin and tonic for me. "How are things in LA?" I ask, returning my attention to her.

"They're good, same old, same old. It's nice to be back. How are you? And the other lifeguards?" she gets the whole sentence out in a rush, stumbling over the last question as a blush fills her cheeks.

"I'm good. Other lifeguards too. Zach is enjoying culinary school," I tell her right as she takes a sip of her drink, and she chokes on said sip when Zach's name comes up.

"Sorry, sorry," she apologizes through a cough as I hand her a napkin to clean her face. "Glad to hear that, his food was delicious," she says, a small amount of pain flashes in her face before she wipes it away.

"Yeah, it is," I agree. "I'll tell him how you're doing—how you're all doing," I correct at the last second when her blush turns a deeper maroon, almost matching the fake blood smeared across her forehead. I make a mental note to tell Zach about this later, but specifically on FaceTime so I can see if he gets as equally flustered. The romantic in me wants to see them reconnect eventually.

Returning to Maeve's side I wonder what we would do if we ended up on different sides of the country. I'd probably do what Zach did and suggest trying long distance—if we were in a real relationship. I run my hands through my hair, rubbing like it will get these thoughts out of my head. Maeve isn't interested in this going longer than this weekend, and I have to remind myself of that.

I try to focus on the conversation happening in the group, but Charlie picks that moment to pick up a microphone and pulls his fiancé to a small stage at the end of the barn. Charlie is dressed in a white long sleeved lace top, with white pants and fake bullets across his chest. I recognize the outfit as the bride from *Ready or Not*, while Logan is in a simple white jumpsuit with a Bride of Frankestein wig. I'm going to have to chastise Maeve later for not telling me about the costumes or I would have also picked a classic Universal monster.

"Attention all!" Charlie yells into the microphone, and

a loud static sound echoes around the room as everyone covers their ears. Charlie winces, moving the mic away from his mouth. "Sorry about that. I wanted to come up here quickly and say thank you to all who have traveled to join us on our special day"—he pauses to kiss Logan on the cheek—"and we have a special surprise for you. Since we've got a smaller crew here compared to tomorrow, we wanted to treat you all to a special keepsake. Over by the far wall please welcome Venus and Emma from Venus Tattoo Company!" he yells, pointing to the area behind all of us, where there are two women smiling and waving.

One is older, with long gray hair and streaks of purple, while the other is in her early twenties with dark hair that looks like it's been dyed one too many times. They're both covered in tattoos and their fair share of piercings, standing in front of a complete area to tattoo people. How did I miss that when we walked in? Looking around, I also missed the fact that there are no kids here, which is probably good considering the tattoos.

"They have a variety of tattoos you can pick from, including one brought to you by our lovely Grams and Gramps." He points to an older couple in the crowd who I recognize from Maeve's PowerPoint. "You can now get the coordinates of the Thousand Islands in their handwriting. So enjoy, get inked, and get drunk!" He cheers, lifting his drink up and finishing it in one sip.

"But please remember to make it to the wedding tomorrow," Logan chimes in, grabbing the microphone in one hand and his fiancé in the other as the crowd around us breaks into conversations.

Maeve has the biggest smile on her face as she grabs the hands of several of her cousins, pulling them closer to her and yelling, "Matching tattoos!" as they all scream in return and I might lose my hearing by the end of this weekend. "You interested in one?" she asks, turning to me as her cousins head toward the tattoo area.

"In matching tattoos? No, I'm good," I laugh, not thinking about the whole tiny-needle-repeatedly-going-into-your-skin thing or I might pass out.

"Well duh, I meant in general?" She playfully hits my arm, which makes me want to pull her to me and kiss her for some unknown reason.

"No, but I'll hold your hand while you get one," I offer, grabbing her hand instead of kissing her. But the feel of her fingers around mine only makes the need grow like it's going to be forever rooted inside of me. And instead of shaking it away, I let it grow as I watch her smile and laugh with her family, realizing she's different here with them compared to at school. I never noticed before how they all look at her when they make jokes or say something, but now I'm finally understanding how easily it is to fall under her spell.

## THIRTY

A peek of sunlight through the curtains wakes me up first, the feeling of arms around my stomach and something poking my back makes my eyes snap open. The memories of last night are a haze of dancing and drinking after everyone got tattoos. Connor loosened up once we were on the dance floor. At first, I assumed the amount of Murphys was too much for him to process. Compared to the small doses of the cousins he usually gets at the campground, being around my entire family in one area can be overwhelming. However, the way he seemed to be holding his breath anytime someone got a tattoo, I'm willing to bet he isn't the biggest fan of needles. That must have been why he was so stressed at the hospital. I pulled him to the dance floor the second my tattoo was completed and it was nice to see him finally relax.

When we got back to the room last night, he insisted on taking the couch, but I told him I didn't mind sharing a bed. Which was true, but now my heart starts pounding as I take in the situation we're in.

We are cuddling.

In the same bed.

And he's *hard*.

My whole body heats up as it reacts to this information. Annoyance washes over me at how easily I can get turned on by him, but lust soon takes over as the ache between my thighs grows with each second I stay wrapped up in his arms. We aren't going to have many more moments like this, and I inhale his ocean and citrus scent as it surrounds me. If I can slip out from under him I can take care of this ache in the shower before he wakes up. It wouldn't take too long and I could start getting ready for the day. Maybe he won't notice if I leave the bed.

The second I move he groans and pulls me closer, my heart feels like it's going to jump out of my chest. His bare chest is warm against my back, and I suddenly wish I slept naked.

"Mhm, you smell so good," Connor mumbles into my hair, brushing his lips over my ear and sending shivers down my spine.

"You're awake?" I ask, making sure he's not talking in his sleep. If he's still asleep I still have a chance of slipping away, because I shouldn't want this as badly as I do. But moments like this cloud my judgment when it feels so right to be in his arms.

"Now I am, are you awake?" he clarifies, pulling me closer to him and twisting my shorts in his hand.

"Connor, what are you doing?" I ask through a breathy gasp knowing full well what he's doing, but needing confirmation that I'm not the only one who needs this.

"Sorry," he apologizes, moving backward and away from me. "I'm just horny. I think I was dreaming of you again. Give me a minute to cool down."

I instantly miss the heat of him behind me, but his

small confession sparks an idea. I spin around to face him, his chest is heaving and his face is beet red.

"Maybe we take care of it now?" I ask, reaching out and brushing a piece of hair behind his ear.

"Are you serious?" His voice is hoarse and it turns me on more than it should.

"Yeah, you're not the only one aching," I admit, moving the comforter down our bodies. "Can I suck your cock?" I ask, too needy to be subtle.

"Fuck, yes, do whatever you want," he says, kicking the comforter off the bed and laying back. His boxers are struggling to keep his erection in and I want to wrap my mouth around his cock and make him fall apart again.

I sit up and run my fingers along the edge of his boxers, his hips coming up off the bed at my touch.

"Maeve," he gasps, his hands running along my back. "Can I eat you out while you do that?"

"You mean you want to—"

"69? Yeah, I'm curious if it's worth the hype," he giggles, covering his face with his other hand as his blush spreads all over his body. I love how he's becoming more comfortable in asking for what he wants, and the blush that usually follows.

"I've never done that before," I tell him, embarrassed at my lack of experience when I'm supposed to be the one showing him things.

"Then we can learn together," he smiles, moving his hand lower on my back.

I've always been curious about this position, and I feel safe trying new things with him. After all, that's what this whole arrangement has become.

"Let's do it," I agree.

We move quickly after that, me pulling his boxers off as

he works my pajamas off my body. He arranges himself on the pillows, and I position myself next to him.

"You sure about this?" I ask, looking back at him. His pupils are blown and he's beautiful laying there, naked and lit by the morning sun.

"So fucking sure, get over here," he grins, pulling my leg over to his other side so I'm above him. "God, you're always so wet. Is this just for me?"

I can feel the heat of his breath, and I lower myself closer to his mouth seeking relief. His cock is jutting straight up from his body and I can see a bit of precum already on the tip that I plan to lick off. "Connor, please," I beg, wrapping my fingers around his shaft and ignoring his question. I don't have time to analyze why he always has me so turned on when I need to come.

"Please what?" he asks through gritted teeth.

"Put your mouth on my clit," I tell him, lowering my face to his tip and taking him into my mouth.

"Fuck, fuck, fuck," he curses, bringing his hands to my hips and pulling my body to his mouth like it's a race between us.

His mouth covers my clit and he licks, causing me to moan around his cock at the pleasure of it. This gets a returning moan from him and it's almost too much at once. I bob up and down, licking around his head and down his shaft. His precum is salty and I want more of it.

I release his cock as his tongue gets sloppier. "Less all over and more focused. And don't be afraid to suck," I direct him before returning to his cock.

He listens and starts to move my hips so I'm rocking over his face as he licks and sucks around my clit. The movement causes me to bob faster over his cock, my hand working in rhythm.

I pop off him, needing a second to swallow and catch

my breath. He keeps moving me and my moans fill the room, but I need more to tip me over the edge.

"Connor," I gasp. "I need you too—fuck that feels good—Connor—fuck—I need you to lick your finger—fuck—and put it in my ass," I manage to finally get out.

He slows down and pulls his mouth away from my pussy, I think he's going to ask questions or judge me. But instead I hear a pop as his finger comes out of his mouth.

He runs it over the tight hole and my heart beats faster at the anticipation.

I return my mouth to his cock, his hips moving to push deeper as he slides one finger into my hole.

The pleasure shoots straight to my pussy and I moan around his cock. Then his mouth is back on my clit, sucking it as he pushes his finger further in.

I gasp at the overwhelming amount of pleasure and pull his cock out of my mouth. Dropping my cheek to his thigh, I move my hips, chasing the orgasms I feel building.

He releases my clit, and stops moving his finger. He tips his hips so his dick taps me in the face. "If you stop, I stop," he growls. "I want us to come together. Can you do that for me?"

"Fuck, Connor, I'm so close. Can you get there?" I ask, looking back at him.

He grins like the little shit he is. "I've been there since I woke up." Then he pulls my pussy back to his mouth and I cry out.

Bringing his cock back to my mouth I wrap my fingers around my thumb and take him the deepest I can, humming around it.

I feel him moan against my clit as he pushes his finger deeper inside of me. He hits that perfect spot and I don't think I'll ever be satisfied with anything else ever again.

I pick up my pace around his cock and his hips thrust

into me. We're both rocking into each other, chasing our orgasms together.

He comes first, his cum filling my mouth as he pulls my orgasm out of me with his tongue and fingers.

Once he's finished, I pop off his cock and fall to the side of him.

"Holy shit," he gasps. "That was so worth it," he laughs, giving my ass a quick slap.

His laughter is infectious, causing me to laugh with him. "So worth it," I agree. Would it be bad to skip my cousin's wedding to stay here all day? That's not a real option, though, so I have to come up with how we can keep doing this past this weekend. A part of me has a feeling he wouldn't be opposed to the idea when I see he's got the widest grin on his face as he runs his hands over my body.

## THIRTY-ONE

## CONNOR

Standing to clap with the rest of the crowd as Charlie and Logan descend the aisle, I should be watching them, but I can't take my eyes away from Maeve thinking about our morning together. If it was up to me I would have locked us in the hotel room and skipped this whole thing.

Unfortunately after breakfast, the day was filled with chaos as we were sent on several last minute errands before the ceremony. Since some of her cousins are in the wedding, we somehow got volunteered to pick up lunch for the wedding party and deliver it. I had a quick run in with Maeve's mom, where she told me she would talk to me later and that scared the shit out of me.

By the time we got ready for the wedding we were rushing so much that I didn't get to take in what Maeve was wearing. It's a chilly day, but it didn't stop her from putting on a sequin pink dress that falls far above her knees. The straps are thin like her dress from the farm, and that must mean she isn't wearing a bra. A detail that will leave me hard if I think about it for too long as I have to keep myself from searching for the outline of her piercings.

Part of me regrets hooking up with her this morning, because now all I want is to drop to my knees and lose myself under her pink dress. The thought of her taste lingers and I'm scanning this venue for hidden spots as we make our way inside before her voice pulls me from my thoughts.

"If I was running this show I would have moved the card box closer to the entrance. All these people are running around looking for it," she says, rolling her eyes and pointing to the people who look confused with cards in their hands.

"Stop, they can hear you," I chastise, glancing over at the employees standing next to us.

"Good, maybe they'll get some good ideas," she says, crossing her arms and standing straighter, like she's testing me to see if I'll push her up against the wall and pull her dress down to suck at her breast. I bite my lip at the image, knowing that's not what she's doing, and frustrated it's all I can think about.

I head to the bar and grab us drinks as she figures out where we're sitting. When I find her again she's in the middle of a conversation with Sidney so I don't interrupt. Handing her the drink I got for her and stepping next to her, I wait patiently for them to finish. She steps closer to me as she talks and her cinnamon scent invades my space. As she's talking to Sidney all I can do is stare at her lips, taking a sip of my drink to distract myself. I want to memorize every last detail of her face when I have the chance to be this close to her. How there's a freckle next to her nose and one on her forehead. As my eyes wander, the strap of her dress falls down her shoulder as she's telling Sidney something and I reach behind her to adjust it.

Hooking two of my fingers in the strap, I pull it over her shoulder and back into place. Time feels like it slows as my fingers graze her skin and send shivers up my arm and down my spine. I see the slight rise of her breasts and hitch in her breath at the touch as I lower my hand and rest it on her hip.

She steps closer to me and they talk for another minute before they move and I follow them to our table. The entire time my eyes are locked on Maeve, and I attempt to focus on what she's saying but I can only think about how right she feels standing next to me. When we arrive at the table I'm grateful to see it's full of her cousins, and hopefully I can distract myself with conversation. I'm next to Finn while Maeve is next to Sidney and her sister, Abby. There's a table next to us with more cousins, and I start to panic when I see Maeve's brother, Ryan, sitting directly across from me.

"Treating her well?" he asks in lieu of a greeting, glancing at his sister as my heart feels like it's about to jump out of my chest. I saw him last night, but we didn't get the chance to speak. He knows about our arrangement, and he wouldn't call us out in front of everyone. Cy has complained about him being an instigator before so I'm also not sure he wouldn't.

Before I can reply, Maeve snaps her head toward him and away from her conversation, "Leave him alone, Ry, I'm capable of taking care of myself. If he wasn't treating me well he wouldn't be here," she clips before returning to her cousins.

He rolls his eyes in the same way she does, and there's no doubt in my mind they're siblings. As we sit through introductions, speeches, and dinner I keep mostly to myself. Occasionally, talking to Finn and Jordan, but mostly watching how they all interact with each other. I've never noticed it before, but they all share similar manner-isms from their laughs to the way their eyes roll. An eye roll that has been slowly growing on me. Sidney, specifically, seems to do a lot of eye rolling and I remember Zach talking about how he missed that once when he was drunk after they broke up.

Being with all of them makes me miss summer and home, and if I close my eyes I can pretend I'm sitting on the beach as they all lounge on the sand next to the life-guard chair. I might not ever tell Maeve this, but I always get excited when her family camps, even if it's only for ten days. They're always so happy to be there, and I can count on them for plenty of entertainment. Cy usually throws parties all summer, but none are ever as memorable compared to when the Murphys are there.

Whether it be Quinn trying to dance on tables or Maeve trying to fight someone to defend her cousin—a fight I luckily pulled her away from—they're always lighting up whatever room they enter. Maeve does that on her own, but when they're all together it's different. Like all the stars are aligned, and I'm grateful to get to spend this extra time with them. They've never made me feel like I don't belong.

"You okay?" Maeve's warm voice pulls me from my thoughts as her hand rests over my knee, giving it a slight comforting squeeze.

"Yeah, just thinking," I tell her, not wanting to admit how much being here with her actually means to me.

"That's dangerous," she teases. "We're going to go dance, want to join?" She nods behind her, where I see most of her cousins have left the table and are making their way to the dance floor. If their wedding dancing is anything like their party dancing, they're going to be out there until the lights go on and the venue tells us to leave.

I grab her hand, standing up and letting her lead us to the dance floor as I see her mom approach us from the corner of my eye. Last night, I was able to avoid the adults since we spent a considerable amount of time over by the tattoo station, and they stayed far away from it as they helped the dinner run smoothly.

I only know this is her mom from the flashcards and the run in earlier, but other than that their features are different. Where Maeve's hair reminds me of chocolate kissed by sunlight, her mom's is darker like a clear night sky. The only similar thing about them is the small waist and larger hip bones, and I'm willing to bet her mom doesn't have nipple piercings. A shudder runs through my body at the thought, and I have to shake the poor mental image out of my head before she reaches us.

"Hi, Connor, lovely to see you again," she says once she's standing in front of us. Her lips are closed together in a thin line as she looks the two of us over. My suit suddenly feels not up to her standards, even though it's the same one I wore to my sister's wedding. The black is classic and the bow tie isn't a clip on but something I learned to tie for the wedding. My dad was nice enough to send it to me before this wedding so I had something nice to wear.

"Nice to see you again, Mrs. Murphy," I say, smiling politely as she turns to her daughter.

"Isn't that dress a little short for a fall wedding? You didn't like any of the dresses I sent you?" she asks, taking a disapproving sip of her drink.

I feel her grip on my hand tighten, and jump in before she can reply. "She looks beautiful, plus she can have my jacket if she gets cold," I say, pulling her to my side and rubbing my hand up her arm. My touch leaves goose-bumps in their wake as she relaxes into me.

"Thanks for the concern, but we are going to go dance.

Join us if you want to," she rushes out, grabbing my hand again and pulling me toward the dance floor. Leaving her mom behind before she can reply. "That woman is going to be the death of me, I swear," she mumbles when we are far enough away.

"Don't worry about her," I tell her, pulling her to me and bringing my other hand to the base of her head. She lets out a gasp when she crashes to my chest. Bringing my lips down to hers, I kiss her quickly before I can get carried away. It's fast, but it lights my whole body on fire. Pulling her face away from mine, I gaze down at her at the shocked expression on her face.

"What was that for?" she smiles as she steps away from me.

"Don't know. Wanted to, I guess," I tell her, shrugging and unable to think of a better excuse.

"Keep that up and people will believe this whole thing. Now let's dance," she says, pulling me into the dancing crowd before I can reply.

Watching her dance, I get lost in the way her dress sparkles under the lights. She moves around the crowd so freely, moving from cousin to cousin and making sure everyone is having fun. Whenever she directs her attention back at me I feel like I've won the lottery.

I don't think about the fact I kissed her because I wanted to, completely forgetting this whole thing is a ruse. I don't think about how I might not get to kiss her again after tonight. I don't think about how I've never felt this way before. And I definitely don't think about the four letter word creeping its way to the front of my brain.

## THIRTY-TWO

MAEVE

It takes all my willpower to pull myself away from the dance floor and to the bathroom. Connor's kiss charged me with sexual energy and I've been trying to dance it off instead of suggesting we go back to the hotel.

When I finally make it into the bathroom stall, I plop down on the toilet with less grace than I'm willing to admit. Connor has been getting me drinks all night, and this is the first time I've stopped moving since getting out on the dance floor. My head feels like a bowling ball on my neck as I sway back and forth on the toilet, throwing my hands against the walls to keep myself still.

I manage to finish and not make a mess, but maybe my next drink needs to be water before anything else. I struggle with the stall lock for what seems like an eternity before heading to the sink to wash my hands. The warm water falls over my hands, and I keep them there soaking in the warmth as I eye the basket on the counter. It's full of supplies someone might need, including bandaids, tampons, gum, floss, and aspirin. I hum at the thoughtfulness of it. Does the men's room have a similar one? Maybe with condoms. A bathroom basket is something I should add to my list of venue decorations for future clients. Focusing back on my hands, I finish washing them and pull a paper towel from the dispenser.

Taking a look at myself in the mirror, I shudder at how drunk I look. My hair is stuck to my forehead from sweating, and my eyes look like part of my soul is missing. Reaching for the aspirin as a precautionary measure, I'm attempting to take the lid off when my mother walks through the door.

"There you are, I was looking for you," she says, her tone patronizing like I'm some type of lost puppy.

"Just going to the bathroom," I grumble, struggling as I push down on the aspirin lid. Why do they make these things so adult proof?

"Here let me," Mom says, grabbing the bottle from my hands and opening it on one try before handing it back to me. "Do you have a headache?" she asks as I pop two pills in my mouth and swallow.

"No, but I'm about to," I mumble, sticking my hand under the sink water to help guide the aspirin down.

"What?" Mom inquires.

"Thank you for opening that, it's just in case," I tell her, wiping my hand on my dress and wincing at the scrape of the sequins. My hand stays wet, but I don't want to waste another paper towel.

"Smart. Are you enjoying the wedding?" she asks.

"Uh-huh, did you need me for something?" I ask, remembering she said she was looking for me.

"I wanted to talk to you about Connor." She whispers his name like he's going to appear in the women's restroom if she says it too loudly.

"What about him?" I instantly get defensive, crossing

my arms and standing as straight as I can without falling over.

"Come on, sweetie, I know you've never liked him. You complain about him every time we go camping. Why would you expect me to believe you're actually dating him?" she says, crossing her arms to match mine.

I catch sight of our reflections in the mirror, and it's eerie how similar our stances are. All my life I've copied what my mom does, maybe even without realizing it. My family has always made fun of me when I say something in the same tone or inflection she does. She's the reason I'm in this sorority—after all she was in the same one when she was in college. She's the reason I'm such a good planner, after watching her plan our camping trip for years that same energy wore off on me. But now? Now I want to find where her influence ends and I begin. I don't need her to hold my hand anymore, and I most definitely don't need her calling my bluff of my relationship with Connor.

Uncrossing my arms, drunk me finds the courage to say something to my mother that I've always thought, but been too afraid to voice. "Why would I expect you to believe me? I don't know, maybe because you should trust your daughter? You know I'm perfectly capable of making my own decisions."

"I didn't say you can't make your own decisions," she defends through a gasp.

"Maybe you didn't say it, but you act like it. You act like I'm still a little kid who needs help in everything. I know you want me to follow the same path you did after college, but believe me when I say I can figure out what's right for me by myself." I'm almost shouting now, and I can feel my heart pounding in my ears. Meanwhile, my stomach is twisting itself in knots that I know aren't from the alcohol.

"I just think—"

"Well stop!" Now I've reached max volume. "Stop helping! I might have complained about Connor in the past, but he's really good to me. He makes me laugh and he makes me mac and cheese and you might not like that I didn't pick your choice, but he's my choice and you're going to have to be okay with that."

"I only want you to be happy, and he hasn't made you happy before," she sighs, dropping her arms and stepping closer to me.

"He does now," I tell her, and my frustration and drunkenness are meeting the tipping point as I struggle to hold back the tears forming in the corner of my eyes. What I'm saying isn't a lie, Connor does make me happy, and maybe I'm crying from admitting that and finally standing up to my mom, or maybe I'm just drunk.

"Oh, sweetie, come here," Mom says, pulling me into her arms, and I don't resist as I let her hold me as the tears slip free. "I didn't mean to upset you." She rubs my back, her nails scratching between my shoulder blades. It soothes me like it always does when she does it, and I take a deep breath willing the tears to stop so I can return to the wedding without looking even worse than I already do.

"I know, I just—" I try to get the words out but a sob interrupts me.

"It's okay, I'm sorry I didn't believe you," she says, continuing to scratch my back.

"I just want you to trust me, okay?" I finally manage, lifting my head up and stepping out of her arms. "Can you do that?"

She sighs, rubbing her hands together and playing with her rings before answering. "I can." She pauses. "But you know I'm always a call away if you need anything."

"I know," I say, carefully rubbing underneath my eyes

so I don't mess up my makeup. I'm clearly not doing a good job because Mom grabs a tissue from the basket on the counter and wipes my cheeks where eyeliner has probably ended up.

"Are you sure you like him?" she checks, tossing the tissue in the trash.

"Mom, please," I groan.

"Sorry, sorry. It's still strange to me. I thought we didn't like him is all," she tells me. How many times have I complained about him while she's been around? Usually, I'm complaining to my cousins, but the adults are always around while camping.

"We do now," I reassure her.

"Okay, I'll have to get used to that. Ready to get back?" She nods toward the bathroom door.

"Definitely," I agree, moving around her to open the door. We re-enter the reception and break apart as she heads toward my dad while I look for the ginger who was almost outed as my fake boyfriend.

I find Connor standing near the dance floor at a cocktail table alone with two drinks and a glass of water. When his eyes find mind they light up as a smile breaks across his face and his hand shoots up in the air to wave me over.

"Everything okay? You were gone for a minute," he says when I reach the table, pushing the glass of water toward me.

I take it, downing half of it in one gulp before replying, "I'm good, talked with my mom."

"How'd that go?" He eyes me cautiously, since I'm usually grumpy any time I talk to her.

"Surprisingly well, but she might be on to us," I whisper, moving closer to him so that our arms brush and the small bit of contact sends shivers down my spine.

"Well we can't have that, now can we?" He leans closer

to me, moving his arm so it's around me as his heat surrounds me.

"No, we can't," I agree, moving to my tiptoes to kiss him. I wobble from the awkward angle, but his free hand moves to cup my jaw as the other slides down to my waist to keep me steady. His hand on my cheek is cold and wet from the condensation from his glass and in direct contrast with the warmth that spreads through my body at his touch.

He tastes like something sweet, and I wonder if the desserts are out as my tongue explores his mouth. His grip around my waist tightens when I bite down on his bottom lip and his small moan threatens to destroy me. Before we can get too far, there's a bang on the table that reverberates through my arms that are still clutching the glass of water.

"Hey, lovebirds," Hannah shouts over the music. "Get back on the dance floor!" Then, she's running away and into the crowd of people, making a beeline for our cousins in the middle of it all.

"Dance?" Connor asks through heavy breaths, picking his drink up off the table.

"Dance," I agree, finishing the water and grabbing my drink before taking his hand in mine and leading him into the chaos.

## THIRTY-THREE

MAEVE

Driving back to school after the wedding is awful. My head was pounding the second I woke up. The precautionary aspirin I took must have lost its luster after I left my mom in the bathroom. After being pulled onto the dance floor with Connor, we were immediately handed shots from Ryan. I'm expecting some type of text from my mom about last night, either to check in or apologize more for making me cry last night. I'm not confident that she'll leave me alone about figuring things out for myself, which makes me want to avoid going home until the end of the semester.

To top off my headache, Hannah won't stop talking the whole drive. Every time I turn around to glare at her she raises her eyebrows and looks at Connor, like I'm supposed to be telling her something. But she didn't say anything about us, instead going through all the photos in the shared album from the night before and recalling all the stupid things we said or did. I don't understand how she can bounce back so well when she did as many shots as

I did. Meanwhile Connor looks like he's trying to focus on driving and not barfing.

At one point last night, the boys all had their shirts undone and their ties on their heads as a dance battle broke out in the center of the dance floor while Connor stayed to the edge of the crowd, never straying too far, simply watching all the chaos unfold. Every time I turned around to make sure he was still there I saw the hunger in his eyes as he watched me dance. With every drink, I swung my hips more to coax a reaction out of him. I was pretty sure if I could push him far enough he would pull me into a dark corner and beg for it.

Instead, we both ended up too drunk. The last thing I remember was cheering at the afterparty when a teenager showed up with an armful of pizza. Connor and I grabbed one and brought it back up to our room, where we immediately passed out if the uneaten pizza on the floor this morning was any indicator.

Finally driving into the Mu Mansion's parking lot, Connor drops me and Hannah off and helps us carry our bags inside. He looks ready to crawl into bed, and I wouldn't be surprised if I didn't hear from him for the rest of the day.

"I'll see you tomorrow morning?" he says, standing at the door and playing with his keys.

"Yeah, we have our sorority meeting tonight so I'm about to sleep until then," I tell him, playing with the hair tie around my wrist, unsure where we go from here. This whole arrangement was dependent on this wedding, and now it's over. I still plan to help him with class, but now I don't know if everything else is over, and I'm too scared to ask. Maybe if we keep this thing going I'll never have to admit these feelings bubbling beneath the surface.

He leans forward like he wants to reach out and kiss

me before he must decide against it, saying goodbye and shutting the apartment door.

Before the disappointment can root itself in my brain, Hannah's voice pierces the quiet of the apartment, "You hooked up with him!"

"I did not," I yell immediately, spinning to face her accusatory glare.

"You so did. There was so much tension in that car, I could cut it better than whoever cut the wedding cake last night," she says, crossing her arms.

"Han, we were fake dating, remember?" I tell her unconvincingly.

It's too bad she can read me like a book, and calls me on my bullshit immediately. "There's nothing fake in the way he looks at you. He's got the look of a man craving something he's not supposed to want."

"Wait. He looks at me like that?" I ask, unsuccessfully hiding the satisfaction in my voice as a blush threatens to break out across my face.

"Maeve," she yells, and I'm starting to hope our sisters don't come barging in here to check on us. They're used to us yelling at each other sometimes, that's the territory that comes with living with family.

My mouth drops open, and I fall over my words as they tumble from my lips without warning, "We might have hooked up and it might not have been the first time and I don't think I told you about how he stayed here during fall break either. Well, stayed in my room if I'm being honest, but not in my bed. He slept on the floor on the air mattress and I got this cute picture of him and Greta I need to show you."

"WHAT?" Hannah yells, running at me and tackling me over the back of the couch while screaming, "Oh my god." Over and over again.

"Um yeah, I should probably fill you in," I say, catching my breath as she crushes me and urging my stomach to not evacuate its contents.

"Tell me everything, don't leave anything out," she says, climbing off me and settling into the other side of the couch as Greta jumps up and onto her lap.

It takes two hours and an order of greasy fast food to tell Hannah everything. My hangover subsides as I talk, not leaving anything out. If I'm going to figure this out, she needs to know everything, including how well he took care of me. She listens the entire time, asking some clarifying questions, but nothing more than that. And right when I think she's not going to ask anything she takes a deep breath and looks at me as I finish my many tales of Connor.

"What does this all mean?" She asks the question out loud that I've been thinking about—well avoiding—for the past week.

"I don't know," I yell, throwing my hands up in the air. "I think it's done? I mean the whole arrangement on my side was only for the wedding."

"Do you want it to be done?" she asks.

"Maybe? Maybe not? I feel like everything from this weekend was a wedding high. And we've never talked about anything long term before. I don't think he'd want that," I tell her, attempting to work out everything going through my head. From what he's said in the past he only wants to use this arrangement to prepare him for future relationships.

"Have you asked him?" she challenges me.

"Not directly…" I trail off, avoiding eye contact with her. I can feel her eyes drilling holes into me, and when I finally look back and see her raised eyebrows I whisper, "I've never felt this way about somebody before, Han."

She leans forward, hands coming to rest on my knees and big green eyes staring up at me. "Talk to him. And if things go poorly, I'll be your buffer when we go camping."

"I don't know if I'm ready," I admit. All of these feelings are new for me. I'm not one to fall for someone this fast, and my longest relationship didn't last more than three months. Connor and I have been doing this for two now and it feels so much more real than anything I've had before. If I open up to him and admit that, then I'm opening myself up to get hurt which is not something I'm interested in. Keeping everything under the umbrella of a deal would make it easier if he decided he was done one day.

She rolls her eyes, and guilt tightens in my gut from the fear of telling Connor about how I'm really feeling and what that might result in. "Then get ready, because this is going to eat at you if you let it fester," she says, and I know she's right.

"I'll tell him soon. Let me see how things go these next few weeks," I say, hoping between now and Thanksgiving I'll be able to find the courage to talk to him. Maybe I'll be able to push this out to Thanksgiving break where I won't see him for a week. If I give myself the opportunity to miss him, maybe that can tell me how I feel because right now I'm nothing but confused. Confused about why he is the one to make me get flustered when he walks into a room. Why he's the first thing I think about when I wake up, and the last thing before I fall asleep. How spending two nights with him led to the best two nights of sleep I've had since fall break. Maybe I'm only comfortable around him and feeling all these things because he's always there.

There to comfort me when I'm not feeling well. There to explore and learn new things. There to encourage me when my mom is being rude. There to step in when I need him, even if it means facing a crowd of college students.

I need to think on this more, so Hannah and I both retreat to our rooms for naps before our weekly sorority meeting later tonight. And right before I fall asleep I feel my phone go off. Hoping it's Connor, I lunge for where I left it next to me only to be disappointed.

MOM

Can you send me pictures from yesterday?

Also I'm sorry for not believing you can do things on your own. I'm so proud of you and all that you do. Love you!

MAEVE

Thanks, mom. I appreciate that. I'll send those now. Love you too

I pull up the shared album and add her to it when a photo I haven't seen yet comes up. It's from the newest batch Sidney added. It's a photo of her and her sister on the dance floor, but what catches my eye is my pink dress behind them.

It's the moment Connor kissed me after we talked to my mom. His hand is wrapped up in my hair, and his arm is around my waist. It looks so effortless and romantic, and there's something about it that looks like we were always meant to do that together.

I screenshot the zoomed in image, opening it and starting a message to Connor, staring at it unsure of what to say. *"Hey we look hot in this photo and I think we might make a cute real couple."* Nope. Definitely can't say that. Canceling the message, I set my phone back down and try to fall asleep.

## THIRTY-FOUR

## CONNOR

Spending the rest of the day yesterday without Maeve made me jittery. I tried to distract myself with video games, calling my parents, and checking in on Cy and Zach but none of it helped. I kept thinking about her, bringing her up, or refreshing Instagram to see if she had posted anything yet. She didn't add me to the shared album, so there was no way for me to see the photos from the wedding. I definitely didn't consider making her my phone wallpaper, because that would be too much.

I was itching to see what photo she would post first. Would it be a family photo? One of Charlie and Logan? A photo of us? You could tell a lot about a person from the order they chose to put their photos in. If she puts us first, I might be brave enough to talk to her about how I'm feeling. But if it's anything besides us I might be able to buy more time.

Sitting in class, I can't stop my knee from bouncing as the time gets closer and closer to eight. Finally, right before class starts, Maeve comes rushing in. She slides into her seat, spinning around to squeeze my hand with a quick "Hi" before Professor Kader starts class.

She reaches into her backpack for her gum, and huffs when she's met with an empty container. Without hesitation, I reach into mine and pull out the gum I bought the week after fall break in case she ever forgot to buy another one again. I've only had one piece, because the second I put it in my mouth I was reminded of the taste on her tongue. That got me too excited thinking about her mouth, so I haven't touched it since. I tap her on the shoulder and hand it over, hoping she doesn't read into this.

When she turns, her face lights up and she takes a few pieces with a whispered "Thank you" before she's turning her back to me again.

For eighty minutes I try to pay attention, but combining the fact that it's Monday and Maeve is in front of me, my efforts are futile. Halfway through class her pink cardigan falls down her shoulder and exposes the tattoo she got this weekend. I've never wanted to bite somebody before, but something about it makes me want to lean forward and sink my teeth into her skin. Maybe I'll get a chance to do that in the future, but I should probably let it heal first.

Before I realize it, class is over and everyone is packing up. I toss all my stuff in my backpack as fast as I can. "Do you want to go get coffee and breakfast?" I stand and step closer to Maeve, pulling her cardigan back into place as she stands up from her seat.

She looks better than she did yesterday morning, like she got a good night's sleep if the sparkle in her hazel eyes says anything. The green and gold are like a gem caught in the sun. Does she regret the shots of Fireball we did at the wedding as much as I do?

"That sounds perfect, I'm starving," she agrees,

adjusting her bag over one shoulder. I sigh in relief, not sure why I was worried she was going to say no. Getting coffee and breakfast after this class is something we both usually do. We don't always sit down and eat together, but today I'm hoping she won't leave right after getting her food. The whole walk there I keep my hands on my backpack, because if I don't I'll reach for her hand, and I'm not sure where we stand. We had said we should start kissing more as a greeting, but I don't think that applies to right now even though I miss the feel of her lips against mine.

She talks about the wedding as we walk and a video sent to all the cousins of Finn throwing up on the side of the road from the morning after, and I have to remember to ask her to add me to the shared album. When we make it to the café, I offer to pay for hers but she insists on paying for herself. I grab us a table while she waits for our food, and I'm drawn to the one where she held her fake dating interviews, to where this whole thing started.

After what I assume is years, she finally sits down and passes me my coffee and sandwich. "Are you okay? You seem distracted," she asks, taking a bite of her croissant.

"I was hoping to talk to you about something, if it's not too early?" I tell her, the different ways I rehearsed this in my head all disappearing into the wind.

"Nope. What's up, buttercup?" She tilts her head to the side, like a puppy does, and I want to forget what I want to talk about and tell her how cute she is for hours.

"I know when we started this arrangement you only needed me for the wedding. But I was thinking, what if we extended it?" I start, and her eyebrows raise as she takes a bite at my suggestion. "Hear me out, the holidays are coming up and that's always prime time for parents to inquire about their kids' love lives. If we extend this, to say the end of the semester, it buys you more time without your mom asking you questions. You can also start planning your event business more and find an internship now that you aren't worried about the talent show," I add the last part and worry it might be laying it on too thick.

Can she tell I'm lying my ass off? That I might want her to be more than my fake girlfriend? By keeping things going I might find the strength to tell her how I really feel, but I'm still not sure if she's interested in a real relationship, let alone one with me. I wait in anticipation as she finishes her current bite, taking a sip of her coffee before answering me.

"Connor O'Shea," she starts, and I might be getting yelled at if she's full naming me. I preferred Big Bird. "That's the smartest thing I've ever heard you say. Plus, I don't think I've taught you everything yet," she says, winking at me and I would have rather had her yell at me. Now I'm thinking about how I never got to get down on my knees for her, and how I very much would like to do that soon.

"You're a menace, Barbie," I tease, not sure what else to say because I can't say *"How about we go fuck right now?"* when I have another class soon.

"But you love it," she says with a smile and another sip of her coffee, reminding me I should probably drink mine since I haven't touched it much since I started talking.

I shake my head at her, not willing to reply to a sentence with love in it because I'm not so sure what it means to her. I'm fairly certain she's messing around, but I'm hoping it was a slip of the tongue and she might be on the same page as me.

"I was also wondering if you would want to come home with me for Thanksgiving?" I ask, and the question surprises me as much as it surprises her. I'm not sure where it came from, it just slipped out. If she says yes I'm going to have to run it by my parents and make sure it's okay. I'm not sure what the protocol there is since I've never brought anyone home before. Before I can panic, her warm voice calms me down with her answer.

"The Thousand Islands in November? Count me in. I've always been curious about it at other times of the year," she says, and I remind myself she's only up there in the summer when tourist season is at its busiest.

"It's pretty boring and slow. But we can walk around town if it's not too cold," I tell her. I know for a fact the whole Murphy family loves hitting up their favorite stores every year, and I'm sure she would be excited to visit places like the cheese shop.

"I could get some cheese," she squeals, and my heart jumps at how well I know her. It's bizarre to realize I know all these facts about her I never realized I was storing in my brain until recently. I also know she'll want to pick up some of the chocolate rocks from the cheese shop. She always brings those to the beach and eats them as she lays out in the sun.

"Perfect, so we have a deal?" I ask, reaching out my hand to make this official, but really just wanting to touch her again.

"Consider our arrangement amended, again," she says, laughing at the alliteration and shaking my hand. There's a spark of electricity and I instantly miss the warmth of her when I pull my hand away. Maybe inviting her home wasn't a good idea, but I can't back out now.

CONNOR

Can you FaceTime?

My leg bounces as I spin in my desk chair and grab a Rubik's Cube to keep my hands busy while I wait for my sister to respond. She should be done working by now, but she's always on the move so if I don't hear from her in the next five minutes I'll assume it's a no.

MORGAN

Call me in 5

I let out a sigh of relief reading the text and set an alarm on my phone, distracting myself with undoing and redoing the cube until the timer goes off.

"What's up, buttercup?" Mo chimes as her face fills my screen. Her brown hair shows tints of red from the lights as she moves around the room before sitting down on what I assume is her couch.

"Are you coming home for Thanksgiving this year?" I ask, not wasting any time.

"What are you a mind reader? Vic and I were literally just talking about that." She laughs, her familiar smile reminding me of our mom.

"Well are you?" I ask, my leg moving faster waiting for her to answer. I'm unsure what I want her answer to be. Do I want her home when I bring Maeve there? Or would it make things infinitely worse?

"Right. I believe we decided yes. Hold on," Mo says, her face moving off the screen as she shouts to her wife, who must be in another room before her attention is back on me. "Yes we are. We did Vic's family last year so we'll be there this year."

"Okay, cool. Very cool. That's good," I ramble, my head bobbing as fast as my leg.

"Why are you being weird?" she asks, getting closer to the screen like that'll give her a better look.

"I'm going to be bringing a girl home," I tell her. "My

girlfriend," I add, letting the lie that doesn't feel like a lie anymore slip from my lips. Mo wasn't there in high school when I had my disastrous girlfriend, and when she found out what happened she said she was going to come home and beat her up. She still jokes about it when we walk around town together, so I'm not sure how she's going to react to this news.

"Oh shit is it the game board girl?" her face lights as she snaps her fingers like she's solved a mystery.

"How do you know about her?" I ask, heat flooding my cheeks as I spin away from the light in my room to hide it.

"Dad told Mom, Mom told me." She rolls her eyes like I'm the idiot for not putting that together fast enough. "What's her name again? Mary? Margaret?"

"It's Maeve," I sigh. "But I just invited her. I didn't ask Mom yet," I tell her.

"So you want me to act like I don't know yet?" she clarifies.

"That would be great. Until I make sure it's okay. I wanted to know if there would be a buffer before I asked them," I explain, my leg finally settling down. Having Mo and Vic there will be good, they can help fill in silences and hopefully my parents won't hound Maeve with too many questions.

"Aw I'm your buffer? How sweet. I can't wait to buffer for my baby bro," she teases, pinching her fingers together close to the camera and I'm grateful my cheeks aren't in the same room as her.

"Will you please not embarrass me?" I plead.

"I make no promises. But I have to go, Vic and I are going to be late for our dinner reservation with our friends," she says.

"Yeah, you go. I've got to eat dinner too. That was all I needed. Thanks for talking. I'll see you at Thanksgiving."

My anxious nod returns as we say our "I love you's" and hang up the phone.

Of course she only had a minute to talk. She's living this amazing life full of friends and dinner reservations. Meanwhile I'm sitting in my bedroom alone, with not a dinner plan in sight. Maeve is probably off with sorority sisters getting dinner too. Maybe if I was brave enough to talk to her about how I was really feeling I wouldn't be eating alone tonight. But that's a worry for another day.

## THIRTY-FIVE

MAEVE

Before I know it, somehow November is almost over and I'm at Connor's house in the Thousand Islands the day before Thanksgiving. My mom was bummed when she heard I wasn't coming home, and my cousins gave me shit, but I don't care. Hannah has been yelling at me almost every day for not talking to him about my feelings and I could use a break from her. My original plan of not spending Thanksgiving with him was thrown out when he asked me to come home with him, and I realized I actually didn't want to spend time without him. I like where we are right now. It's simple. I've been able to do more research about opening my business and I've had two interviews with a wedding planner for an internship next semester. Instead of using that time to worry about a real relationship and what I should be doing with that person.

Connor and I see each other for classes and studying, and the occasional meal. Every time we study it seems like we sit closer and closer together, and I'm not complaining. There's no pressure to constantly be with him or be texting him, and it's been such a relief.

I've focused so much on myself that we haven't done much outside of school. I would have assumed by now we would have hooked up again, but there's also no pressure to meet a certain arbitrary number of times a week. Instead, I find myself thinking more and more about the possibility of what it would be like to make this a real thing. But I don't know if it would be as easy as it is now. Making this thing real might backfire and I could fall back into feeling perceived obligations to make time for the other person. Where we are now is perfect, and I don't want to change that.

On the drive, Connor gave me a run down of who would be attending Thanksgiving. Even though his family is much smaller than mine, my nerves are making my heart pound in my chest. His family doesn't know our relationship is fake, so we're going to be pretending all weekend to keep this up like we agreed. Even though it doesn't fully matter if they believe us or not. But I'm excited at the prospect of getting to touch him whenever I want now that he's given us more time. It's probably going to be the last time for something like this, so I'm going to have to enjoy it while I can.

Heading up to his house, he grabs my hand and reassures me it's going to be okay. But I'm unsteady, and the déjà vu of driving through the Islands is throwing me off. The usual sun I'm used to is replaced by cloudy skies and cold weather. And driving through the town to get to his house there's noticeably fewer cars and people, compared to the hussle of summertime. Being here during the winter feels wrong when all our interactions in the Islands have previously been accompanied by warm weather and sunshine, but being here with Connor makes the cold not matter at all.

The second we step through the door, I'm overwhelmed with comfort. There's loud instrumental music coming from down the hall and the air smells like apple pie. I follow his lead as he removes his shoes, dropping our bags next to the stairs and heading down the hallway.

I take in the family photos on the walls as we pass them, while still managing to keep up with him. The biggest one is a family portrait, with a tiny redhead sucking his thumb and resting his head on his mom's shoulder. It's adorable and I'll be returning to take a picture of it later. I don't have time to look at everyone else in the photo before we step into the kitchen.

"Hey, Mom! We're here," Connor shouts over the music toward a tall woman with graying hair who's cutting a pie while swaying her hips.

"Honey," she shouts, dropping the knife and throwing her arms up in the air as she rushes over to him. She wraps him in a tight hug before pulling away and turning her attention toward me. "Hi dear, I'm Michelle. It's so nice to meet you. I've hardly heard anything about you," she says, giving her son a side eye. "I'm a hugger, if you don't mind?" she asks, holding her arms out toward me.

"It's nice to meet you too," I say, stepping into a quick hug. "He doesn't talk enough, does he?" I elbow Connor in the side, and his cheeks turn a light pink.

"He really doesn't. It's a shame, when he was a kid I could barely get his thumb out of his mouth so he talked even less," she teases, and his blush darkens.

"Can we please not?" he groans next to me, and I can't help the giggle that escapes.

"Sorry, honey. It's nice to have you home. Your sister and Victoria are staying in her room so the two of you will be in your room. I've blown up an air mattress and put it next to your bed since you both won't fit on the twin bed. Why don't you go get settled and then come downstairs for pie? Dad will be home in a few hours, and your sister should be here by seven," she tells us, spinning us by our shoulders and pushing us toward the hallway.

Connor leads us back down to the hall, picking up both of our bags and heading up the stairs. We're staying here for four nights before going back to school, and I did my best not to overpack, but my duffle bag looks like it's holding on for its life.

The walls leading upstairs are filled with more pictures from family vacations to graduation photos. He's the spitting image of his dad, and I can't wait to meet him. Meanwhile his sister has darker hair, but the same light green eyes that they all have.

When we make it to a door with a handmade sign that says 'Connor's Room' that looks like something you would purchase at an arts festival, he pauses before opening it. "You can't laugh or make fun of what you're about to see," he warns.

"Me? Make fun? I would never," I feign innocence as he rolls his eyes and opens the door.

Stepping in, I expect to see something embarrassing like posters from a teen magazine hung up all over the walls or a race car bed. Instead, the room is painted a deep green and a clear theme of horror monsters is prevalent. There's a twin bed in the corner with black sheets and green drawings of monsters covering the entire thing. Old horror movie posters decorate the walls and there are several shelves of action figures and boxed Funko Pops while board games and old binders cover his desk.

Turning to face Connor, he's looking at me like he's been holding his breath for the last minute. Part of me wants to tease him, but another part wants to put him out of his misery. "This is cool, why would I make fun of you?"

"Why wouldn't you?" he asks, clearly confused.

"Why is your room decorated like this?" I ask instead of answering him.

"Because I like horror monsters. These figurines are ones I painted with my dad while watching movies. And these posters we found at the antique shop after someone donated their whole poster collection. It's all kind of dorky, isn't it?"

"I don't think so, it's cute. But these monster figurines might give me nightmares," I say, pointing to a particularly scary one on his dresser.

"That's the Creature from the Black Lagoon. I'll protect you tonight, don't worry," he says, stepping closer to me and kissing my forehead.

"From a separate bed?" I laugh, gesturing to the twin sized air mattress next to his bed.

"You want to squeeze in my twin bed, Barbie?" he teases, wrapping an arm around me and pulling me to his side. The warmth of him around me is comforting, and I wouldn't be opposed to sleeping next to him again.

"Only if I get scared," I tease back, moving to the tips of my toes to give him a peck on the cheek.

He takes that moment to cup my face in his other hand, keeping me close to him and bringing his lips to mine. It's a kiss I've been craving since the wedding, and I melt at the feel of the familiar touch. I wrap my arms around his neck and let him hold me, ignoring the fact that I'm in Connor O'Shea's childhood bedroom.

He holds me tighter as I run my tongue along his lips, requesting access. When he opens for me, a moan escapes from his lips and I swallow every sound like my life depends on it. And when my fingers twist in his hair, nails scraping at his scalp, he moves to push me up against the wall. I gasp when my back hits the wall, breaking our kiss.

He pauses, looking down at me as I catch my breath. "We should go back downstairs," he pants, my leggings bunching under his fist.

"Right, apple pie," I say, remembering his mom is waiting for us.

"But later?" he asks, a glint of hope shining in his eyes —they are somehow the darkest I've seen them in this green room.

"Later," I agree, nodding my head and willing my heart to return to a normal pace.

"You're not sleeping on that air mattress, Barbie. Not when I want to wake up with you tucked against me. I've been dreaming about waking up like that again and getting lost between your legs. Does that sound like something you want?" he asks, dropping his head and whispering in my ear. His breath causing goosebumps to break out along my skin.

"Who taught you to talk like that?" I laugh, dropping my head back to the wall and rubbing my hands over my face as my heartbeat does the opposite of what I want.

"What? You don't like it? Fuck, I didn't—"

"Connor, stop," I interrupt him, rubbing his arms in reassurance. "It's perfect. I do want that, but not right now. Let's go get pie with you *mother*," I emphasize the last word, reminding him that his mom is in the same house before taking his hand and leading us out of the room.

## THIRTY-SIX

# CONNOR

E ating pie in my kitchen with Maeve and my mom while waiting for my dad to get home from work is something I never would have guessed as a possibility at the beginning of this year. Mom fills us in on all the latest, from her plans for tomorrow to the most recent town gossip.

Growing up in a small town like Black Willow Bay always meant everyone seemed to know everything about everyone. And I'm reminded of that when I check my phone and see several texts from a while ago.

### BAYWATCH BOIS

CY

Connor did I see you driving through town with Maeve??

ZACH

He WHAT

CY

GIRL! AT! HIS! HOUSE!

ZACH

CONNOR ANSWER YOUR PHONE RN

CONNOR

Can you two fuck off? I'm trying to enjoy Thanksgiving with my family

I laugh to myself at their obvious distress. Taking a picture of my mom and Maeve, who are focused on their conversation, I send it to them and then mute the chat before pocketing my phone.

I listen to them chat, and it's not long before Dad comes through the door and immediately goes for a slice of pie before saying hi.

"How about saying hello to your son first?" Mom clips from the table.

"But, Michelle, your pie is one of my favorite things. How could I walk in and not go to it first?" he teases, moving over to the table with his plate and kissing my mom on her forehead before turning his attention to us and exchanging a quick handshake with me. "Maeve, right? It's a pleasure to meet you in person," he says, reaching his hand out to her next.

She's already smiling from trying not to laugh at him, reaching her hand out to shake his. "It's lovely to officially meet you too. I love your watch."

His face instantly lights up at the complement as he takes a seat and launches into something I've heard a million times before. "This old thing? It was my father's, it was a gift from my mother on their fifty year wedding anniversary. When he passed away, it was one of the things he left to me. It doesn't work right now. It needs a new battery or something else, I haven't taken it in yet," he tells her, poking the watch's face like it will magically come to life.

"That's so sweet, I love it," Maeve swoons, as her hand comes to rest on my knee under the table. I'm not sure if she's doing it out of instinct, but I'm sure it's not because she's thinking about relationships—or us in a relationship. Meanwhile, an image of an older version of us on our wedding anniversary creeps into my mind, but I know she's not thinking that. I'm not the type of guy someone picks to end up with, I'm only a friend type.

"When's Mo getting here?" Dad's question breaks my train of thought as I look at Mom for the answer I already know.

"Around seven, so I thought we could wait for dinner. I was going to start preparing it soon," she tells him.

"I can help you with dinner, Mrs. O'Shea," Maeve chimes in and I get ready for Mom's usual answer of not needing any help.

"Call me Michelle, darling. And that would be wonderful, thank you," she replies, and I exchanged a confused look with my dad as soon we both get an idea at the same time.

"*Wingspan?*" we say in unison, mine louder than his which is through a bite of pie.

"That was freaky." Maeve's gaze bounces between the two of us before the whole table erupts into laughter and my heart warms at the familiarity and ease of being home.

Hours later, we've survived dinner and more pie is being devoured as my sister tells another story about me. Morgan and Victoria arrived right when dinner was ready and Maeve and Mo acted like instant besties, sending my nerves into overdrive. By the time we sat down to eat she had already told a story about me getting a LEGO piece stuck in my ear when I was a kid. And by the fourth story, I gave up trying to stop her after Vic said it was no use once she got started.

I've lost track of how many she's told now, but getting to hear Maeve's laughter mixed with my family's is worth it. She blends in so well here, the perfect splash of pink. How am I supposed to end this like we planned when I want more of this?

"Want to see the newest game I got?" Dad leans over and whispers to me, nodding down to the basement where all the board games are. Earlier, he ran downstairs and grabbed *Wingspan* to play at the table while Mom and Maeve cooked. Maeve kept coming over to see how it was going, and when I told her I was winning she said she was proud of me. Which caused my face to blaze red, but I didn't care.

"Please I can't take another second of this," I reply, rolling my eyes at my sister.

She pauses her story to stick her tongue out at me before focusing her attention back on Maeve who is fully invested in the story about how I mistook a toilet in the store as a functioning toilet while potty training.

I follow Dad to the basement, where there's a large board game table in front of a wall full of games. He shows me a new expansion pack of *Eldritch Horror*, telling me we can play tomorrow or another time this weekend. I suggest Maeve might be into that, too, since she's now played with me a few times, which makes him smile.

"Speaking of Maeve, what do you think?" I ask, since he'll tell me the truth.

"I like her more than you, already," he teases, laughing at his own joke. "Tell me how's school going?"

"Good, really well. Starting to feel better about my classes and grades," I tell him, grateful for Maeve and saving me from the awkward conversation of telling my dad I was failing.

"Great. I'm proud of you for getting help, glad we picked that school for you," he says, and my heart warms at his approval while I try not to hint at who is really helping me.

"Me too, now to survive the rest of this year and next," I joke, hoping I won't need help next year.

"Well when you graduate, my firm said they would love to interview you for a position. And if you decide to not move back here, I have a few other connections I could send your way," he tells me, and I'll be forever grateful to him for helping me with this. I imagine us working side by side in matching sweater vests Mom had gotten us for Christmas. It's not a bad image.

"Thanks, Dad," I say, hoping I don't need to tell him how grateful I am, and that he knows.

"Yeah, of course. Hey, have I ever told you about how I knew I was in love with your mother?" he asks, and the abrupt change of conversations catches me off guard.

"No, I don't think so," I reply, my heartbeat picking up because if he asks me if I'm in love with Maeve I don't know if I can lie to him.

"We weren't dating yet, but I could tell pretty early on with her. In high school I wasn't the coolest person, and I had a hard time making friends. One day at lunch, she came over and sat with me. You know how she is, always taking care of people. She started talking to me, but it took a while for me to give her more than one word answers. After about a week of her sitting with me, I started to open up. Thank god for her patience," he teases, and we both laugh knowing we're both the ones to test her patience.

"Then what happened?" I ask, wanting to hear the rest of the story.

"After a few months, I finally asked her to hang out outside of school. I was so nervous to invite her over, I took three showers before she got there because I was sweating so much. It wasn't an official date, but it was to me. When she got to my house, I asked if she was interested in playing a board game with me, fully prepared for her to roll her eyes, make fun of me, and leave. But instead, she agreed and listened to all my pitches for each game. We ended up playing Risk, and she kicked my ass, but that's not important. The point is, she never once teased me like the other kids at school did. And as I opened up to her more about games and other things like horror movies, her smile got bigger and bigger. Never making me feel bad for being excited about things I liked, no matter how weird they seemed."

"Is that when you knew you were in love?" I ask.

Dad takes a deep breath, scratching at the stubble on his chin before answering. "No, it was a random Monday. She came into school with a game she bought over the weekend because it seemed like something I would like. I'm surprised I didn't ask her to marry me right then and there, but we were in high school so that wouldn't have gone over well."

"Why are you telling me all this now?" I ask, unsure if I want to hear the answer.

"Think about it, you'll figure it out. But let's go back upstairs before your sister breaks out the photo albums," he says, resting his hand on my shoulder with a light squeeze.

Following him back upstairs, Maeve perks up the second she spots me. "New game was cool?" she asks as I sit back down next to her.

"Yeah, it was an *Eldritch* expansion," I tell her, resting my arm on the back of her chair.

"One you have or one we should get?" she asks, leaning closer and putting her hand on my knee like earlier.

"I'll have to get it," I tell her, willing my heart to stop racing and stop focusing on her causal use of 'we' and how closely it relates to Dad's story. Hearing him talk about my mom only conjured Maeve to the forefront of my brain. It felt like he was telling me about us, and now I need to figure out what the fuck I'm going to do about it. Right now, I'm happy to take whatever she'll give me. If I say something first I'll only end up hurt, for all I know she might not feel the same way.

## THIRTY-SEVEN

## MAEVE

I loved every second of Thanksgiving with Connor's family. His sister is one of my new favorite people, and she sent me some of her favorite makeup brands to try. Getting to talk to his dad was strange, since it was like looking at a spitting image of an older Connor. His grandparents were adorable, and told me more stories about baby Connor. Once they left, his dad convinced everyone to watch a new horror movie and Connor held my hand through the whole thing because I was jumping at almost every strange sound.

I was starting to think fake dating was a bad idea because I didn't have a real relationship in my plans for the year, but being here makes me not care at all about my plans. He makes me feel like I'm the only person that matters to him, and we've snuck kisses here and there, but his family has been around the whole time. I almost wish we had stayed at school and spent the holiday in my apartment, where these feelings wouldn't be surfacing and I could focus on making him lose his mind instead. Last year,

I avoided any feelings by sleeping with people who would never be interested in a relationship.

We unsuccessfully tried to sleep in the twin bed together the first night, but it was so small that we both barely fit, and I rolled onto the air mattress after he fell asleep. We've got two days left here, and tonight his dad said we are playing board games after his mom and sister get back from Black Friday shopping at the nearest mall half an hour away.

"I'm going to head to Grandpa's and help him fix their porch. The railing is getting loose and I don't want either of them falling down the steps," Mr. O'Shea tells us as we wash the breakfast dishes. "Did you two want to come with me?"

"We're all set, we are going to hang out here," Connor quickly answers before I can, winking at me when his dad looks away.

"Okay, I will see you both later," he says, turning and heading for the garage.

We resume washing the dishes, me rinsing and him putting them into the dishwasher. With each dish, he steps closer to me until we're touching. When the loud whirl of the garage door stops, Connor turns off the water and spins me around, trapping me between the sink and him. I drop the plastic cup in my hands and gasp as his hands cup my face.

"We're finally alone." He smirks, leaning closer to me until his mouth is a whisper away from mine. "Want to go upstairs?" he asks against my lips, and I'm lucky he's got me pinned upright or else my knees might give out.

"Lead the way, red," I tell him, lifting my head to kiss the tip of his nose.

He quickly shuts the dishwasher and grabs my hand, practically sprinting out of the kitchen and up the stairs.

The second we get into his room, he slams the door shut and falls against it. His chest is heaving from how fast he's breathing, the blush I've come to adore already creeping up from under his T-shirt. We stand staring at each other for a minute until he lunges himself off the door and at me.

We're a tangle of limbs as his hands come to my face again, pulling me into a kiss as he walks us backward to the bed. He tastes like coffee when his tongue slips into my mouth and I moan as we fall onto the bed.

He breaks the kiss first, lifting off me and looking down. "What do you want to do?" he asks, and my mind runs rampant at all the things I want to do to him and vice versa.

"You tell me," I say, wanting to only do what he's ready for.

He sighs, sitting back on his heels and opening my legs around him. His fingers travel up my legs and over my center, causing my hips to lift seeking the friction they've been craving from him for weeks. "As much as I want to peel these leggings off you and taste you again, I won't last. I already feel like I'm about to come from simply seeing you on my bed, and I have something else in mind. I want you to fuck me," he says, and I groan at the idea of having him inside of me.

"Are you sure?" I ask, moving to my elbows.

"One hundred percent. Show me what it's like," he says, pulling his shirt up and over his head. I've seen Connor shirtless plenty of times before; he's practically shirtless every summer working at the beach. But I've never been this turned on by him being shirtless before. I want to explore every ridge and valley with my mouth until he's pleading for me to touch his cock, but that can wait.

"Lay down, and take off your pants," I tell him, snapping the waistband of his sweatpants on his skin with a loud snap as I jump off the bed and over to my bag.

"Where are you going?" he pleads behind me, and when I turn around with a condom in my hand I swear I see his dick twitch. He's laying on the bed, taking up the frame from top to bottom, with his cock at full attention in the middle. The trail of hair that runs from his stomach to his cock is like an arrow pointing me to where I want to be the most.

"Don't worry, I'm grabbing protection," I tell him, slowly making my way back to the bed. Before climbing on top of him, I set the condom down next to him and slowly pull down my leggings and underwear. His green eyes are caves of darkness, and his hand wraps around himself with quick pumps. Reaching out, I pull his hand off his dick. "Not yet, not until I say."

"Fuck, please, Maeve, get over here," he pleads. The itch to tease him and make him beg more fights the need to feel him inside of me. I want this as equally as he does, if the wetness pooling between my legs is any indication.

Climbing onto the bed, I settle over him with my legs on either side, not quite lowering myself all the way down. Staring down at him, I pull my shirt over my head as his fists curl in the sheets. Reaching behind me, I unhook my bra and let it fall onto the floor. He groans, tossing his head back as his whole body strains below me.

"Oh god, please, can I touch you?" he gasps between breaths.

"Go ahead," I drawl, reaching for the condom and opening it.

His hands release the grip of the sheets and start roaming over my body, and I can't stop the moan when one slips between my legs and into me.

"So fucking wet, we're not going to need any lube are

we?" he muses, pumping another finger into me as his thumb brushes over my clit.

I lose all function, and rock into his hand like my body has a mind of its own. Intent on regaining control, I lift up on my knees causing his fingers to slip out of me. Wasting no time, I take his cock in my hand and roll the condom down as he gasps at the touch.

Lowering myself, I pin his cock to his stomach, grinding and coating it in my wetness. If I keep up the right pace I could come like this, the head of his cock hitting my clit in the perfect way each time I reach it, but it's not about me right now and I want his first time to be perfect.

He's biting his lip as his hands move up to my breast to play with the piercings there. I gasp when he pinches one as my clit rolls over the head of his cock. He lifts his hips and moans, "Please, let me feel you."

Lifting up, I line the head of his cock at my entrance and watch him as I start to slide him into me. He mutters a combination of swears and praises as I slowly lower myself completely, giving myself some time to adjust to having him in me. It's a fullness I haven't felt in months, but somehow it feels different from all the other partners I've had. Like we were made to fit together.

I start to rock over him, and his hands come to my hips to guide me. His nails dig into my sides, surely leaving marks so later when I ask myself if this was a dream I'll know it wasn't. I try to set an even rhythm, but every time I think he's got it, he either pushes me the wrong way or lunges up at the wrong time.

"You have to stop." I bite my tongue to hold back a laugh, stopping and pinning his hands next to his head. We are definitely going to need more practice, but I don't want him to lose his confidence right now. I'm closer to his face now, and I can see how wide his pupils are blown. But there's a hint of sadness in them when I remember he can't read my mind.

Before I can speak, he asks, "Is this not working for you? What should I do?"

"Let me set the rhythm, let me take care of you. Okay?" I clarify, making sure he knows I don't want us to stop what we're doing and hoping to lessen his worry.

"What do I do with my hands?" he asks, and I wish I had brought a scarf with me. Looking up the slats on his head board, I move his hands above his head and around them.

"Hold on to the headboard, and let yourself feel," I tell him, pushing myself back up and resting my hands on his chest. I start slowly, rocking a few times to let him get used to the new rhythm. His knuckles are white around the wooden slats and he looks like he's holding his breath.

"Connor, breathe," I tell him, picking up my pace.

When he does, his moan is the loudest I've heard. "This is fucking incredible, but I'm about to come," he gasps.

"Do it, come for me," I encourage, moving faster since he's almost there.

When he comes it's with a loud groan and more curses mixed with praises as I slow my movements over him.

Slipping off him, I lay down next to him and rest my head on his chest as his hand releases the headboard and wraps around me to keep me on the bed.

"Wait, but you have to finish," he says, turning his head to look at me.

"It's okay I don't need to, it was your first time, this was for you," I tell him, and I'm surprised when I realize it's not a lie. Getting to be with him was enough, and I don't mind that I didn't finish.

"But you should finish," he argues, furrowing his eyebrows.

"Don't worry," I reassure him, pushing the space between his brows to relax his face before running my nails through his hair.

"Ohmygod that was amazing," he says in disbelief, holding me tighter to him.

"I know. Imagine the next time we do it," I say through a laugh as his eyes shut at my touch.

"Next time?" he mumbles.

"Duh, you didn't think we would be one and done, did you?" I ask, knowing I would keep going now if he was ready.

"I guess I didn't think anything, I can't think at all right now to be honest." He chuckles before his eyes spring open. "But if they're still not home we totally could. Let me clean up, get a cup of water and a snack, and let's do it again." He jumps up from the bed and trips over our discarded clothes as he makes his way to the bathroom. I can't help but laugh at the clumsiness of it and how I love everything about him, and how I don't mind that I'm letting myself think that. Looking around his room before I get up and follow him, I notice all the small things that would have annoyed me a few months ago.

All the monster posters and memorabilia intrigues me instead of making me roll my eyes, because I know it makes him happy and I want to understand why. His closet is slightly open and I can see his lifeguard hat shoved at the top. Would he notice if I took it home with me? There's also a familiar navy New York State Parks hoodie that I recognize from the colder days at the beach. I never would have guessed I would be seeing it again so soon, but now I'm warming up to the idea of being honest with him, and myself, about my feelings.

## THIRTY-EIGHT

"Wait, what?" my brother's voice echoes through the phone during our weekly check-in call.

Since I missed Thanksgiving with our family, he's filled me in on anything I need to know. Like how Liam kept defending his girlfriend was real and not made up—a fact we were pretty sure was true but it was too easy to tease him about it since no one had ever met or seen her in person. Ryan also let me know how Grandpa fell asleep on the couch the second he was done with dinner, and half the family spent the rest of the night preparing for Black Friday shopping.

"I slept with Connor," I repeat. The admission comes after he finishes rambling on about our family because I can't hold it in any longer.

"*Why* on earth are you telling me this?" Ryan yells, emphasizing the beginning of his question. We're close, since we're only two years apart, but I usually spare him the details of my sex life. He's not getting all the details now either. Like how we managed to have sex multiple times while staying at his house. Including him slipping into me one morning after waking up tucked into him. He thrust into me while covering my mouth and burying his face in my hair so neither of us made a sound, and I can't wait to do it again.

"Because I need your advice," I tell him. Last night when Connor dropped me off, I talked to Hannah about it, but she only repeated what she told me after the wedding. The easiest way to figure everything out would be to talk to Connor, but I need to make sure that's the right move before I embarrass myself and risk heartbreak. If Ryan repeats the same thing Hannah has been saying, I have no choice but to talk to Connor. Of course another option is I never talk to him, and keep pushing my feelings further and further down until summer comes and we both go home. Maybe we'd fall into a relationship or fall out of touch and I'd never have to admit anything ever. But that's not realistic.

"Can you erase my memory so I don't remember you told me that?" he asks with all seriousness.

"Ry, I'm serious. I'm only telling you this because you should have the full picture before I tell you I think you were right," I admit, even though it pains me to say those words to him.

"Hold on, what? Can you repeat that? I need to record this," he teases, and he's lucky we're not in person or else I would be hitting him right now.

"For fucks sake, will you be serious?" I groan, wanting to get this over with.

"Fine, fine. I was right, what was I right about? Wait," he pauses, realization finally hitting him, "you actually like him? Don't you?"

"Unfortunately, I do," I tell him, ready for his gloating and teasing when all I've done for the past five years is say negative things about Connor.

"Why's that unfortunate? It seemed like he was pretty into you at the wedding. Like Hannah and I knew you were supposed to be faking it, but it didn't feel that way," he says, and my brain is slowly working out what he means. I fully expected him to laugh at me and convince me I didn't, not be supportive about the potential of a real relationship between us.

"You and Hannah talked about me behind my back? Rude," I say instead, filling the silence with anything besides my new feelings for Connor.

"Not the point, Sis. I've known him for as long as you have, but I've had more conversations with him compared to you. I know what he thought of you before, he never hid an eye roll anytime you spoke or came into a room shouting at the top of your lungs."

"Now it seems like you're trying to hurt my feelings," I interrupt. "Where are you going with this?" I ask, wondering why he's only insulting me.

He groans, and I snap my mouth shut. "What I'm trying to tell you, is he didn't do any of that at the wedding. It was honestly disgusting the way he was looking at you, he had this love-sick puppy dog look on his face the whole time. Everyone noticed it, and people kept asking me about it all night. It was actually pretty annoying. Like why can't our family ask the person they have a question about to that person directly? Why do they have to always ask someone else? That's how things get miscommunicated and I think—"

"Ryan," I interrupt again before he gets on a soapbox about how our whole family could communicate better.

"Right, sorry. Anyway, I hate to break it to you, but your scheming failed you big time. Cause you were looking at him the same way," he says with a finality I need to hear.

"So you think it's okay?" I ask, still feeling like I did something wrong by allowing myself to fall this far.

"Why wouldn't it be? I feel like you're overthinking this. It's pretty obvious to me you've both gotten to know each other these last few months. You know it's okay to change your opinion on someone after getting to know them, right? I've been waiting for you to finally say something about him, but you avoid the topic each week. When you told me you weren't coming home for Thanksgiving, I was sure you were going to tell me then, but you didn't," he says, and I struggle to process everything he's telling me.

"Ry, it's more than that," I whisper into the phone like Connor is going to come barging around the corner at any moment, even though he's at his apartment.

"Dude, do you *love* him?" he whispers back.

"Yeah. I love him," I say, finally voicing the words I've been too scared to say out loud. Memories of the semester flashing through my brain like a movie montage. From seeing him in class the first day and being furious about it, to seeing him in class this morning and wishing we had more time during break. In the span of a semester, he's altered everything I know about relationships, and we aren't technically in one. He's treated me better than anyone else has in the past, and he didn't have to do any of that.

He never signed up to pick me up when I was drunk, or take me to the hospital, or make me mac and cheese. I never signed up to let him slowly break down the walls around my heart that I've spent so much time building these past few years. And I definitely never signed up to allow him to take my breath away with every kiss, every touch, and every whispered word of praise in my ear. But now, I don't want to know what it would be like to live without any of that.

I want him there when I'm at my worst, and when I'm at my best. And I want to be there for him when he needs me the most, I just have to tell him.

"Maeve? You still there?" Ryan's voice cuts through my thoughts as a tear falls from the corner of my eye.

"Yeah, just processing," I tell him, wiping my face. "I have to tell him, don't I?" I ask, even though I know the answer.

"That's the only next step, or you have to let him go," he says, and my chest tightens when he mentions letting him go.

"Thanks, Ry. I have to go to class. But thanks for this, I love you," I tell him, wiping another tear as it falls.

"Of course, talk to you next week. Love you," he says before ending the call.

Instead of getting up and heading to class, I sit there and stare at the wall. I have to talk to Connor about how I'm feeling. But we only have two more weeks left in the semester, and then finals. He barely needs me to help him anymore, and our study sessions have become more of a set time to work on assignments and papers. If I tell him now, and he doesn't feel the same way I do I'll have to suffer through the two weeks of seeing him. I'd rather tell him after finals, that way if my feelings are stronger I can drive home and cry about it there instead of being awkward for two weeks.

Deciding I'm going to wait until finals, I stand up and head to my night class, hoping I made the right decision and he doesn't break my heart.

## THIRTY-NINE

CONNOR

Today during our study session there was something wrong with Maeve. All day I was looking forward to seeing her again, it felt like the only thing getting me through my classes. But when I got to the study room she was back on the other side of the table, instead of at the end like the last few weeks. Her head was down and she barely said hi when I walked in.

Her nose was buried in her laptop, typing away, and I sat down and started working on a final paper due next week. We didn't talk much, but made plans to have dinner later this week, and I could sense something was wrong. It might be nerves for finals, but instead of asking I ignored it.

Sitting in my room playing video games, I can't get my mind off her. Spending the holiday at my house with her exceeded my wildest expectations. I never expected her to fit in so well with my family. My dad had texted me when we left that she was invited to Christmas and every other holiday unless I mess it up. What he told me about him and my mom lingers in the back of my mind. Do I love

Maeve in the same way? I'm pretty sure the answer is yes, but it won't be real until I tell someone else before I tell her. What if I tell her I fell in love with her these last few months? That having sex with her wasn't just because I wanted to learn, but because I couldn't imagine doing it with anyone else.

Throwing my controller to the side I pick up my phone and open my text messages.

**BAYWATCH BOIS**

CONNOR

SOS anyone free?

CY

Give me two minutes

ZACH

I'm off today, what's up?

I hit the FaceTime button, knowing it will be more useful to talk through things compared to text.

Zach's face fills the screen right away, and I can tell he's in his apartment based on the couch and the Thousand Islands map behind him. One that Cy and I gifted to him when he went away to culinary school so he wouldn't feel too homesick.

"Are you okay? What's up?" Zach asks rapidly. "Is it Maeve? You've been kind of radio silent since the wedding. I saw the photos they all posted though, you looked very handsome," he says, and I can't help the blush on my cheeks from being called handsome. Zach's unapologetic unfiltered compliments are something I've gotten used to, and grown to love. Compared to me, he's much more comfortable in his skin and expressing his feelings.

"Shit that reminds me, I forgot to update you. Sidney

says hi and she's doing well in LA," I tell him. How did I forget to call him after the wedding? It's been a busy month for all of us and we haven't had the time to talk to each other as much. The second I mention Sidney's name, Zach's phone takes a tumble as I see nothing but his ceiling.

"Fuck, shit, sorry," he mumbles as his face fills the screen again and I do everything in my power to contain my laughter. "You talked to Sidney?" he asks, and the hope in his voice makes me feel guilty for messing with him.

"I mean, yeah, she was there so I said hi to her. She asked how everyone was doing."

"What did you say?" he gets out before I finish my sentence.

"That everyone was good and you were enjoying culinary school," I say, remembering what she said about his food and the look in her eyes, but I don't want to make him feel bad about picking his career over someone he knew for ten days.

Zach looks like he's about to ask more before Cy joins the call with a, "What's up motherfuckers?" He must still be at work if the bookshelves behind him are any indication.

"I need your advice, again," I tell them.

"What? Did you go and fall in love with Maeve?" Cy quips, taking a bite of a beef jerky stick.

"Yeah, I did." The admission comes easier than I expected with the direct question being asked first, and I can see my whole face turn bright red in the small frame of the phone. Cy chokes on his snack and Zach drops his phone again as I wait for them to say anything.

"I mean I definitely saw this coming but I'm still surprised," Zach says, propping his phone on what I assume is his coffee table, so he can stop dropping it left and right.

"It was either this or she was going to kill him," Cy laughs, taking a sip of water to wash down his snack.

"The problem is I don't know if she feels the same way. She's been acting weird since we got back from Thanksgiving. I was planning to talk to her today, maybe ask her to officially be my girlfriend, but it didn't feel right. Everything seems good between us, but I'm worried I fucked this up when we had sex," I say everything while staring at myself on the phone, not wanting to see how they're both reacting to this.

"YOU HAD SEX?!" They both yell in unison, and I remember I haven't updated them in a while.

"We did," I say, not being able to contain the giggle that slips from my lips and I cover my face with my hands, feeling the heat from my cheeks on my palms.

"Shit I need to make you something." Zach's voice is still loud, but not yelling. "Do you want dinner? Maybe a dessert? Should I send you a cake? Or do you like tiramisu?"

"You don't have to make me a sex dessert," I laugh, imagining the *'Congrats on the Sex'* cake from The Lonely Island's song.

"Yes, I do," Zach argues.

"He does," Cy agrees as I roll my eyes at them. "But please elaborate on the situation."

"Right, so let me fill you in on the last month," I say, running my hand through my hair and willing my face to stop acting like I'm lit on fire from within. I run through all the updates from the hospital to Thanksgiving. Telling them about how we extended our agreement and how we've fallen into this comfortableness that I don't know if I want to give up. I tell them everything my dad said to me, and how it got me thinking. How I feel safe with her and how I can't stop thinking about her. How every pumpkin I see reminds me of our date and how I'll never be able to look at the color pink or gum the same ever again. How I don't know if telling her all this will ruin things, thinking maybe I should wait. When I finish they both are staring at me with matching devilish grins.

"Oh, you're down bad," Zach says.

"Like real bad," Cy agrees.

"What do I do about it?" I ask, annoyed they're repeating each other.

"You need to talk to her, that's literally the only way you will know if she wants to officially date you," Zach tells me, and I wish he could send some of his confidence through the phone.

"Or you could wait until the semester is over, and talk to her then," Cy counters, repeating my idea of waiting.

"That's not a good idea," Zach says firmly.

"But what if it is a good idea?" I say, pointing to Cy, but he probably can't tell that.

"You can still have fun until then, just don't drop the L-bomb until you know you might not need to see her for a while. That way, if she does laugh in your face you can come home and I'll make you soup," Cy offers, and I burst out laughing.

"I've never seen you cook, and I don't know if I'd need soup," I tease.

"I could make soup. You only warm it up," he defends himself.

"I'll tell you what," Zach interrupts our bickering. "You two use this stupid plan to wait, don't listen to me. But when it blows up in your face, I'll see if I can leave for a few days and I'll make you food to dull the pain in addition to your sex dessert. Don't let Cy cook anything."

"Okay, so I'm waiting," I say as Cy mutters curses about how he swears he can cook. "That's the right call, it's only two more weeks. I can not say 'I love you' for two weeks."

"Sure you can, whatever you say." Zach rolls his eyes and Cy gives me a thumbs up.

"Make sure you actually update us this time," Cy reminds me before they both hang up, and I assure them I will. Now I only need to survive through finals without scaring her away and hoping she isn't done with me.

## FORTY

MAEVE

Sitting in my apartment with my feet on Connor's lap, I try to distract us from our impending final grades by lightly running my foot along his dick through his sweatpants. His knuckles go white around his phone as his head drops backward with a groan and I feel him harden beneath my touch.

"Stop refreshing the page, she said they were going to be posted at one. She probably needs someone to help her since she's so bad at technology," I remind him, glancing at the time and seeing we still have five minutes. My stomach is a mess of knots, and it's not from waiting for our grades but what I have to do after.

"Yeah, but maybe she'll post them early," he says, finger hitting the screen where the refresh button is as he moves his body away from my foot.

"Why do you want to see it so badly?" I ask and stop trying to distract us. Yesterday after the test he told me how well he thought he did. He was so excited he understood the questions, pulling me into a big hug and thanking me for helping him. He didn't have any reason to be nervous about getting our grades. Meanwhile, I'm a mess. Knowing once we have these grades I have no more excuses for not telling him how I feel.

"I need visual confirmation I did it—*we* did it," he corrects himself at the last second.

"Don't give me credit, you did most of it yourself," I say, as his hand comes and rests on my ankle. The touch sends a tingle all the way up my leg and through my spine, and I suppress the full body shiver that accompanies it.

"Seventy-thirty," he laughs, rubbing his thumb along my skin and making my stomach twist in more knots that this could be the last time we sit like this. Comfortable and together. In several minutes there are three possibilities that could happen, and they all play out in my head in slow motion. One, I tell him how I feel, he feels the same way, and I finally venture to my Facebook page I haven't seen since my last birthday to make it official. Two, I tell him and he laughs in my face and I employ Hannah as a shield every summer until Connor is no longer a lifeguard. Lastly, he fails the final and I forget all my plans and never tell him. I'm not sure which one I'm hoping for, because one and three both sound appealing, while two would be painful and ultimately crush me for eternity.

I snap my gum and attempt small talk to pass the time. "Do you think you'll go to the Learning Center next semester?" I ask him, not sure if he's confident in his classes next semester. I've noticed how he struggles more than usual, but I've kept myself from researching anything about it.

"You know I was thinking about that," he says, setting his phone on his lap. "I've been meaning to look into it more. I did some research and I think I might have some type of learning disorder."

"I think you might be right," I agree, glad I didn't have to be the one to say it. Sometimes people can get defensive about this type of thing. What scares me most is that I know him well enough to notice it. "I can go with you if you want," I offer, not sure what I'm doing. If this whole thing is about to end, that offer is going to be invalid.

"I'd really love that." He smiles back at me, and I have to hold back shouting *"Well I love you so why wouldn't I come with you?"*

A silence falls over us as he picks his phone back up, hitting the refresh button. "Shit, they're posted," he shouts after a fairly aggressive tap. Both of our spines straighten and as his eyes widen and wrinkle at the corners as a smile envelops his face. "Eighty-three! I passed the whole class!" he shouts, dropping his phone and tackling me back to the couch.

My head hits the pillow as his scent surrounds me. His weight over me makes it harder to breathe, but I don't mind. His hands bracket my head as he pushes up and gazes down at me. There's so many emotions in his bright green eyes and I'm not sure which to analyze first. The sparkle of joy, the wonder of surprise, or something else I can't pinpoint. Before I can figure it out, he's lowering his body again and his lips are on mine.

It's frantic and messy as I open myself to him, the plunge of his tongue into my mouth welcome. He kisses me like it's the first time after we won the game, but I kiss him like it might be the last time. Because if this is the last time I want to remember it. So I take my time remembering every detail. The softness of the couch below me, and the hardness of him above me. I can feel his pulse beating when I reach up to cup his face and run my thumb over his neck. The light brush of facial hair that only grows on his jaw line and needs to be shaved tickles my fingertips.

Moving to the top of his head I finally take hold of his soft hair and swallow his moan like I'll be able to bottle it inside me for safekeeping.

He smells like his deodorant but my shampoo since he took a shower here over the weekend. The taste of mac and cheese lingers on his tongue from our lunch together. I'm not sure what he does to my boxed mac and cheese, but even in the remnants of his mouth, he makes it taste better. I want nothing more than to have him make all my future boxed macaroni.

I take my time tracing his teeth with my tongue, memorizing every ridge and surface as he starts grinding into me. Opening my legs, I make room for him to get closer and gasp as he settles between them. His hard cock is evident through our clothes, and I feel like I'm in high school again about to be caught by parents.

We continue like that as I keep his mouth on mine. Could I give him one last orgasm before messing this whole thing up? There's a chance he still views this whole thing as practice, and I'm the only one who caught feelings. I try not to overthink this, and simply feel him rocking into me, and how good it feels even with so many layers between us. When he breaks the kiss to move down to my neck, I focus on the way his lips are soft against my skin and how his moans of pleasure are in sync with the head of his cock being pressed against me.

Right when I expect him to finally reach down and rake his hands over my body, someone in the hallway passes by making too much noise, and that has him pushing up and off me. No doubt afraid someone might walk in on us dry humping on my couch. The air is cold as he sits back on his heels and his hair is messier than a minute ago. He breathes heavily, and instead of waiting for him to say something I jump in with the first thing in my head that isn't *"I love you."*

"I'm so proud of you," I tell him.

"Thanks, now let's hope I passed the rest of my classes," he says with a self-deprecating laugh.

"You know Hannah and I are coming back here the weekend after Christmas. Some of the cousins are going to come and stay here for New Year's. I'm not sure what your Christmas plans are, but you're always welcome to come." The invitation spills from lips, and it's only because I have no clue how to start telling him how I feel. I'm stalling and I know it, but ripping off the Band-Aid might be the only way I can get this out. "I was thinking we could—"

"I want to talk to you about—"

Our overlapping sentences are interrupted by the ring of his phone. His eyebrows furrow with confusion at the peculiar ringtone as my mind runs wild with what he could want to talk about. Does he feel the same way? Or is he planning to end this and was waiting for his grades to come in? Did he spend time memorizing all the details about me while we were kissing like I did with him?

"Hold on, it's my sister. She never calls so I should probably answer this," he says, picking it up and answering it. I want to tell him to ignore it and finish what he was saying, but I can't do that. I don't say anything as he talks to her, but his phone isn't loud enough that I can make out what she's saying. His cheeks are still tinted pink, lips swollen from our kisses as he stands up and starts pacing in front of the couch. Moving to sit up, he passes in front of me, then turns and comes back toward me as I start to get nervous for a completely different reason.

Then, in the blink of an eye, all the color on his face disappears. Connor's pale Irish skin goes the whitest I've ever seen it, like a ghost. He stops moving and stares straight ahead, and I can't tell if he's still breathing. Something is wrong and my feet are taking over, standing to move toward him. He drops his phone and I see his body start to shrink to the floor. I manage to wrap my arms around him before he can hit the ground, holding him as he screams.

## FORTY-ONE

## CONNOR

Some people's favorite parts of their childhood are the big memories. Winning whatever sports championship they were in, going on vacation to Disney World, or holidays like Christmas. Mine aren't big at all, they're the tiniest of moments, scattered throughout time to make up an unforgettable childhood. But they all center around one person, my dad.

Him picking me up from school and taking me to the McDonald's half an hour away when my mom and sister were busy, and me promising not to tell my mom about it because she didn't want me having fast food too much. Walking to the game store with him on a Saturday after Mom made her famous French toast. Spending the following Sunday night playing whatever we bought the previous day after dinner was done and cleaned up. Putting in an old Universal Horror movie whenever a storm would come through, the black and white of the movies were always the perfect choice for bad weather. Eventually we had to get a replacement for Dracula since we wore out our first VHS copy. Those were the loudest memories in my mind. But now, sitting in my room with the lights off, I'll never experience anything like that again.

Because I'm not a kid, and my dad isn't here anymore.

Morgan said it was a heart attack. It came out of nowhere, and the paramedics did everything they could. But it wasn't enough, and he was gone. He is gone and I am hours away. We both are. She said she and Vic are leaving as soon as they can to go be with Mom, but I don't have to leave right away.

They are going to take care of all the arrangements, and the funeral is on Sunday. Which gives me four days to get home. I came in here to pack hours ago, but once I sat on my bed I couldn't move. The only reason I know time has passed is because the darkness coating my room must mean the sun has set. It's a darkness I welcome and crave, hoping this feeling of emptiness can be satisfied long enough to let me stand and get something done.

I've thought about texting Dad to talk to him, but I'm worried Mom already called the phone company and canceled his phone line. Part of me wants to ask her to keep it on the family plan, and I'll pay for it. So that I never have to worry about texting him and getting a text back from a stranger. I called his phone late last night because I thought maybe the phone call with Morgan was a dream, and that he would be on the other end wondering why I was waking him up at 2:00 a.m. But all I got was his voicemail, and the second I heard his voice I hung up the phone. Now I want to call back again to hear from him. There are several voicemails on my phone, but I'm too nervous to listen to those ones again. I don't know how I'm supposed to keep moving on when he isn't here. He's the one I ask for advice from, and I never thought I'd be wishing I could ask him how I keep going after he's gone.

A knock at my door breaks me out of my thoughts as

I look up and see Maeve standing there. When did she get here? She doesn't belong here. Not when I'm like this. The brightness and joy of her pink outfit and aura are in direct contrast with the despair and loss of my own life. She shouldn't see this, but I also don't want her to leave.

"Hey, I texted you but you didn't answer," she says softly and at a volume I'm not used to hearing from her. It's one that could put me to sleep, but it's not right because it's too low for her. I bet I look pathetic sitting here in the dark. I'm not sure why she's here when we didn't have plans for anything.

I scan the room for my phone, and find it sitting face down next to me. A memory of the notifications lighting up the screen and pissing me off surfaces and I remember why I put it face down. Can't people leave me alone? I don't know how many times I can thank somebody for their condolences. After the first few generic messages I started copying and pasting my response so people would stop, but the texts kept coming. I didn't know that many people had my number. I didn't know that many people cared about me.

"Did you get packed?" she asks when I don't reply, setting my phone face down again. I'll deal with those messages later. Or maybe never.

I don't know how to tell her I haven't done anything all day, so I simply shake my head. Then she's in front of me kneeling and placing her hands on my knees. The warmth of her seeps through my pants and I'm suddenly freezing. I must shiver because she brings a blanket around my shoulders.

"Have you eaten today? Or had water?" she asks another question that I'm embarrassed to answer, so I don't. I can't bring myself to shake my head. "Okay, well lay down. I'll be right back," she says, standing and leaving the room.

I'm not sure how much time passes, but it must be at least twenty minutes because the next time Maeve enters my room she's carrying a bag of food. The smell of French fries permeates the air and my stomach grumbles. The empty feeling comes back and I might throw up. I'm glad the food isn't McDonald's, knowing if she brought that I'd probably sob through eating it because of memories of my dad. I'm not sure where it's from. Did she drive to Bud and Honey's? The bag is unlabeled, but the food tastes familiar, comforting.

"Eat this, and I'll pack for you," she says, taking the food out and setting it on my nightstand. I manage to sit up and wince when she turns the light on, my eyes not ready to adjust to the intrusion. It makes me think of how pirates wear an eye patch so they can see below deck in the dark by moving it to their other eye. That's something my dad told me when we were playing a game with pirates once, and tears threaten to break out at the memory of him wielding a plastic sword.

Meanwhile, Maeve moves around my room like she knows where everything is, which isn't hard since I don't have much in here. It's nothing like my bedroom at home, the bedroom I built with my dad. Everything in my room will always remind me of him, hell I can connect anything back to my dad probably. Maybe that's good, maybe he'll always be with me in that way. But right now, it just hurts.

Suddenly, she drops the duffle bag she's holding and climbs into the bed next to me. When she reaches up to touch my face I flinch before I register what she's doing. Relaxing into her touch as she swipes a finger over the corner of my eye to remove the water escaping them. My vision becomes blurry as I pull the burger away from my face, my nose pinching as the tears become the only thing I can focus on.

She pulls me to her, my head falling to her shoulder as her arm wraps around me and into my hair. Her whispering, "I know" and "It's okay" only make the tears fall harder. I'm not sure how long she holds me, but it's long enough to let the food get cold. When the tears finally run dry I manage to sit up and eat as she finishes packing my bag.

"Thank you," I whisper, my throat sore from crying.

"Of course. I'm here to help in any way I can. Do you want me to drive you home? I already talked to Hannah and she's willing to take my car home and pick me up if needed," she says.

"No that's okay," I say through a cough, grabbing the glass of water she got me. "That's so much extra driving for both of you. You go home and enjoy Christmas with your family."

"Are you sure? I don't mind doing it."

"Yeah, I just want to drive home and be with my family. My sister should already be there, and she told me I didn't need to rush home, but I don't feel right sitting here," I tell her. I wish I could teleport there. The four hour drive is going to be brutal and no part of me is looking forward to it. If Maeve was my real girlfriend I would take her up on the offer, but she's not, and I don't want to put that burden on her. It's bad enough that she's here now taking care of me.

"Okay, but you know I'm here, right?" she asks, stopping with a pair of my pants in her arms and staring at me. I nod to confirm and she continues, "But you're not driving tonight, and I'm almost done here. Do you want to watch a movie? Horror?" she suggests. Would now be a bad time to ask her to be my girlfriend? Tell her that I love her. And *this* is why. But it doesn't feel right to do that now. Like she would have no choice but to say yes out of pity.

Instead I focus on why I love her. She's not asking how I'm doing, because it's obvious the answer is "not okay." She's still here despite the fact we're technically not together. She didn't need to check in on me, help me, or even care. But she does, and she knows exactly how to make me feel a little bit better. Even if it means watching something that she probably won't enjoy. And that's why I'm in love with her, and that's why I can save it for later.

"That would be perfect." I nod, and move the food wrappers off my bed to make space for her.

I get my laptop out and get a movie cued up as she puts the final things in my duffle bag and tosses it by my door. I want to put on an old Universal one, but they're not streaming anywhere and I don't own them digitally, so I settle on one I've seen a million times before and won't scare her too bad. When she climbs into the bed with me, she pulls the covers over her body as her legs tangle with mine. She's my own personal space heater here to keep me going. The smell of her shampoo is familiar and comforting when she rests her head on my shoulder. She fits perfectly beside me, not knocking my laptop out of the way or taking up too much space.

At some point during the movie, the dramatic notes of the score and Maeve's breathing mix together. As exhaustion takes over, I can't tell the difference between the two. A horror movie score would wake most people up, but for me they're soothing. My eyelids are heavy as I struggle to stay awake for the rest of the movie, but I finally give in and close my eyes as I fall asleep with Maeve wrapped around me.

CONNOR

The last few days have gone by in a blur. From driving home on auto pilot to crying with my family and planning the funeral, I feel like a shell of myself.

Staring at myself in the funeral home's bathroom mirror, I splash cold water on my face to help wake me up. The bags under my eyes stand out against my light skin and there's a pimple forming on my jaw. I wish I had Maeve here to give me one of those star patches. Not being with her for a few days has made me realize I've started to relate things to her almost as much as my dad. Yesterday Mo made us mac and cheese for lunch, and I could only think about how Maeve always asks me to make it for her. And how I learned to make it from Mo, who always throws in extra cheese when no one is watching.

Straightening, I take a deep breath and make sure everything is in place. My sports jacket feels too big, like I shouldn't be wearing it yet. I attempt to adjust it, shaking my shoulders, but nothing helps. The bright light of the bathroom bounces off the glass on my watch as I move the jacket out of the way to see it. The feeling of having it on my wrist is foreign, and I rub my finger under the bottom of it to give my skin a break. It still doesn't work, but that's not why I'm wearing it.

Taking a deep breath, I suck back the tears threatening to escape my eyes and turn to leave the bathroom. At some point I thought the tears would stop given how much I've cried, but my body always seems to find more whenever I sit with my thoughts for too long. We're halfway through the calling hours now and there's a small service once they end. Dad wanted to be cremated, so he's not actually here with us, which feels wrong. But Mom wanted to do this before Christmas which I understand. What I don't understand is how the fuck I'm supposed to get through Christimas without him.

The voices of the crowd grow louder as I get closer to the room everyone's in. I'm sick of thanking people for coming. I want this all to be over. I want to go home and look through pictures and videos with my sister. I don't know who half of these people are, and I'm over pretending to care.

Entering the room, my feet take me to where Cy and Zach are standing. I told Zach he didn't have to come, but he didn't listen to me. They're both dressed in slacks and dress shirts with jackets, but theirs look like they fit.

"You good?" Cy asks when I stop next to them.

"Yeah, just"—I gesture around the room like that will suffice—"it's a lot."

"Yeah, I get it." Cy nods with sympathy in his eyes. He lost both his parents last winter to a case of black ice, and I remember how hard that was for him.

"Does this get any easier? Missing them?" I ask them. It hasn't even been a week, but it feels like it's been a lifetime.

"Honestly?" Cy starts, sighing and wiping his hand

over his face. "No. But some days are good and some days are bad. There's always going to be part of you that misses them, and that's okay. Your grief is going to look different every day, and you have to know when to recognize the bad days and ask for help if you need it."

"I lost my mom when I was a kid and I still think of her any time I see roses," Zach chimes in, and glances at his tattoo sleeve that's only roses, barely poking out under his shirt sleeves. "I've learned it's not about focusing on the fact that you miss them, but celebrating their memory by honoring them. Even if it's in the smallest way. But that also took me several years to realize, so if you don't get there right away don't feel guilty. As long as you don't lock yourself in your room and disappear on us," he teases, nudging my shoulder with his.

"Thanks guys, and I won't. Feel free to yell at me if I do," I tell them, worried that could very well happen.

"Obviously. Plus now you get a membership to the dead dad's club. We meet at the bookstore on the third Tuesday of every month. Bring a dish to pass," Cy jokes, and the laughter helps ease the pain if only for a moment.

"Is Maeve coming?" Zach asks, pivoting the subject to something brighter.

"No, I told her she didn't have to. I also haven't talked to her yet about everything, so she's got no reason to."

"You sure about that?" Cy asks as his gaze moves to something behind me.

I don't have to turn around to know what he's looking at. I can sense it in the air. The way my chest already feels lighter and the space around me knows it's missing something key. I turn around to confirm what I already know, Maeve is here.

She's standing at the front of the room, wearing a long sleeved floor length black dress. All of her hair is draped over one of her shoulders in a braid tied together with a black ribbon and she's stunning. Tears well up in my eyes at the sight of her, and intensifies when Hannah comes up behind her, hooking their arms together and giving me a slight nod. *She isn't alone.* That's when I see the rest of Murphy cousins pile in through the door. It's only nine of them, but that's nine more than I expected. I'd much rather have them here compared to people I don't know. It's not a short trip up here, and they didn't even know my dad. Maeve is the only one who met him. Did they really come up here for *me* in the middle of winter?

Before I can make sense of all the emotions my feet take over and I'm headed her way, leaving Cy and Zach behind me. Hannah steps away as I wrap my arms around Maeve and pull her close.

I close my eyes and breathe in the scent of her, spicy and sweet, and she holds me tight. Her arms feel like a shield blocking me from all the sadness from today. Like everything about today is a little bit easier with her here by my side.

"I told you not to come," I say, pulling away from her.

"I know." She shrugs. "But when have I ever listened to you?"

I want to make a joke, return to our usual banter, act like everything is normal. But I can't. No one outside my family has ever gone out of their way to show up for me like this when they didn't have to—minus Cy and Zach. I pull her back into my arms, my fingers finding their way into her hair. I hold her as close as I can get without fusing our bodies together.

"Thank you. Thank you so much. I love—that you all came," I trip over my words as I whisper into her hair as tears spill from my eyes, almost telling her that I love her but hoping she thinks I was just getting choked up.

"Of course, and sorry for the extras. They insisted on tagging along." She pulls away, taking my hands in hers and nodding toward her cousins who are all talking to my family.

"Don't worry, there's plenty of room. Sidney's not here? I could use a distraction and Zach's here." I nod behind me to where Cy and Zach are eying the group of Murphys.

"No, she couldn't get her flight moved. She's home in a few days for Christmas," Maeve tells me. "But Ry is here, so at least we can watch him and Cy act like idiots." She smiles at me as she rolls her eyes. We haven't talked much about our overlapping lives, stuck in the bubble of college, like if we talk too much about anything outside of college this whole thing might collapse. But the way we both understand what we're referencing and the ease of it makes me curious about how well we could function as a real couple.

"Are you staying here tonight? All of you are welcome at my house after the service for dinner. Mom is heating up all the food people have given us and the rest of my family is coming over. It's like people only know how to make lasagna and casseroles, is that common?" I attempt to joke, feeling comfortable enough with her to try when I'm supposed to be sad.

"I'm not sure, but that's what my mom always makes for someone after a loss. It must be an unspoken rule we don't know about." She laughs, dropping my hand and playing with her hair. Wrapping her finger around the ribbon at the end, her classic gum is absent from her mouth. "We're driving back home tonight. We don't want to impose on your family, so we're going to stop at the diner for dinner first."

"You'd never be an imposition, but I understand." I'm

not lying either, she'd never be an imposition. Not even her family. They're an extension of her and helped shape and create her, and I want them around if it means she'll be around. Having a constant crowd of Murphys around would bring a much needed laughter to today, but we don't have room for all of them to sleep at my house. Instead of telling her I never want her to leave my side I ask, "Will you sit with me during the service?"

Surprise flashes over her face before she wipes it away and returns her hands to mine. The feel of her skin on mine again grounds me, and even if she says no I'll be okay if she keeps holding my hand for now. "Of course I will," she says, squeezing. And I might be able to make it through the rest of today without crying in public.

She doesn't let go of my hand as she leads me over to my family, where the Murphys have my mom and sister laughing. It's good to see them smiling again, even if the look in their eyes is still empty. The rest of the Murphys take their time saying hi to me, offering condolences, and hugging me. Then scatter around the room, looking at the various photo collages and memorabilia honoring my dad before gathering in a corner where I glance to every now and then to make sure Maeve is still there.

When it comes time to gather in the other room for the service, Maeve finds me and takes my hand again as we enter the small interfaith chapel. The pews fill up quickly, and my mom makes sure to get my grandparents to the front of the room. I sit down next to my sister, who grabs my free hand. Various people get up in the front of the room and tell stories, but when my mom finally gets up and speaks I can't hold back the tears.

Sitting there with Maeve, Mo, and Vic, I let the tears stream down my face as all our hands stay locked together. I don't break the chain to wipe them. Instead I focus on my mom, and how she retells their story. It's almost the same as the one dad told me, but it turns out mom was smitten from the beginning too. She recalls their honeymoon when they went to Hawai'i and it was like the universe was against them with several canceled flights. They ended up spending a night in New York City where she swears she had the best pizza from a random pizza shop she can't remember the name of. The crowd laughs at the appropriate amount of times, but I can hear the sniffles filling the room, and I'm glad I'm not the only one crying. Mo's eyes are red and her cheeks are tear stained as Vic rests her head on her shoulder.

After the service ends, everyone filters out and the Murphys say goodbye. Maeve hugs me one last time, and when she goes to pull away I don't let her. Keeping her close to me for a few more seconds, breathing in the scent of her before she's gone.

She leaves with her cousins and I return home with my family. My house quickly fills up with other family and friends. Cy and Zach help me unload all the things from the funeral home from Mo's car. When we finally sit down to eat my thoughts drift to Maeve. Is she still at the diner? What did she order? Did she get a burger like our first date, or something different? Before I can chicken out I pick up my phone and text her.

CONNOR

Thanks for coming today

Hope you got the burger, they're so good there

BARBIE

Of course, it was a lovely service

And of course I got the burger

A picture of her comes through next. A selfie with the burger in her mouth. One of her eyes is pinched shut, and her lip is turned up in the corner like she's growling as she bites the burger. Warmth spreads through me as I save it to my phone and return to my lasagna.

## FORTY-THREE

## MAEVE

"Who are you sending that to?" Hannah asks across from me as I send my burger selfie to Connor. It's a cute selfie, and the diner's wooden planked booth and cream wall make it obvious where I'm at. It's our favorite place to eat in Black Willow Bay. If we end up in town during vacation, there's a high chance we are stopping here for lunch. Their fries are thin and the perfect amount of crispy, and this whole place reminds me of being a kid. It's one of the first memories I have of the Thousand Islands. Being here now is different though, without any of the adults. For one, we are all going to have to actually pay this time. We're at the biggest table in here, half booth and half chairs, since there are so many of us, and I wish it was for a different reason.

"She's so sending that to Connor," Abby chimes in from next to me, ratting me out.

"No, I'm not." I get defensive immediately as I turn my phone away from her line of sight, the heat in my cheeks increasing as I hold in the urge to reach up and cool them down.

"What's going on there?" Liam mumbles through a bite of his burger as my heartbeat picks up at the idea of talking about Connor.

"Liam, please, mouth closed for fuck's sake," Finn mumbles from across him and next to me. "But what is going on there? Were you going to tell us you've been faking it or not?" he asks, turning to me and popping a fry in his mouth when he's finished.

My head snaps to Hannah as her eyes go wide. "Did you tell him?" I whisper-yell, trying to not cause a scene in our favorite diner because I might have to fight my family.

"To be fair I only told Abby," she defends, throwing her hands up in the air. "Finn was coming around the corner and then it spiraled from there." She throws an accusatory finger his way.

"It's not my fault you can't whisper," he yells, pointing back at her.

"Wait so everyone knows?" I ask, catching up as they yell at each other and toss the blame around. Then, eight pairs of eyes are staring at me as they all nod their heads. It's creepy how they all do the same nod, like I'm in some type of horror movie where everyone is possessed. A thought I normally wouldn't have, but I've seen so many with Connor that I can't help make the comparison. "How long?" I ask.

"Since Thanksgiving, and I would like it noted I didn't spill the beans," Ry says from the end of the table. I can picture them at Thanksgiving, all huddled up and whispering about me as the news slowly spread. I'm hoping none of the aunts or uncles overhead them because I don't want to explain this to my mom.

"And none of you said anything?" I ask, glancing around at the others who didn't know.

"We were planning to ask at Christmas," Quinn says with a shrug.

"We were all kind of suspicious when you two started dating, I mean you never said a nice thing to each other ever," Lucy says, and everyone asking me questions and giving their input is too much. There's too many thoughts, too many opinions, too many Murphys.

Dropping my head to the table, I let out a low groan before taking a deep breath and telling them the whole story. I run through a spark notes version of the semester, leaving out all the sexual details since I don't need this diner knowing my sexual history. Plus Ry would yell at me if I went through it again. I talk about how we slowly became friends and how he apologized for being mean and vice versa. I don't explain why he was so mean to me, or discuss his demisexuality, because those aren't my things to tell. But the point comes across just as effectively without mentioning it. They all listen and eat as I talk, sometimes asking clarifying questions. By the time I'm wrapping up, all of their meals are done and mine is still half eaten. But I don't know if I would be able to eat anymore with how anxious I'm feeling after telling them everything.

"So yeah, basically the point is I was about to tell him I love him and then his dad died so now I don't know what to do," I finish, taking a deep breath and grabbing my water because my mouth is dry from talking so much.

"Shit, that's totally not awesome," Finn mutters, and the rest of the table agrees with murmurs and nods.

"Maybe give it a few weeks? But if you told him now it would also be okay. We all agree the way he looks at you is a complete switch from this summer," Abby suggests.

"Glad to know you've all discussed my love life without me," I groan, not sure if I want to yell at them or thank them for their observance. Even though I've heard it before from Hannah and Ry, it's comforting to hear it again and my hopes rise at the prospect of a real relationship with Connor. "When did you all notice this?" I ask, curious to hear their views on the situation. If they have noticed a change in him, then maybe I'm not making up all this in my head. Plus I like hearing how he looks at me when I'm not looking.

"The wedding," they all say at the same time, and I let out the loudest and most giddy cackle I've ever made—like a little girl meeting her favorite boy band.

Throwing my hand over my mouth in surprise, I mumble through my hand, "I'm so fucked, aren't I?"

"Yes, but it's a good thing. I asked Cy about it and he thinks you should tell him too," Abby says, resting her hand on my shoulder as she tries to hold back her laughter. If she starts laughing I'm going to start laughing and it feels like the type that could turn into the uncontrollable unable to stop type.

"When did you talk to Cy?" Ry asks quickly, and we all turn our heads his way.

"Literally today, when we saw him. You still need to apologize to him by the way. You were a real ass this summer," Abby says, pointing her finger at him. I'm happy to let them fight if it means this conversation shifts from my feelings about Connor.

"What? I was not," he tries to defend himself.

"This isn't about you, Ryan. Please focus on the situation at hand." Hannah snaps her fingers in front of him, and I have to hold back laughter and the annoyed look on his face. "Maeve, you love him right?" she asks me, turning her attention my way and I'm not surprised I'm not getting out of this.

"Yes," I answer instantly as various "aws" ring out amongst the group.

"Do you want to tell him before we leave?" she follows up.

"No. I can't. Not today. I want to focus on helping him grieve," I answer, the guilt of making today about me twists in my stomach and there's no way I could take away from today.

"Okay, so stop freaking out, babe. You'll be okay. We're all very excited about this development," Hannah reassures me. "We'll go home for Christmas, and you can figure it out after. There's no need for you to have answers right now. You've got this." She reaches across the table and wraps her hands around mine.

"Can we stop talking about it now?" I ask, ready to stop dwelling on something I can't change today. "I want to stop by the cheese shop and go home."

"Yes. I need to get some for Sidney," Abby says, slapping her hands down on the table and making all the silverware clatter.

"I'm going to eat a whole brick on the drive home," Liam says, rubbing his hands together. "Ryan, you've got the check right? You're the finance bro and I'm *bro*-ke."

"I mean, I guess I'll use my card for the points but you all need to pay me back," he groans, pulling his wallet out from his back pocket.

"Sure thing, thanks, Dad," Liam jokes, patting Ry on the shoulder.

We all head out of the diner as Ry goes up to the counter to pay. Hannah hooks one of my arms with Abby on the other side, and I feel like a weight has been lifted off my shoulder knowing I don't have to pretend around them anymore.

No more pretending like my relationship with Connor hasn't progressed into something more. No more pretending this whole thing was only an arrangement. No more pretending I don't love him. Next time I see him, I'm telling him the truth. Hopefully it isn't too late for us to make our relationship real and he's open to hearing me out.

# FORTY-FOUR

# MAEVE

**Thu, Dec 25** at 9:00 AM

MAEVE

I got Ry a board game and had to tell you.
He suggested playing it tonight! How's your
Christmas?

CONNOR MY FAVORITE LIFEGUARD

It's strange, but okay. Watching all dad's
favorite holiday movies. I hope your family
enjoys the game

MAEVE

I'll let you know how it goes, I'm
determined to beat him

CONNOR MY FAVORITE LIFEGUARD

I have faith in you, Barbie

MAEVE

Thanks, red

CONNOR MY FAVORITE LIFEGUARD

Is red your official nickname for me?

I thought you didn't repeat them

MAEVE

It's a classic pick, I like the classics

CONNOR MY FAVORITE LIFEGUARD

Me too

**Thu, Dec 25** at 8:53 PM

MAEVE

FYI I beat him!! He's pouting in an ugly Christmas sweater. It's hilarious

CONNOR MY FAVORITE LIFEGUARD

Pic or it didn't happen

MAEVE

<Image: a dining room table with a board game. Close to the camera are Mahjong-like tiles on a board. Across the table a white male with shaggy brown hair sits with his arms crossed in a light up Christmas sweater with gingerbreads that says "I eat ass and cookies.">

CONNOR MY FAVORITE LIFEGUARD

Oh shit I love Dragon Castle!

Proud of you. Hope you told Ryan to suck it

MAEVE

Don't worry I did 😊

**Fri, Dec 26** at 11:00 AM

CONNOR MY FAVORITE LIFEGUARD

The invite for new year's still open?

MAEVE

Yeah, han and I are headed back tomorrow

The front door buzzer goes off suddenly, and Hannah and I let out twin shrieks causing Greta to jump off the couch and run toward Hannah's room.

"Who's here?" she asks, since the Mu Mansion is practically empty besides us and a few sisters here for the New Year's party in a few days. The party is a tradition for one of the frats and open to anyone staying on campus between the semesters. We went last year, and it was fun to celebrate with people our own age instead of my parents who wanted to go to bed the second midnight hit.

"Maybe it's Connor? I thought he would have texted me though," I say, checking our texts to make sure I didn't miss one from him.

"Sweet, I'm going to go to my room in case you two want to *talk*." She emphasizes the last word, raising her eyebrows at me.

"Yeah, yeah. I'll talk to him, go away." I roll my eyes at her, shooing her off down the hall after Greta.

I buzz hopefully Connor in and wait for them to come to the door. After another minute, there's a knock and I open the door to the tall ginger I've been waiting for. But he's holding his duffle bag and his eyes are red. There's bags under them like at the funeral and I can tell he's been picking at the pimple on the side of his face.

"Hey, um, can I stay here?" he sputters through his words as his eyes get glossier.

"Of course, come here," I say, pulling him into the apartment and into my arms. I guide his head to my shoulder like after our first quiz. Rubbing my hand up and down his back as he drops the duffle bag and holds me tight.

"I can't do it, Maeve. I can't go anywhere without thinking of him," he cries into my shoulder. "At home, everywhere I looked I saw him. I thought coming back here would be helpful, getting away from all those reminders. But my apartment does the same thing. There's pieces of him everywhere and I can't stop reminding myself that he's gone." He's sobbing now, and I feel a tear slip from the corner of my eye and down my face.

"You can stay here as long as you need, I'm here for you. No matter what," I reassure him and I stand there holding him until he's ready to let go. It's still not the right time to tell him how I feel, but I hope holding him is proof enough how much I love him.

The next few days pass by slowly. Connor doesn't do much besides sleep and hang out on the couch while we watch TV. Greta has gravitated toward him again like she did the first time he spent the weekend here. Hannah pretends to pout about it, but she keeps sending me pictures of Connor holding Greta like a security blanket even though I'm sitting right next to him. I'm making sure he eats every day, but sometimes he isn't hungry. I'm not sure what else to do besides be there for him, and for now that's what I'll do.

I was grateful when my mom sent me money, even though I was confused at first. She didn't send it with any message so I ended up calling her.

*"What did you send me money for?"* I had asked her.

*"I heard Connor was staying with you and it was the least I could do to help after his father passed away. Since we didn't go to the funeral with you. Are you taking care of him?"* she said, and I remember convincing her to stay home while we all went to the funeral.

*She had so much to do to get ready for Christmas and I didn't want to overwhelm Connor with my entire family again.*

*"Yeah, I am," I told her.*

*"Good. Is he doing okay?" she asked.*

*"I mean, his dad just died. Would you be okay?" I countered as I fought back tears.*

*"That's true. I'm glad he has you," she told me through a sigh, and it almost made me cry more.*

*"Me too," I agreed. "Thank you for the money."*

*"Of course. And tell him he's welcome here any time," she told me, and I had to move to the bathroom so Connor wouldn't come out of my room and see me crying.*

I suck in a deep breath at the memory and focus on the now. Last night, Connor was asleep when all my cousins got here for New Year's and now he's still asleep as we all have breakfast. It's a smaller crowd compared to the funeral—well, one person less since Quinn is with her boyfriend and Sidney went back to LA after Christmas.

The air mattress is blown up and in the middle of the room for the boys. Originally, Abby was going to sleep in my bed. But since Connor is here, she and Lucy managed to squeeze into Hannah's bed. It reminds me of sleepovers at my grandparents, something we haven't done since we were kids.

Everyone has messy hair from sleeping, and there are blankets scattered around the living room as everyone slowly wakes up. There's a half eaten pizza from last night on the kitchen table that was ordered sometime after everyone returned from the bars. I'm not sure how Connor slept through all that, but he didn't make a peep when I finally went to bed next to him. Greta was asleep on his chest and I felt bad disturbing them.

When Connor finally emerges, he comes down the hall

rubbing his eyes and is clearly not paying attention when everyone greets him at once.

"Hi, Connor!" Lucy shouts.

"Want a bagel?" From Liam as he picks up a bag of extra food we got.

"There's leftover pizza too." From Finn.

"Come hang with us!" From Jordan.

He looks shocked as he falls over his words. "I just want water, but thanks."

I jump off the kitchen stool and over to him, turning back to my family. "Leave him alone. He can do whatever he wants," I chastise before focusing on Connor. "Sorry about them, let me get you a glass of water and some toast so you've got something in your stomach." I grab his hand and lead him into the kitchen.

"Thanks, toast sounds good. Is it New Year's Eve already?" he asks, rubbing his eyes more. The bags are a bit better, and his face is clear thanks to the patches he let me put on him. I've also started introducing him to a nightly skin care routine, including some under eye patches to help with his bags and puffiness.

"Yeah, everyone is going to be here for a few days," I tell him.

"Cool, cool." He nods, coming up behind me and pulling me into him as I pop the bread in the toaster. His arms wrap around my chest and he buries his face in my hair. I hear him take a deep breath, his exhale tickling the skin on my neck as he whispers, "Seriously, thank you."

I reach up behind me and rake my fingers through his hair. "You're welcome." I hold the confession of love back, but it's getting harder to not tell him the longer he lets me hold him.

The rest of the day is calm as everyone recovers from the previous night, and more pizza is ordered for dinner before we start getting ready for the party tonight. The Mu Mansion has slowly gotten louder, since a majority of the sisters decided to come back today. The underclassmen are all here, too, since the dorms are closed between each semester. Every door is open with different music filling the hallways. My queer pop playlist is on full volume in the living room. Finn and Jordan have disappeared, and I assume they're in a different apartment. Hopefully not hooking up with any of the sisters and causing future problems for me and Hannah.

Connor is in my room watching older seasons of the dating show we got him sucked into. He keeps saying he likes the background noise, but he must be getting invested since he keeps asking if the couples are still together. I felt bad when I told him most couples from those shows weren't together and his "oh" sounded so defeated.

Walking back into my room, I grab the same pink sparkly dress I wore to the wedding.

"You're wearing that one tonight?" Connor asks, pausing the show on my laptop and sitting up in the bed as Greta rearranges herself next to him.

"Yeah, what do you think?" I ask, holding it up in front of me.

"It's perfect. I love it on you," he says, and I try not to focus on the use of the word love. He's done it several times now since he's been here and I don't know if he realizes he's doing it. First it was how he loved the smell of my shampoo, shampoo he was going to need to replace after using so much of it. Then he told me he loved my laugh when I attempted to cover it up after an embarrassingly loud cackle at something stupid on the dating show. And now he loves this dress.

"And you don't mind that I go?" I check again. I've

probably checked too many times today, but I don't want to leave him alone on New Year's if he wants me here.

"I don't mind. Go out and have fun, maybe I'll make mac and cheese if I'm still up when you get back. Do you have enough boxes for all of you?" he asks, and my heart strings pull that he would do that. I hope this means he's doing a bit better than yesterday.

"We should, do you need anything?" I check to make sure he's good.

"No, you just get ready and come say bye before you leave," he says, smiling at me.

I change in front of him, and catch him peeking up from the laptop to watch me. But the heat I'm used to seeing is absent from his eyes, instead replaced with the same sadness that's been there since he returned. I want to go over and kiss him so badly, even just a peck, but I don't know if I can yet. We haven't kissed since before his dad died and I'm not going to be the one to force him to do something he doesn't want to.

I'm in and out of my room as everyone gets ready. Grabbing different make up, clothes, and shoe options for everyone since no one seemed to pack anything they liked. Lucy has changed three times, only to settle on the first pair of overalls and crop top she tried on. Every time I came into my room, Connor's eyes tracked me until I left.

Before we leave, I check with him one last time in case he changes his mind. But he doesn't, so I give in to what I want slightly and kiss his forehead when I say goodbye. Leaving him in my room, and heading into the cold winter air I ignore the guilt in the pit of my stomach and focus on having fun with my cousins.

CONNOR

When I got back to campus I was grateful Maeve was okay with me staying with her. Hannah, too, since I was also encroaching on her space. Maeve doesn't constantly ask me how I'm doing like my family. It felt like they were all focusing on taking care of me instead of each other. Like if they all put their efforts into making sure the baby of the family didn't cry, then they wouldn't cry. Combined with the fact that everything reminded me of my dad, I had to get out of there before I had a full breakdown.

Another episode of this horribly addictive TV show plays, but I don't bother to turn it off. Instead, I burrow further under Maeve's covers. There's something about the drama that's comforting, and it definitely doesn't remind me of my dad. Like yes, I might be slowly falling apart, but at least I'm not falling apart on national TV in a bathing suit for millions of people to see and judge.

The Mu Mansion is quieter, and everyone seems to have gone to the party. The music in the building has stopped and there's no more yelling and slamming doors. I can hear the faint sound of Greta's snores from the end of the bed and the tick of the clock on her wall.

Picking up my phone, I scroll back in my photos for old New Year's ones. We always ended up at my aunt's house in our pajamas, taking pictures on her couch in front of a handmade sign with the new year on it. One year Mo couldn't make it because of work and I held up a picture of her. Things were easier back then. I only worried about how to convince my parents to let me stay up past my bedtime. Now everything is harder, and I wish I could rewind time and spend one more day with my dad. Play one more game. Get advice one last time.

I scroll so far back that I make it to when I was eight. I've never scrolled back this far before, these memories have been at fingertips the entire time. A memory of Mom talking about digitizing all our photos and videos flashes through my mind, so it makes sense that I have access to them. My fingers freeze over a video with a freeze frame of me sitting on my dad's lap.

I hesitate as my thumb hovers over the video, before I finally hit play. My screen fills with us at my aunt's dining room table. We're wearing matching black pajamas with "Happy New Year!" on the chest. The video is slightly grainy from how old it is, but there's no mistaking the cards in my hands. It must have been the New Year's before I went to magic camp, since I tried to learn tricks on my own.

*"You can do it, bud. Try again,"* my dad encourages me. Tears gather in the corner of my eyes at his voice.

*"What are you two trying to do?"* Mom's voice comes in from behind the camera.

*"Connor learned a trick from the book I got him for Christmas. Want to see it?"* he asks her.

*"Of course I want to see it!"*

*"You want to try the trick again for Mom?" He focuses his attention on me, and I can see myself shrinking and shaking my head no. "Give us one second, Michelle." He puts one finger up to my mom, but she doesn't step too far away, keeping the camera on us. "What's wrong, bud?"*

*"I'm bad at it," eight-year-old me says.* I can barely hear myself with how low I'm talking, so I turn it up. *"I already messed up, what if I mess up again?"*

*"If you mess up, you try again. That's how you learn. It's okay to mess up. The key is believing in yourself. You have to tell yourself you can do this, and then you will. Plus I believe you can do it, I think you can do anything you set your mind to. Now straighten your shoulders and try again," he says, sitting up straighter to show me what he means.*

*"Okay. Mom, I'm ready," I tell her, turning to the camera. "Please pick a card," I say, holding out the deck.*

I watch as I fumble over my words and I remember this being the first trick I mastered. I mess it up here though, since I had only gotten the magic book a few days prior. But my parents encourage me every step of the way, and tell me to keep practicing. Then the video ends and I have to take a deep breath since the tears have escaped from my eyes all the way down my neck.

I hit replay and watch it again. And again. And again. Every time, watching my dad. He always believed in me, even when I was clearly not good at something or clearly struggling like this semester.

"Hey, Dad," I say to the screen. "I wanted to let you know I passed that class. I never got to tell you. You were right, I definitely needed a tutor. But I'm kind of glad I didn't go get one right away, since I never would have roped Maeve into helping me if I had gotten one the first week. Thanks for always believing in me and being there for me," I pause, zooming in on the screen so it's only his face. "Most of all, I'm glad I got to hear about you and mom last month. And I'm glad you got to meet Maeve, I have a feeling she might stick around for a while," I tell him, and I know I'm not wrong.

Then, it's like I've run head first into a brick wall as I sit up in the dark room and realization hits me. Greta gets scared and jumps off the bed, running into the hallway as I pick up my phone again.

"Wait. What the fuck am I doing?" I yell into my phone as I close the app and open my texts. Maeve's contact sits there and my thumbs hover the buttons. If I want her to stick around I should tell her I love her. I have been over the last few days, and I've been doing it indirectly. But I didn't want to lose her yet if she didn't feel the same way, and was simply taking care of her friend.

What Dad said about Mom comes flooding back as the pieces come together. I'm stupid to think she doesn't at least *really* like me. She might not love me fully yet, but I love her. And I need to tell her. I can't text her that when she's at a party though, that's no way to tell her this. It needs to be in person, and it needs to be now before I lose the courage. In my heart I know if I called my dad right now he would encourage me to talk to her. He basically was telling me I loved her last month, and he always wanted me to be happy, so why wouldn't he be rooting for us?

I glance up at the time and see it's eleven thirty. I have enough time to make it to the party before midnight. Jumping out of bed, I run down the hall and into the living room. There are shoes everywhere and it takes me a minute to locate my sneakers. But once I do I'm throwing open the door and running down the stairs.

Right as I round the corner I almost run over Casey.

"Fuck, Casey, I'm sorry," I shout, grabbing her arms to make sure she doesn't fall down the stairs.

"You're good, why are you running down the stairs?" she asks, stepping back a step.

"I was going to go find Maeve, and shit, actually I don't know where she is," I say, running my hands through my hair at the realization I have no idea what party they all went to.

"I can take you there, just let me run into my apartment. I forgot my ID and had to come grab it, silly me." She shakes her head and steps around me, heading up the stairs to her apartment.

I tap the hand rail until she returns and leads me out the front door.

"It's only a ten minute walk this way," she says, pointing toward the area where most of the fraternity 'houses' are. Memories of my only frat party this semester come back, and I hope none of these assholes try to test me tonight because I might end up being the one to fight them.

"You're sure she's there?" I ask, making sure Casey is taking me to the right party.

"Hundred percent, it's one of the only parties tonight." She nods. "You two are cute together. I'm happy to see her happy again. Last year she smiled, but this year it's different. Brighter, and that's because of you," she says, as I resist the urge to ask her to run with me. Instead, I walk at her pace and nod along to whatever she's talking about. But I'm not really paying attention since she's leading me toward the rest of my life. Casey might not know it, but she's going to get a huge shoutout when I tell this story to my dad later.

## FORTY-SIX

CONNOR

"She's around here somewhere, good luck finding her!" Casey shouts over the music as we enter the house. I check my phone and see there's only seven minutes left now, ten minute walk my ass.

Looking around, I trust my gut and turn into the room to the right. The whole house is dark, with neon lights and strobe lights going off everywhere. The floor is sticky as I push through the crowd, and I almost slip on what I hope is a spilled drink and not something else.

"Connorrrrr!" A familiar voice slurs from in front of me as Finn and Jordan come into view. "You made it ou —" Finn tries to say but hiccups on the last word.

"Do you know where Maeve is?" I yell over the music.

"I think that way," Jordan points into another room and I sigh, heading that way.

Pushing through the packed crowd, I run into Liam and Lucy who are playing beer pong against two of Maeve's sorority sisters. "Do you know where Maeve is?" I lean in and ask them when they spot me.

"No, but if you find her tell her if she wants to play she

should come by soon. We're almost done kicking their asses," Liam calls out, as the sisters flip him off.

"Will do." I nod, but I don't plan to tell her that when I have something much more important to say. I continue to push through the crowd and run into every Murphy but the one I'm looking for when I finally spot Hannah.

"Connor!" she shouts, followed by "Holy shit, Connor!" from Abby.

"In the flesh, have either of you seen Maeve?" I ask, hoping that they have some answers since no one else has.

"Yes!" They both shout and point to the staircase behind them.

"She went upstairs, said she needed to take care of something," Abby yells, but it's practically a screech as she bounces in place.

My feet take me to the stairs, and I ignore the 'NO ONE upstairs' sign as I start to climb them.

"Hey Connor," Hannah shouts from below.

"I know, no one upstairs, I'll be quick," I tell her, sure she's probably about to yell about the sign.

"No, I don't care"—she waves her hand in the air—"Don't mess this up, okay? We believe in you too much," she says pointing at me to emphasize how serious she is, and I have to hold back a laugh, wondering how long they've all been waiting for me to do this.

"Don't worry, I won't," I reassure her as my dad's same sentiment fills my head. When I finally reach the top of the stairs I look around but don't see her. All the doors are shut and it's darker up here, the neons and strobe lights noticeably absent. I walk down the hallway, and around a corner until I finally see a sparkly pink dress lit by the street light shining through the window.

For a moment I don't move, watching her as she peers out the window to the street and taking in the beauty of her. Her phone is clutched in her hand, the screen lighting her up with a FaceTime screen as it rings and rings.

Becoming aware of my phone again, I pull it out of my pocket and see her name on my screen and swipe to answer it. Her face fills my screen in an instant, the glow of the street light on her showcasing her tear stained cheeks and watery eyes. The sound of the music echoes through the phones as she stares at the screen.

"Connor? Wait what the fuck?" she asks, eyebrows coming together and creating a valley between them that I've grown to love. "Where are you?" She pauses again. "Why is this echoing?"

"Turn around, Barbie," I chuckle, looking up from my phone to see her spin in place.

I don't have time to register what's happening until she is crashing into me, sending me several feet back. My arms wrap around her to keep us upright as she holds me tight.

"I was calling to countdown with you," she says into my chest, and I'm grateful the music isn't as loud up here.

"I'm here because I have something to tell you," I say, pulling her away from me so I can look at her. Her eyes still watery as more tears fall from them. "Why are you crying?"

"I don't know," she says, ending the FaceTime call still going. "You weren't answering. And I had some drinks, so I'm more susceptible to crying."

"Are you drunk?" I ask her, wanting to make sure she remembers this tomorrow.

"No, maybe tipsy." She shakes her head and holds up her cup. "I'm drinking water now."

"Okay, so I can tell you something?" I ask as my hands make their home on her shoulders. "It's a few things actually, so stick with me here," I tell her, and she nods. "First, you're amazing and thank you for taking care of me."

"You've said that before," she reminds me.

"And I'll say it a million more times. Second, I should have come with you tonight," I admit. Knowing if she had asked me more I probably would have still said no.

"You really didn't have to come. I mean you've been through a lot recently," she argues.

"That's the thing though, you want to know what I realized?" I ask, even though I'm going to tell her anyway.

"What?" She tilts her head slightly as one of my palms moves to cup her face, the warmth and familiarity of her skin giving me courage.

"I realized my grief can live in harmony with my joy. Just because I'm choosing to experience joy by being here with you doesn't lessen my grief or how much I miss my dad. And by allowing myself that grace, maybe being here with you will make it hurt less."

Another tear falls from her eyes as I brush it away with my thumb. "Is that all?" she asks through a sniffle.

"No, it's not. There's one more thing. When we were at my house for Thanksgiving my dad told me how he knew he was in love with Mom. About how she always took an interest in his hobbies. At first, I didn't know why he was telling me. But then I realized it's because he knew how badly I needed to hear it. He could see how much I loved you, even if I couldn't. He even bought a set of pink dice for you, for Christmas I think. I found them in the basement when I was home, but I wasn't sure when to give them to you. I've spent the last few weeks replaying his story over in my head a million times, and I've loved you for a while now. I love the way you aren't afraid to call me on my bullshit or challenge me if I'm wrong. I love the way you care for your family and show up for the people that need you. I love the way you laugh and how your eyes sparkle whenever I bring up making mac and cheese. But most of all, I love the way you make me feel. Like I'm perfect just the way I am, and how you welcome that. Because I think you love me too," I finish as the crowd downstairs starts to countdown from ten. Maeve's eyes are glossy, and a tear slips from the corner and rolls down her cheek. Bringing my thumb up to wipe it off her cheek, she leans into my touch before taking a deep breath.

"I do, and I tried to stop it, but I couldn't. Every day it became harder and harder not to love you. I've wanted to tell you for so long, but I was scared you didn't love me back," she says, as the crowd downstairs gets to one and cheers fill the space around us.

"Trust me, I tried not to love you either, but you're too damn loveable, Maeve Murphy," I say, bringing my other hand to her face and pulling her closer to me.

"I'm sorry," she laughs and the warmth of her breath covers my lips as our foreheads connect. "But really, I'm not sorry at all," she whispers, dropping her cup some-where and throwing her arms around my neck as she kisses me.

Relief floods over me as her taste overwhelms my senses. I hold her tight as she opens for me and our tongues meet in the middle, both eager to take control after being away from each other for too long. I let her take over, giving myself over to her like she's my salvation and when she pulls away I'm left panting in front of her.

"Happy New Year, Connor," she says, smiling at me with swollen lips.

"Happy New Year, Maeve," I say, pulling her to me one last time and kissing the tip of her nose. My hands wander down to her hands, taking her phone and putting it in my pocket for her.

"Does this mean we're officially boyfriend and girl-friend?" she asks, giggling like she's in middle school.

"If that's okay with you, I'd love to be your official non-fake boyfriend," I tell as her infectious giggles take over my system.

"They're going to be so happy," she giggles more.

"Who?" I ask, not sure who she's talking about.

"Everyone! My family, your family, your dad," she says.

"He did say he likes you more than me," I laugh, repeating what he told me at Thanksgiving.

"Obviously," she says, rolling her eyes. "I'm awesome."

"You are," I agree. "Now let's go tell everyone and let them act surprised. Plus Liam said you were up on the table next," I tell her, remembering what he told me.

"Will you be my partner?" she asks, squeezing my hands.

"I'll always be your partner," I tell her, letting her lead us back down the stairs and into the unknown. But that doesn't scare me as much as I thought it would, not with her by my side.

# EPILOGUE - MAEVE
## 1 ½ YEARS LATER

"Excuse me! Move! Out of the way please!" I yell, dodging idiots who have clearly never walked on a sidewalk before. What kind of people take up this much space to walk anyway? Don't they know to keep to one side?

I'm already running late after the repair shop called me at the last minute to pick up my order and my Uber had trouble getting into campus. The order was supposed to be ready two days ago, but the part they needed got delayed and a bunch of other bullshit I didn't understand.

My gown flows in the wind, and I'm glad I glued this cap to a headband so it stays in place as I run into the fieldhouse. I make my way through the crowd and to the floor where everyone is seated. It's a sea of navy and everyone looks the same. Slowing my pace so I'm not sprinting down the aisle, I scan the crowd as the first speaker reaches the podium and starts speaking. But I'm not listening.

Making it halfway down the first side, I spot the two

familiar caps I helped decorate last week. One on a blonde I could pick out of anywhere, and the other on a red head I've become fairly fond of over the last two years.

I shuffle down the row, remaining low so everyone can see and so I don't stick out, clearly late to graduation. Finally, I spot the empty seat next to Connor, sitting down with a sigh.

"Way to run late." Hannah leans over and hits my leg.

"Yeah, where were you?" Connor asks, grabbing my hand and giving it a kiss.

"I had to get something for you," I tell him, reaching into the pocket of my dress and pulling out the watch. He doesn't wear it much since it didn't work, so sneaking it out of his apartment was easy enough.

"What—wait is this working?" he asks, mouth hung open as he takes the watch from my hand.

"Yeah, I had it fixed for you. I wanted to make sure your dad was here with us," I tell him, taking the watch and putting it on his wrist. He holds his arm out for me as I clasp it and turn it back over so he can see it ticking away.

"I—you—Dad—" he sputters as tears form in the corner of his eyes.

"You're welcome," I laugh, wiping the tears away and kissing his cheek. "Now pay attention," I tease, pointing to the stage in front of us.

A century goes by before we finally make it outside of the arena, blank diploma holders in hand.

"They're over here," Hannah says, with her phone to her ear.

I pull Connor behind me as we follow her through the crowd to where our families are. They're taking up a huge space on the grass with almost too many people to count between mine and Hannah's family, then Connor's too. Finn and Jordan are holding up a giant cardboard cutout of Hannah's face as they cheer for her.

"Fucking told them not to do that," she mumbles under her breath, as we reach them.

There's hugs and congratulations, as the three of us make our rounds saying hello to our people. Even Cy is here for Connor, which makes me tear up because I know how sad he is that his dad isn't here. Zach said he wanted to be here, but he couldn't make it since he just opened his restaurant in LA. But that's okay because we plan to Face-Time with him later. Plus it will let me say hi to Sidney, since her and Zach reconnected last month and are now dating. Things are finally starting to come together for everyone, and sometimes I still can't believe I'm in love with Connor.

"Okay pictures," my mom calls out, holding up her phone and snapping me out of my daydreaming and bringing me back to the present. "Only the graduates first," she says, grabbing the back of my dad's shirt and pulling him behind her as he steps forward.

We cycle through different pairings as my mom takes a million photos, switching with Connor's mom and Hannah's dads when they want to be in them. Finn, Jordan, and Ry insist on lifting me and Hannah on their shoulders, and when Connor jokes about making a full pyramid, I have to threaten breaking his favorite board game to make him drop it. I don't want him falling and busting his nose before we take pictures together.

Connor and I are next, and part of me thinks he might take this opportunity to propose. We've talked about our future before, things we would want at our wedding and how we would raise kids, so I wouldn't be surprised if he did it. Two years ago that was the last thing I wanted, desperately trying to avoid doing what my mom wanted. But ever since I've been with Connor she's let me figure things out on my own, so I don't mind following in her footsteps anymore. But it's also too soon for us, and while I do love the attention, I want something like that to be more intimate. Which isn't something I've told Connor before. When he backs up from me my heart stops for a second because I think he's getting down on his knee when he starts to bend. Instead, he scoops me up in his arms as a squeal slips from my lips.

"Careful! Don't drop me!" I yell, throwing my arms around his neck.

"I'd never drop you, Barbie. Now smile," he says through a laugh before smiling for our moms who are laughing as I kick one of my feet in the air and one of my arms in the opposite direction for the perfect photo.

I already know I'm going to have a hard time picking which photo of us I'll want to hang in our new apartment, because I love every photo of us together. We work so well together, even when we're both covered in pimple patches and face masks, something he now buys from the store since he loves them as much as I do.

Whenever we do face masks he acts like a middle school kid at a sleepover, insisting we take pictures and making funny faces as soon as the masks are on. I plan to make a collage of them somehow and hang it in our bathroom.

After our moms are satisfied with pictures of us, Connor's mom requests pictures of their family. One of Hannah's dads takes over being the photographer as I step next to my mom.

Her arm swings around my shoulders and pulls me close to her. "I'm so proud of you, sweetheart," she whispers into my ear.

"Thanks, Mom. And thanks for letting me figure things out on my own," I tell her. After Connor and I officially got together, I brought him home for a long weekend. He and Mom ended up bonding over the dating show I had him hooked on. I had no idea my mom was also into it. From there, she became less pushy and let me do my own thing. Instead of telling me what she thought I should be doing, she let me tell her about my plans and encouraged me as I found an internship with a local wedding planner and got my business off the ground. I've already got a lead on my first client for a small backyard wedding this summer where the couple isn't interested in having a long engagement or a big party. It's the perfect place to start building my own portfolio for bigger clients.

Mom ends up jumping next to Hannah to get more pictures as I make my way over to Ry and Cy. "He's not, like, going to propose or anything right?" I lean in and whisper, if Connor talked about that with anyone it would be them. And I need to know if I need to be prepared to act surprised.

"No, he's not," Ry reassures me.

"I'm not saying he's talked about something more low key, but I'm also not not saying that," Cy chimes in, winking like he thinks he's being subtle about it.

"Good, because I do not want proposal pictures in this outfit," I joke, pointing to the cap and gown. I did my best to spruce them up, but they're still the worst.

"When are you moving again?" Cy asks, as a set of familiar arms wraps around my chest.

"Next week," Connor offers the answer on the tip of my lips. "Ready to take on a new adventure," he says, leaning forward to look at me.

Next week is when we finally move in together not far from where Quinn, Liam, and Lucy have an apartment back home. I'll be running my event planning business from there, and Connor was able to find an accounting job at a place nearby thanks to connections from his dad's old firm.

We had a long talk with his mom about not living in Black Willow Bay, and she was more than understanding. Meanwhile, I think if I didn't move back home my mom would have cried for hours.

Connor and I have been happily dating for the past year and a half, and sometimes I still can't believe we made it this far. He's gotten me more into horror movies and board games, and I've shown him how to dance and add color into his wardrobe. Gone are the days of black sweatpants and hoodies in public.

Now we get to tackle living together, even though we basically do now. What I'm most stressed about is agreeing on how to decorate the apartment. He constantly shoots down my pink options, and I'm shooting down his life sized replicas of monsters. I'm almost ready to give up and split the apartment in half, but I'm sure we'll be able to figure something out.

"You all ready to head to dinner?" Hannah pops up from behind us. "Our reservations are in half an hour, so we can run home and drop off our gowns."

"If you hurry, we have a bucket of Fireball shots in the car." Finn comes up behind her, almost knocking her over.

Both Connor and I wince, and bet he's thinking about Charlie's wedding where we both had too many Fireball shots. We haven't touched it since, and it doesn't sound appealing now.

"I'm going to pass on the shots, but running to the apartment first sounds perfect," I say, turning in his arms to face him. "You want to drive me to the mansion one last time?"

"For you, I'd drive anywhere," he says, smiling and bending down to kiss me. My cap falls from my head as he dips me as everyone hollers around us. But I don't care because I'm only thinking about Connor and our next adventure together.

**THE END**

For anyone looking to know when open-door scenes occur,
including one intense make-out scene, they can be found in
the following chapters:

- Sixteen
- Twenty
- Twenty-Eight
- Thirty
- Thirty-Seven

# ACKNOWLEDGEMENTS

To my husband, thank you for being my board game and horror sensitivity reader. This story feels like a 300 page love letter to you in multiple ways. I can't wait to raise our daughter on old horror movies and Disney board games. I'm forever grateful for all your support on this author journey.

To Chelsea L, Hannah B, Jordana S, Katie G, Lauren B, Lauren S, Megan G, Megan V, Paula S, Rebecca B, and Sophia, thank you for making this story the best it could be. Without all of your insights and suggestions, this book is simply nothing.

To my editor Kristen, thank you for making sure all my commas were used correctly. I'll never fully understand those rules, and this book wouldn't have gotten that extra finishing touch without you.

To Paige and Jordan, thank you for creating the most beautiful cover and illustrations for this book! I'm obsessed with everything you both do.

To you, the reader, thank you for getting this far and taking a chance on Roll of the Dice. I hope you enjoyed Maeve & Connor's story, and I hope I made you want to play a board game or watch a horror movie. I know how many books are out there, and it means the world to me that you chose to spend your time reading mine.

# ABOUT THE AUTHOR

Kayla Martin (she/her) lives in Upstate New York with her husband and Neptune—her tuxedo cat and writing assistant. As an avid reader and audiobook lover, Kayla loves to write swoon-worthy stories that will pull at your heartstrings. Using her big family as inspiration, there is no shortage of hijinks and family meddling involved in each character's story. She believes in writing love stories that help you find joy while also exploring different human experiences about sexuality, mental health, and everything in between.

Connect with Kayla on her website at www.kaylamartinauthor.com to sign up for her newsletter and get early access to news about her latest book! Find Kayla on the following platforms:

# ALSO BY KAYLA MARTIN

*Murphy Family Series*

**Book #1: A Thousand Sunsets:** A shy recent college grad is looking forward to a calm family vacation in the Thousand Islands until a game of twenty questions with the new tall, dark, and tattooed lifeguard goes further than either of them intended in this bi4bi hot summer rom-com.

*Evergreen Lake: Under the Mistletoe Series*

**Book #2: Sprinkle All the Way:** Two ex-best friends put aside their eight year silent streak to join forces and reopen their small town's local cookie shop in this swoony romance story set during the town's annual Christmas Festival.